WHEN YOU LOOK AT ME

Cover Photo by Al-Khabir Richardson

Cover Layout & Design by Amiyr Barclift
    for A-Train Studios

Additional Editing provided by Judy Salcedo

Biggs, Undra E., 1966-
    When you look at me / Undra E. Biggs.
        p. cm.
        ISBN 0-9647635-6-7 (pbk. :alk. Paper)
            1.   Afro-American teenage mothers—Fiction. 2. Single-
        parent families—Fiction 3. Drug traffic—Fiction. I. Title

PS3552.I435 W47 2000
813'.6—dc21

                                                    00-35214

La Caille Nous Publishing Company, Inc.
PO Box 1004
Riverdale, MD 20738
www.lcnpub.com

Media contact:
328 Flatbush Avenue
    Suite 240
Brooklyn, NY 11238
212-726-1293

When You Look At Me

Undra E. Biggs

La Caille Nous
Publishing Company,
Inc.

AKNOWLEDGEMETS

Aknowledgements to those who have been instrumental in assisting me through life and with my writing career:

First and foremost GOD from whom all Blessings flow!!! To my home town Trenton, NJ which I love with all my heart Husband: Alvin Biggs, Sr., Children: Miya S. Jones-Biggs and Alvin Biggs, Jr., Parents: Charles and Dolly Clay, Family: William, Stella and Josephine Biggs, Brenda & Kenneth McLeon, Keneisha McLeon-Roberts, Kenny McLeon, Lewis family, Clay family, Pollard family, Simmons family, Williams family, Thomas family, Francis family, Andrea Seay, Donna Williams, McLeon Family

Friends: MY BEST-BEST BUDDY John Wu, Norma Kalibbala, Shirley Jones-love you, Archie B.-Thanks for looking out, Michael Miller, Gary Johnson, Mary Chmielewski, Robert Mapp, Jr., Michael Jackson, Tracy Brown, The Ooow Crew, M&IAU, my OMB family, Stacy Barksdale-Jones, Yolanda Zayas, Carla Shabazz-Logan, Seay-McCarthy family, Towanda White, Denson family, Hicks family, Agron family, Ross family, Jerry DeLorenzo, Doughtry Long, Judith Williams, J. Freeman, H.J. Lee, Sharon Mitchel, Dwaine Williamson, Jack Washington, Kitsy Waterson, Fred Gerald, Anthony Logan, Brenda Pinkston

Technical Support: Sandy Payton, C. Knight, Mrs. T. Banks, V. Rushmore, C. Wilson, Tracy Waters, K. Lewis, Shirley Hailstock. Organizations: Harvest Productions, Trenton Writers' Guild, Inc., Black Women In Publishing, Toastmasters, Yes M'AM Story Development Team

Special Thanks to my editor, Guichard Cadet and La Caille Nous (our house) for seeing and developing my potential. For all of the patience and knowledge you shared. And for giving my writing a home.

DEDICATION

If my pen can write
What my mind imagines

What my eyes see and
What my heart feels
Then let the experiences of my being
Be an open book

In hopes that HE will say, Well done.

ON MY OWN

Knowing my days of calling this house home were numbered made walking through the front door especially painful. For the last seventeen years, it is the only home I've ever known. Last week, my mom told me that my time here was up. Losing my virginity and becoming a teenage mother has changed the path of my life drastically. My head dropped, as tears swelled in the rims of my eyes and my stomach churned from a bad case of the nerves. I put my three-month old daughter Tianna on mom's lap, dropped the diaper bag on the floor next to the couch, and started toward the steps. Kiara, my one-year old flopped her sleepy little self on the floor next to mom's feet. The babies and I were all tired after being at the welfare office for over seven hours. We had to get assigned an apartment.

General Hospital was on, and if you were going to die, you'd better not do it during a weekday between three o'clock and four o'clock or your butt would definitely be S.O.L, shit out of luck. What hurt me most was that my brother Tim had his twenty-one-year-old, out-of-work behind parked next to her, watching the soap. Yeah, I understood I had to get out, but why did he get to stay?

"Tammy, did you find an apartment?" mom asked during the commercial. I ignored her question and continued up to my room. I still couldn't believe my parents were throwing me and my children out of our home. I could hardly take care of myself, and was scared to death of being on my own. How was I going to take care of my babies? There is still so much I don't know. What if they got sick? How am I suppose to pay for rent, diapers, and food for them? Budgeting money was never on my list of to-dos. And what about furniture? I guess they just expected us to sleep on the damn floor. No, I can't do this! Stopping half way up the stairs, I yelled, "You wanted me and my kids out of your house, and we're gettin' out!" I didn't mean it to come out like that, but I wasn't exactly in the best state of mind.

"Don't you raise your voice at me little girl, and don't you dare catch no attitude either!" Mom jumped up off of the couch with the baby in her arms storming behind me as I made my way to my room. "You made your bed, now you have to lie in it!" She yelled behind me.

"Yeah right," I grumbled under my breath.

"Tammy, I love you and my grandbabies." Mom stormed through my bedroom door with Tianna tucked under her arm like a football. "...but I told you, me and your father, we told you that after you had Kiara we would help you and stand by you, long as you stayed in school and didn't have no more babies. You were the one who ran around with that damned boy and got *yourself* knocked up again. Then to top it off you went and quit school. Now Mark's tired ass done gone and left you here looking mighty stupid with two kids!" She added waving her finger in my face.

"Ma, why you got to talk to me like that?" Tears shattered my vision. And *excuse me*, but what did she mean I had to lie in the bed I made? I have been lying in it and damn it feels like a bed of nails. I hate to admit it, but she's right. They did warn me, but at the time I was blind, deaf *and* dumb.

When I started going with Mark, my life was going through some serious changes. Being the middle child of five siblings, with two older brothers and two younger sisters, wasn't always the easiest job in the world. Even though my parents were wonderful at giving us all their love, sometimes in a family as big as ours one could get lost in the shuffle. It was a big responsibility to help mom cook and clean. I also had to tutor my younger sisters and keep my own grades above average.

My parents were strict, not on the boys, just on us girls. That always made me angry. It wasn't right. Tim is only three years older than me. Jimmy has me by five years. The things they were allowed to do at an early age, like go to the mall by themselves and hang out with their friends, at that same age, we girls didn't dare ask. Mom wasn't having it. She would make us sit on the porch, bored to tears as she preached on about how it wasn't proper for young girls to be out running the streets like they ain't have *proper* home training. My life was so tedious, so predictable, and at that time, I even bored myself. But when puberty came knocking, whether mom was ready for me to grow up or not, whether I was ready or not for that matter, changes started happening.

Both socially *and* physically, I was a late bloomer. Being a petite 5'5" and one hundred and ten pounds soaking wet, I didn't start developing breast until I was fifteen, and then my hips and butt started to round out. All of a sudden, dudes were noticing me in a different kind of way-- saying that I was fine and that I had it goin' on. Strange. Even though I looked different, I still felt the same on the inside, and *pretty* sure wasn't how I felt...well, not until Mark came into my life. He became to me the early morning sunshine which flooded the dark rooms in my life. He took me out of the *'some old thing, day after day blues'*.

We met in Trenton High where we attended school. Even though a lot females jockeyed for Mark's attention, he wanted me. He was fine as wine, light-skinned, soft baby hair that he wore in either braids or a fro. His b boy style was hype. Mark didn't play sports or anything. He didn't have to. He just walked the halls being a pretty boy.

He made me feel special because, no one else had ever given me so much attention. The first time we cut school, I knew it was wrong, but it felt so right. Skipping class was scary at first, but after a few times with no repercussions, it became easier. His mom would be at work until four o'clock and I'd be long gone by then.

Eight weeks after we started going out, he asked me to go all the way. Nervous, yes, but I was ready. Many times I wondered what it would feel like to be in a room, alone, together flesh to flesh. I had never seen a naked man before. I was *green* to the third power. Mark thought it was funny that nowadays there was someone in high school who was as inexperienced as I was. But then, in his tiny overcrowded bedroom with our clothes off, I wasn't so sure if I was ready after all.

Knowing that I was a virgin, he promised not to hurt me, and Mark kept his promise. He took his time trying unsuccessfully for three separate days before he was able to penetrate me. We'd go at it for hours, then I'd make him stop. The next day he'd meet me at my locker in school and then we'd catch the bus to his house and try it again...until at last, on that third day, it felt comfortable and I was able to take him fully inside.

I guess I mistook his patience for love. But, *oh my goodness!* I had never experienced anything that felt like sex in my life. Sure, I've touched myself a hundred time in the privacy of my own room, but masturbation was such a controlled act. There was no surprise to it. I knew what was going to happen every step of the way. Making love to Mark was like jumping out of an airplane and free falling amongst the clouds. For the first time in my life someone let it be all about me. It wasn't Tammy do this or Tammy do that. When I was in Mark's bed I would close my eyes and all of my pressures would just disappear. In my own realm, I could hear nothing but Mark's breath in my ears and my own moans, and it sounded so pretty. Just like he made me feel. There was nothing simple about it. *He turned me out!* In Mark's house, in Mark's bedroom, in Mark's bed, in Mark's arms, Mark inside of me was all I thought about. He took me away often, to that place in my mind where everything was *pretty*, where things felt so good, and where it was all about me.

By the time the disciplinary reports from school started rolling in, my grades had already started to plunge. It had been a long time since my mom raised her hand to me, but when she took a look at my attendance record and my grades for the semester, she slapped me right across the face. She was furious. Needless to say, there was a lot of stress at home. I shaped up, enough to stifle the tension between my parents and me, but I wasn't trying to let Mark go. In fact, the only thing I understood was Mark's thick, pink lips forming the words, *"Let's get out of here and go back to my place."*

My mom was a stickler about keeping track of her daughters' periods. She wrote on her calendar in three different color marker, one for each one of us, the date of our menstruation. When a whole month went by and my name didn't appear on the calendar, all hell broke loose. We all were in a state of shock! Mama cried and screamed. Daddy was the quiet type. He seldom yelled about anything unless you pushed him way past his limits. Even though he didn't say one single word to me, I knew he was hurt. He would stare at me deep in thought, like he could look right through me. After a few days when mom's pressure returned to normal she, daddy and I had another talk. They told me that as a Christian family, abortion was not an option, but they expected me to stay in school and forbade me from seeing Mark. There were a lot of tears shed, but after the shock wore off, all of my family supported me and waited for my new arrival. But I still needed to see Mark and he told me he needed to see me too.

He was there for me, although it was on the down low. I told him about my parents demanding that we not see each other. Mark didn't press the issue about playing a roll in the baby's life. At the time I thought he was being respectful to me by not causing any trouble between me and my parents. After Kiara was born, Mark was excited. He was all up on me to let him spend time with his daughter. The only way I knew how to get them together without my parents finding out was to sneak her over to his house. I would bundle her up, and instead of taking her to the sitter's so I could go to school, I'd go to Mark's house. He looked so proud that he had this beautiful baby girl. We'd lay her at the top of his bed, and we'd be at the bottom fuckin' our brains out. That's when I became pregnant with Tianna, and my entire life fell to pieces.

Mark told me that if I didn't have an abortion, we were through. Just like that!!! He told me that he could get the money and it would be over before anyone even knew I was pregnant again. I didn't want to believe that he was saying those words to me. What a rude awakening. All the beauty he showed me was just an illusion. It wasn't really there. What I thought was, *all about me*, was actually all about him. *He*, had to have it and I was the stupid one he got it from. Now *that* was the only simple thing about the whole affair.

I stayed in school walking the halls with my head hung low, all by my damn self. And it hurt like hell when I see him turn and walk the other way when he saw my face. I knew the other students were laughing at me. I felt the stares and heard the rumors. Yes, I was ashamed of myself, but abortion just wasn't for me. It was bad enough I was pregnant in the eleventh grade at age sixteen. Then there I was pregnant at the age of seventeen for my senior year too. There was no way that I was going to stay in school pregnant for the second time. I couldn't handle it. I hung in there until I started to show, then five months into my senior year I quit, breaking yet another demand that my parents laid down to me- that I stay in school. Eleven months after Kiara was born, I gave birth to Tianna. On several occasions, since the second pregnancy, my mother had threatened to throw me out when the baby was old enough. Who knew she was serious?

Mom sat down on the bed and put Tianna next to her. "Don't you think this hurts me, Tamlyn? You're my first daughter. You always were a very smart girl, until you started with that Mark boy, and from that point on, you just act like you ain't have a damn mind of your own. Skippin' school, havin' sex, all the things you know you were not suppose to do." Mom crossed her plump legs and straightened her skirt over her knee. She looked at me intensely to make sure that I understood. "Your father and I feel that as long as you stay here with us, you'll never grow up. So whether you like it or not, baby, you have put yourself in this position and need to grow up much quicker than you are ready to. You're now a mother of two, a woman, and you have to act like it. You need your own space for you and your children, so that you can raise them as you see fit. And besides, I still have two other young ladies who I have to set an example for."

"But Ma, I'm scared. I've never lived by myself before."

"I know you're scared 'cause I'm scared for you, but I know, once you get yourself together, you'll do just fine." Mom patted the bed, gesturing for me to sit down beside her. "Your daddy and I, we'll help you," she said putting her arms around me, pulling me into her size forty-D breasts. Where is your new apartment?"

"Domtar Courts."

Mom grew quiet. Domtar Courts was one of several public housing tenements in the city, notorious for drugs and crime. To hear me say that's where the children and I were moving must have been unsettling for her.

"Did they say when the apartment would be ready?"

"In two weeks. The maintenance people have to paint it first." Mom picked up Tianna in her arms, kissed her gently on the side of her head, then went back downstairs.

Cleaning my room, I started separating the things that I wanted to take with me from the things that I would leave behind. I loved this room, this house. Mom was a seamstress. She had a shop set up in the basement, where she made everything from drapes for the house to clothes for her customers. Every room bore her special touch. When I was eleven, she took me and my younger sister Kiesha, who was the second oldest daughter, and also shared my room, to the fabric store. Mom let us pick out our own material. We picked out this wild purple and green material with big flowers outlined in black. Mom asked us at least five times if we were sure about our decision. There was no changing our minds. Mom came home, and within the week she had created a work of art. She had sewn a comforter, a pair of drapes and two matching lamp shades. It was beautiful. Mom paid a little extra and had a purple carpet laid down. Our room had sort of a jungle look to it. Kiesha and I spent weeks in our room, refusing to leave. As much as I loved it then, I love it more now. It's a little different with the crib and the babies things in here, but it still has the same flavor.

In two weeks, I received a call from Domtar Courts that my unit was ready. My oldest brother, Jimmy drove me over there to get the keys. Mom came along. She held Kiara on her lap in the front seat while I nervously fed Tianna a bottle in the back. It was so quiet in Jimmy's car. It felt like we were going to a funeral or something- my funeral. Domtar Court's rental office was located in a basement unit of Tower B. Inside looked like an old school principal's office. The walls were cinder block, painted aqua blue on the bottom and white on top. The furniture was of old but sturdy wood with names and years carved into them. The windows were barred and ragged and needed to be replaced. It smelled like a laundromat. I wondered why, until the manager pointed out that there was a washing area down the hall.

"Your apartment is on the 9th floor, number 917 in Tower A. It's all ready for you to move into. Your rent is due on the first of the month, and after the fifth there is a ten dollar late charge." He went on about the rules and regulations of Domtar Courts. "We have apartment inspections once a year, no washing machines allowed inside the apartments, no one who is not on the lease can live in the apartment without our consent. If your income changes we need to know about it, so your rent can be adjusted." He handed me my keys and said, "Welcome to Domtar Courts," like I was moving into The Ritz-Carlton.

We walked out of the management office and nobody said a word. It was like we were from a foreign land, another planet, the planet *Middle Class*.

I felt both scared and a little excited. I've always heard how awful it was to live in the projects with the drugs, the violence and the wild people. But it was the unexpected that frightened me the most. As Tower A came into view, it looked like a big dog waiting to devour me. I wasn't ready for this.

Scratching my scalp, I thought to myself, 'Dag, look at all those mismatched curtains'. I hated ugly dressed windows, and this place was full of them. There was all kinds of junk up to the window perpetrating as decor- sheets, curtains tied into knots, some even had two different colored panels to the same window.

There weren't a lot of people outside, just a few kids hangin'" out listening to Heavy D, blastin' on the boom box. They should have been in school. It was Friday morning in May.

"It's funny," I said breaking the silence, "Whenever I rode by this neighborhood, I'd point and say, *that's one place I'd never want to live*. And now, here I am." The lobby was disgusting. I held Kiara's hand tight to make sure that she didn't fall and end up on this nasty floor. Graffiti covered the walls. While we were waiting for the elevator, three guys sitting in a window checked us out. They made the hair on the back of my neck stand up. My pulse was racing. Mom and Jimmy shot doubtful looks back and forth at each other. A bell chimed, then half of an "L" lit up above the elevator. The doors opened up, and the rank smell of urine burst out. In disgust, I shook my head. "I can't believe that this trifling place is my new home."

We got off at the ninth floor and headed down the long, dimly lit, narrow hallway.

The aroma of fried bacon filled the air. While searching for 917, a door swung open and two kids ran past us. A voice yelled behind them, "How many time I got to tell y'all to close the damn door?"

Unsure of what would be behind the door when I opened it, I put the key in the lock. Envisioning dog sized rats and rat sized roaches, I swear I was sick to my stomach. Once inside, it wasn't too bad though. I did see some roaches dart behind the refrigerator when I went into the kitchen. I'd just have to remember to bring the bug spray with me when I moved in. The tile floors were clean, even though there were a couple pieces missing. The walls were white, and overall, the place was clean.

The apartment was small, yet big enough for me and my two children. It had a small kitchen with an eat-in area, a small living room, one bath, and two small bedrooms.

"What do you think baby?" mom asked with Tianna in her arms as she opened up the yellow steel kitchen cabinets.

Walking over to the window, I looked all the way down at the cars in the parking lot. "It's alright. It's a lot better than what I thought it was gonna be," I smiled as Kiara ran through the apartment.

"Y'all ready to go?" Jimmy had his hand on the door knob. I could tell that he was upset, and didn't like this place at all.

Jimmy was five-ten, and very meticulous about his compact, muscular, physique and the way he carried himself in general. If I didn't know him on a personal level, I would probably think he was the most stuck up person alive. Everything in his surroundings had to be in order. His clothes were always the best quality and he went to the barbershop every single Friday to get his hair, as he put it, tightened up. But Jimmy was way deeper than that. Out of all of us siblings, he was the one most influenced by my mother. Everything she ever told him to do, he took to heart and put into practice. I believe that's why he's as disciplined and for the most part as successful as he is. By successful I mean he's a family man - has his head on straight, knew what he wanted to be in life and he went after it. Jimmy finished college, worked as a computer analyst, has a wife, house in the suburbs, children, dog, and even drives a foreign car. I admire that about him, and once upon a time thought that would be me as well. That's why I could overlook the bad vibes he was dishing out; he wanted more for me.

"Ma, I don't have any furniture," I said ignoring Jimmy.

"Don't you worry about that. You can have your bedroom set from the house, and tomorrow we'll go around and see what we can find to make do."

Inside the bathroom, there was a white toilet with a pink sink propped up on two rusting silver poles. Leaning over in the tub, I turned on the water and it blasted out full strength. A smile crept on my lips as I imagined how it would be to take a bubble bath in my own tub, with no one banging on the door telling me to hurry up. Maybe that was one of the perks of being kicked out of mom's house. I turned off the water and opened the medicine cabinet, "Ugh!" There was a dead roach on it's back with all them icky legs tangled together. Slamming the door shut, I overheard mom and Jimmy talking. He sounded aggravated, "You really gonna let her move in here?"

"Yes, Jimmy. Your father and I already discussed this, and we decided that, yes, it's time for her to move."

"This doesn't make any sense. She's seventeen years-old, and she has two babies. She needs to be home with you. She needs help, and this damn sure ain't no place to raise no kids."

"James! I think you best remember who the parents are around here. Now, me and your father have made a decision and that's that. Tammy is not going to be alone. We're still family."

Mom has been saying 'your father and me' ever since we were kids, and all of us know that 'your father and me' means that it was her idea, and he's just going along so he don't have to hear her mouth.

On Saturday morning, I woke up to the smell of homemade biscuits. Mom was up fixing breakfast for us. We had to fuel up. Our mission today was to hit every second-hand store and yard sale in town. When I woke up, I had a whole new attitude. Waltzing into the kitchen fully dressed, I walked over to mom, and gave her a big kiss on the face. Maybe living on my own might be nice, I thought.

"Good morning, Ma."

My tone must have surprised her. "You look mighty happy this morning. What a beautiful smile you're wearing," she said squeezing my chin.

"Ma, I'm starting to get excited now. It's just starting to hit me that I'm gonna have my own apartment."

"Now don't you go getting too excited. I don't wanna know that you'll be havin' wild parties," mom said wiping her hand on her apron, and getting the eggs out of the fridge.

We both started laughing. From the cupboard, I got some plates and started setting the table.

"Kiara and Tianna are gonna stay home with Nichole, til we get back. I told her I'll pay her later."

"Now you know you shouldn't have to pay your own sister to look after your kids. That's what family is for. I don't know where y'all got that from, cause you didn't learn it from me."

"I don't mind paying her when I have it. This way she'll have some spending money."

"Don't fool yourself, that child got mo' money than all of us put together," mom said smiling, flipping those eggs in the pan like a chef.

"Is daddy up already?"

"Yeah, he's already been out and gassed his truck up."

Daddy was a big man, well over six feet. He reminded me of a black lumberjack 'cause of his big build, and he always wore flannel shirts and blue jeans. Tim was the only one of us who took height after him. My dad is my heart and the words daddy's girl always brought a smile to my face. He worked at General Motors for twenty-one years and has been retired now for eight years, but he still works harder than ever. He has a junky old, red truck that he hauls stuff around in to make a little extra money, and 'to stay out of Annita's way,' he says.

After breakfast mom, dad, Keisha, and I were off. The first second-hand store we went to, we found a small dinette set that was just the right size for my kitchen. Mom bought me a toaster, an iron, an ironing board and two nice lamps. Dad threw our findings onto the back of his truck. We drove around to several other second hand stores, and yard sales in the township, picking up odds and ends. Not until we came to the last stop did we find suitable things for the living room. None of the chairs matched, but daddy said that they were sturdy, and that's all that mattered.

On the way back, daddy pulled into McDonald's and brought us all lunch. Riding with all that stuff sticking out of his beat-up old truck was embarrassing. Felt like we were the Beverly Hill Billies, or something.

It was every bit of 2:00 P.M. when we headed for Domtar Courts. The weather was surprisingly cool, after a week of temperatures in the eighties. It was really cloudy out, too. When we got to my apartment I was so elated I didn't even notice that Domtar Courts was such a shit hole. All that was on my mind was that I couldn't wait to get inside my own place and put my furniture any damn place I wanted to. I felt kinda' free, kinda' grown up.

Dad stopped at a pay phone to call Jimmy. He and Tim came and helped dad unload the furniture. Mom and dad paid under two hundred dollars for everything. If mom couldn't do anything else, she sure knew how to stretch a dollar. With all of us kids to raise, she had plenty of practice. After they moved everything from the truck into the apartment, my father and brothers went back to the house. They picked up the bedroom furniture and the girls' bedding. While they were gone mom, Keisha, and I sat on the couch and talked.

The apartment had potential, but at the moment, everything was in disarray. There were boxes and furniture all over the place, windows to be washed and curtains to be hung.

"This furniture stinks. It smells like mildew."

"That comes from being in the second-hand store for so long. You're gonna need upholstery cleaner to spray it down real good," mom said. "You know what I'm gonna do for you? I'm gonna make you some covers for these chairs and some curtains to match. But for now just clean them and put sheets over them. What color do you want it to be?"

"Uhm...I want it to be blue. I like blue."

Mom smiled at me. "We better get started washing and putting up these dishes and getting some of this stuff in order."

After the men came back with the bedroom sets, daddy pulled me over to the side and put his arm around me, "Look sugar, I'm goin' on home so I can get Kiara and Tianna and bring them here. I'm not coming back up. I'm just gonna send them up with Nichole." He kissed my forehead. "You enjoy your little place here. You know I love you, don't you?"

I gave him a tight hug. "I love you too daddy, and thanks for helping me."

It was getting late and mom, Keisha, and I had put the apartment into some kind of functioning order. We had straightened up the kitchen, bedrooms, and the bathroom enough to use.

After Nichole dropped off my little ones and everyone left, I felt strange in this new place. It was too quiet. Back home, something was always going on.

It was just about midnight and the babies were in their room sleeping. Exhausted, I had also fallen off to sleep, but for some reason I became wide awake. Afraid to be in the apartment, my heart started pounding erratically, and I couldn't stop looking around. My mind started wondering all of this crazy stuff like, *what if someone tried to break in?* The saying is true, 'you never know what you have until it's gone,' and I definitely missed having mom and dad and the rest of the family in the next rooms while I slept. Now they were all the way across town.

On the edge of my bed I sat and looked out of the window, even though it was late, I could still see some of the fellahs playing basketball on the court under the street light, and people were hanging out on the corner.

Up and around the apartment, I turned on all of the lights, then checked on the girls to see if they were alright. I walked around, and paced around until I couldn't take it any longer. Paranoia had me in its grips. Throwing on some clothes, I hurried out in the hallway to the apartment next to mine and banged on the door. I knew that knocking on a stranger's door in the wee hours of the night was dumb, but fright will make you do some crazy things.

"Who the fuck is it knocking on my door at this time o' night?" a female voice yelled.

I thought about running back into my apartment, but my feet wouldn't move, "It's Tammy from next door. Can I use your phone to call my mother? It's important." A slender dark-skinned female opened the door with this quizzical look on her face. "Hi, I'm Tammy. I moved into 917 today." I was a bit chocked up and wishing that I'd stayed in bed, 'cause I didn't like the way she was looking at me. "I just have to call home, right across town. I'll make it quick." She moved to the side and let me in.

"Phone's over on the table" She was fully dressed, like she had just come from a party or something. Her apartment, to my surprise was rather decent. In my mind I had this stereotypical image of the project trife life, but in here was nothing like what I had imagined. There was an old couch and love seat, and somehow in this tiny space, there was a china closet stuck in a corner, stacked with dishes. In the small kitchen, on top of a frayed piece of shag carpet was a dinner table that matched the maple wood china closet and four, worn, high back chairs which spilled over into the living room. Everything was tight, but polished and cozy.

Tim answered the phone. "What's up?"

"Tim, I'm alright, but can you come over here with me?" One thing I knew about my brother was he's very unpredictable. Tonight, I just hoped he was in an agreeable mood.

"Girl, it's almost one o'clock in the morning. Are you out of your fucking head? Go back to bed."

"Come on, Tim," I whispered into the phone, "I'm scared."

"Look, I ain't walking all the way over there. Don't nobody want your ass. Just go to sleep, and before you know it, it'll be morning. You can't be scared forever. I gotta go, Rachel's on the other line." Tim hung up. He makes me sick sometimes with his old skinny body built like a string bean. Yeah, he got abs and definition but if it wasn't for those singers who made the anorexia look popular, Tim wouldn't have a prayer. Can't tell him that though, what his body lacked in size, his *big head* made up for with ego. He thinks he's every woman's fantasy. I was crushed but I played it off.

"Thanks for letting me use your phone."

"Yeah, sure anytime. By the way I'm Jeannette Ford," she said.

Just as I was leaving a big, tall, jet black skinned man came out of the bathroom with a towel wrapped around his waist. He looked like a body builder. Even his muscles had muscles. He looked at me and nodded his head.

"Hi," I responded.

"Tammy this is Bull. Tammy just moved into 917 today," she told him.

Bull, what an appropriate name, I thought. "Thanks again."

Back at my apartment, I got into bed and stared out the window. The next thing I knew I was awakened by the sun beaming on my face, and Tianna was crying for me to come and get her.

As the weeks progressed, I became more and more comfortable living on my own. Mom came through again. She made me the blue curtains and chair covers like she promised. My living room took on a nice, homey look.

Not having a phone was a major inconvenience, because I couldn't speak with my family as often as I would have liked. Jeannette, although a little rough around the edges, was gracious about me using hers whenever I needed. And that girl sure had the gift of gab! Each time I need to make a quick call, I just prepared myself to stay and listen to her talk for the next half hour.

She was older than me, twenty-three, but we had some good talks. She told me that she grew up in that apartment, and for the life of me, I couldn't imagine that. The semi-detached colonial style house I grew up in had four bedrooms, an attic, a basement, and a large kitchen. We had a front yard and a back yard where mom grew flowers and vegetables. That's how you were suppose to grow up, or so I thought. Her mom and little brother moved out and left everything to her. That explained the mature decor of her apartment.

Two months after I moved into the apartment I answered the door and couldn't believe who was on the other side. How he found out where I lived was a mystery to me.

"Hey Tammy," Mark said with his high-yellow self. He was now a little taller and heavier at around five-nine and one hundred sixty-five pounds. He sported an Orlando Magic baseball cap, over his soft, black wavy hair. His khaki shorts were baggy and hung around his hips revealing the top of his sky blue boxers. And he wore black combat boots with white calf high, crew sox. His style used to drive me sexually crazy. He looked down at me with his chinky eyes, but they didn't look so good to me today. They just looked like trouble.

"What do you want?" Throwing my hands on my hips, I was thoroughly disgusted at the sight of him.

"I just stopped by to see how you were doing."

Mark stepped into the apartment. I despised him, but I allowed him to come into my home because I had a point to prove. He didn't ruin me, and the girls and I were fine without him. He looked at Kiara sitting on the floor playing with her colorful blocks. He went over and picked her up kissing her on the face.

"Where's the baby?"

"She's in the room sleeping." I pointed to the children's room. Mark walked, with Kiara in-arm, into the bedroom to look at Tianna. The girls looked just like Mark; Kiara had his eyes, and Tianna had his light complexion. They both had his beautiful hair.

"You got a nice place, Tammy. How you been making out? I see you still looking good with your pretty brown self." Mark put Kiara back on the floor with her blocks and walked up close to me.

"I've been fine." With folded arms, I looked up at him from the corner of my eyes.

"Tammy, I been thinking. Since you got your own place and everything, you know, why don't you let me move in here and take care of y'all?"

When he said those words, I nearly gagged, "No, you didn't say that to *me,* Mark. Take care of *us*! It's because of you that my parents kicked me out of my home in the first place. And instead of being by my side, you told your mother that Kiara and Tianna weren't even yours. Now that I got my own place, you talking about us getting back together. *Hell, no!*"

"I ain't never tell my moms that Kiara and Tianna weren't mine!"

"Yes you did, Mark, because she told me you did!"

"No, she didn't."

"Look, whatever. I ain't gonna stand here and argue with you. Just get your sorry butt up out of my house. And when you see me in the street, act like you don't know me. Okay."

"You ain't all that, Tammy!"

"Oh yeah, well why you trying it, if I ain't? Just get out, cause you ain't *none* of that!"

He had a damned nerve. I guess he figured I'd be his fool forever. Not this time around. The only thing Mark was good for was making pretty babies. Not taking care of them, just making them.

A PROMISE

Every six months, I would receive notification in the mail that I had to come to the welfare office to be requalified for my monthly check and food stamps. When I got there they would ask me the same old questions and I would give them the same old answers. As I waited in the crowded waiting area, my case worker, Jerry DeVello appeared holding a folder in his hands. He was a handsome, slender Italian man. Always a casual dresser, he was sporting beige Dockers, a striped Polo shirt, and Hush Puppy shoes.

"Tamlyn Blake," he called, motioning for me to follow him. I got up and gathered my belongings from the chair next to me, propped Tianna in her stroller, and grabbed Kiara's hand. We followed Jerry into a small room and sat down.

"Hi, Kiara. Are you being a good girl for your mom?" Kiara smiled and shook her head. I coaxed her to speak. In a shy little voice she said, "yes," and giggled softly. Even though my oldest baby was a year old, some words she pronounced clearly, the rest she simply made up. But whatever the case, my Kiara sure loved to talk.

"So how is the apartment coming along? I know that's a pretty tough neighborhood, but are you alright?"

"Yes, we're fine."

"Are you back in school yet?"

"No, not yet," I admitted shamefully.

"And why not, Tamlyn? You're a smart girl, and I know you can do better than just sitting home all day waiting to collect a check." He cocked his head to the side waiting for an answer.

"Jerry, I don't have any one to watch my kids during the day. And I can't trust just anyone with them." My words were, half truth, half excuse.

His eyes caught mine. Collecting his thoughts, he ran his fingers through his wavy black hair and leaned his elbow on the table.

"I'm going to talk to you off-the-record for a moment. I wish I had a dollar for every person coming in here who has said what you just said. This is nonsense, Tamlyn. You're young. Eighteen years old, right? You have your whole life ahead of you. It gets me sick to my stomach to see the hundreds of young girls, just like you, come in here and make this system their whole life. But you're different, I really believe that. I called your counselor, Mrs. Palmer," he said checking his notes. "She said you were a good student until you became pregnant with your first child. I know you had to have dreams, and I know that the life you're leading is not it." He reached down and touched Tianna's hand, "You can still have your dreams, even with your children. But you just have to be willing to work a little harder to make those dreams come true."

He saw something in me, what it was, I didn't have a clue. All I knew was that I didn't want to let *him* down. After he requalified me for my welfare benefits, Jerry strongly urged me to go back to school. Besides, I knew I had to.

My first experience with the welfare system had been awful. While pregnant with Kiara, about four different examiners interviewed me, one after the other. Each one treated me like I was just another dumb-ass teen who fucked up her life and expected society and them personally to pay for it. The first woman, a sistah at that, came in playing this head game with me asking me all these questions, then after what seemed like an hour- tells me that I didn't qualify. Didn't qualify...for welfare? Hopeless and humiliated, tears rolled down my face as she stood up getting ready to walk out of the room. Was it my tears, or my bare-assed emotions which compelled her to sit back down at the table and decide that I was actually indeed *qualified for welfare*. After she walked out, an elementary school teacher of mine walked through the door. *Vapor*, I remember the word going through my mind. *God, please turn me into vapor so I can just disappear and float away.* The shinning star pupil, the kid with all the potential being interviewed to *qualify for welfare* by my former teacher. For him, being at the welfare office was an upward career change. For me, it was a downward life change. What do you see when you look at me, I wanted to ask him, but I didn't. His ignoring our past and acting like I was a total stranger told me everything I needed to know. He didn't acknowledge me as his shinning star third grade student, and I didn't acknowledge him either. After all those years, was it possible that he simply forgot who I was? Maybe, but the way he avoided my eyes and the cold tension between us told me- he knew exactly who I was. Just like I knew him. By the time the third examiner came through the door, stripped was how I felt. Stripped of self, stripped of pride, even stripped of memory cause I really don't even remember the interview. That part remains a blank.

Then there was Jerry! At the end of a long and grueling course of examinations, Jerry walked through the door. He shook my hand, introduced himself, and treated me like a person who deserved respect. He was pleasant, encouraging, and someone I felt I could trust. Right off the bat, he made me feel like somebody. One thing he wasn't was showy. He didn't flash the teeth or put forth any additional effort to have the effect that he had on me. He was quite the professional. But from the moment he walked into the room, looked at me and shook my hand, we connected. I will always be thankful to him for that.

By the time I left his office, I had agreed to go back to school. Before I could back out, Jerry made a phone call to my school counselor, Mrs. Palmer, who would prepare the necessary forms. He told her that I'd be right over to register for my last year of high school. "I want you to go on out there and make us all proud. I know you can do it Tamlyn, and deep down inside you know it too."

The weight of the world seemed as if it were on my shoulders. Could I be both mom and student? Would my babies suffer if they didn't have my full attention?

"Do you have a ride?"

"No, we're gonna catch the bus."

"I'll send you over," Jerry winked at me and dialed for a cab.

When I got to Mrs. Palmer's office, all of the registration papers were ready for me. "Have a seat, Tamlyn. It's good to see you again," Mrs. Palmer said with a smile. "Are these your daughters? They're so adorable." Mrs. Palmer was a big, beautiful woman. Everything about her was big–her body, her jewelry, her perfume, her sculptured nails, even her hairdo. "Before we get started, I must tell you how fortunate you are to have Jerry DeVello as your social worker. He's a good man."

Nodding my head I agreed, "Yeah, he is nice."

"He has saved many young people from taking the wrong road in life. He is one of those rare people in the business who truly cares about young people. Tamlyn, like Jerry, I am here for you. I want to see you succeed. With your living on your own, and with all of your responsibilities, these next few months are going to be tough, but I want you to make a promise now."

Staring at her I felt quite overwhelmed. Waking up this morning, I knew I'd make a trip to the welfare office to requalify for my benefits, but I had no idea that I would be standing in Mrs. Palmer's office committing myself back into school.

"I want you to promise that if things get too tough for you, you'll come and talk to me first before you make any major decisions. Is it a deal?"

Feeling numb and confused, I agreed. "Yes, it's a deal."

Mrs. Palmer extended her large hand and gave me a firm hand shake. "Great, I'll see you in the morning then."

BACK TO SCHOOL

Mom and dad were so happy to learn that I would finally get my diploma. They believed their strategy to have me move out on my own was working.

For two weeks now I had been in school, and I wasn't so sure this would work. It felt strange to be older than my classmates, but a promise was a promise. While my classmates dreamt about the future, my future was now. The other seniors talked about parties, getting some play for the weekend, the senior prom, what college they would attend, and stuff like that. The only thing I worried about was graduating in June and finding a job so I could get off welfare and support my two children.

Most of my first periods, I spent staring out of the window trying not to fall asleep. Today, the sun was shining so brightly, all I could think about was if my daughters were missing me as much as I missed them. When the dismissal bell finally rang signaling the end of the day, I packed up my homework and slung my bag over my back. Squeezing my way through the crowd of students to reach my locker brought back memories of how Mark use to wait for me between classes.

Once outside, there was no warmth to accompany the bright November sun. The library was only three blocks away, but the walk was so cold that when I entered the building, my toes and fingers stung like crazy. Rubbing my hands together, I blew hot air from my mouth to warm them.

There was a table in a secluded corner that would become my favorite place because it was far away from everyone else. A grand old painting of George Washington crossing the Delaware River hung above my chair. This is where I studied, because at my apartment it was impossible to do homework. Too many distractions: my kids, the neighbors shouting and running through the hallway, chores to be done. The library became my home away from home.

Being back at school was more than I had bargained for. It was a lot of work, and sometimes I wondered if I had the stamina to see this through. But, I had to admit though, I felt pretty good about myself, even though keeping track of time was one of my problems. Engrossed in a geometry equation, I looked up to discover that it was after six, "Oh shit!" I had ten minutes to pack up and get down the street to catch my bus. Slamming my book shut, I shoved my things into my bag, and hauled ass out the door and down the street. The bus was on the corner, but I still was half a block away.

"Hey! Hey! Hold that bus! Hold that bus!" Hearing my desperate plea, a guy who had just stepped off the bus quickly turned and caught the driver's attention.

"Thanks," I said trying to catch my breath as I climbed on, fumbling for my bus pass. Flopping down in my seat, I rolled my eyes up in my head. If I had missed this bus, I would have had to wait another hour for the next one.

The bus dropped me off in front of Kim's Korean Mini Market, which was the neighborhood store. On the front door, there was a bold sign that read, *No Loitering*, but that's where all the action was. I was steppin' fast. It was too dark and too cold to be messin' around out here. Them druggies must have antifreeze, instead of blood, in their veins to survive such temperatures night after night.

In the Domtar lobby, my neighbor, Ms. Evette was standing at the elevator with her blue grocery cart. She had carted four huge bags of groceries that she must have paid a fortune for. Kim's charges three times what the supermarkets charged.

"Hey, Ms. Evette."

She shook her head in disgust. "I been standing here almost ten minutes waiting for this damn elevator. Ain't nothin' but them ole ig'nant fools up there holdin' it up. You think they care!" Ms Evette was pissed. "You just comin' fum school?"

"Yeah, and I'm so tired. I just want to go to sleep," I said ramming the up button. "I wonder when they're gonna' fix the other elevator. It's been broke for two weeks now."

"And it's gonna be another two weeks before them ole heffas fix it too," she said, shifting her weight from one orthopedic shoe to the other. "If they wanna office, they should go get a real damn job. Never min' usin' the elevator for they bizniss." Two minutes later, an empty, smoke-filled elevator opened onto the lobby.

When I finally opened my apartment door, I flipped on the lights, and there was no place in the world that I would have rather been. Suddenly I remembered that I hadn't been to the bathroom since I left school before three o'clock. My coat went flying as I ran into the bathroom and took a *long* overdue pee. My clothes weren't even pulled up over my behind good when there was a knock on the door. Knowing who it was, I rushed to finish, then opened the door. I took Tianna, my chunky nine-month-old from daddy's arms, and Kiara ran into the apartment past me.

"Thanks, daddy," I said giving him a kiss on the cheek.

"Your mama said to tell you that Kiara ate good, but you might have to feed Tianna again."

"Okay, dad, tell her thanks."

He kissed me on the cheek, "I'm gonna get on home. I'll see you tomorrow when I drop the kids off to you."

I was so thankful to my parents for helping me with my girls. Daddy was faithful about picking them up from daycare. Mom would feed them dinner, then daddy would bring them home to me in the evenings. Sometimes he would come in and we'd talk, but most of the times we'd both be so exhausted from our day the only thing we had strength for was a quick hug.

Closing the door, I put my mommy hat on. "Hey, stinkies. How's mommy's babies?" Kiara spent the next half hour, *in her own words*, telling me what she did today. She was so animated, using her little hands and moving all around when she spoke. But Tianna wasn't feeling well. She was cranky and felt a little warm. I put them both in a warm soapy bubble bath. It worked to soothe Kiara. She fell right to sleep.

Tianna was another story. She wouldn't eat for me either. She kept pushing the spoon from her mouth with her little dimpled hands, crying and drooling down her little neck. Nothing I did was working to soothe her. While she cried, she moaned over and over, "da da, da da, da da," and I said, "Yes, I'm here baby." This went on for almost two hours straight. From the long day and need for sleep, I had a freakin' massive headache. I was hungry, but Tianna wouldn't let me put her down long enough to make myself anything. When I thought I couldn't take another minute, she dropped off to sleep. Maybe a tooth was breaking through her gum. With my finger I fished around in her mouth, and sure enough I felt it. Tianna was teething.

I put her in her crib before wheeling the TV into my bedroom. The television use to belong to my dad. It was old as sin, with the flip channels- one for UHF and one for VHF stations. Thrown in the storage space of my parents' basement, no one was using it, so I asked if I could have it. With a coat hanger for an antenna, it didn't pick up anything but the local stations. But hey, something was better than nothing. Looking down at my feet, I noticed that I hadn't even taken my shoes off yet. Exhausted, I went into the kitchen and took two aspirins to hush the freakin' pain screaming in my head. Maybe taking a shower and getting something to eat would relax me, I thought ready to drop. The pill didn't get down my throat when Tianna began fussin' *again,* and I fell apart. All the hustle bustle had caught up with me and tears began to roll.

"Why are you doing this to me?" I yelled at God. Didn't He know I was doing the best I could? My legs buckled as all my strength seemed to dissipate. Sitting on the kitchen floor with my arms wrapped around my knees I cried and cried as Tianna screamed in the background. Completely used up, *I had no more to give.* Purging and purging, I continued to cry until I had no more tears. I sat there wishing that I had help. My mind wondered to Mark and how nice it would have been if he really meant he wanted to take care of us. When I was finished feeling sorry for myself I got up and made Tianna a bottle. I brought her to the bed with me. The next thing I knew, it was six o'clock in the morning and my alarm clock was sounding off. Propped up on my elbows, I tried to open my heavy eyes. Focusing in on my feet, I couldn't believe it, I was still fully dressed from the night before, with my shoes on! Tianna was sprawled out across my bed, asleep with her mouth wide open.

It was seven o'clock before my eyes opened officially to start another hectic day.

PLAY ANOTHER SLOW JAM

Classes were the upside. All of my teachers were telling me how pleased they were with my academic performance. They said that if I kept it up, college would be a definite possibility.

Depression was the down. When I wasn't being *mommy*, I was studying my butt off. Sometimes I got so lonely, I could die. I'm not the jealous type, but when I saw Jeannette and Bull together, or my brother Jimmy with his wife Sharon, or Tim with one of his girlfriends, or any couple for that matter, I felt so incomplete. I wished I had a man.

The guys at school be tryin' it, but those young boys couldn't handle what I had. I was a package deal, kids and all. No time for childish head games. Besides, I didn't know too many guys who would want an eighteen year-old female with not one, but two babies, anyway.

During the day I was fine, but at night, that's when the dull pain of loneliness became unbearable. It was as if someone had cut off my air supply, leaving me only a trickle to fight like hell for. And I would inhale and inhale and inhale to fill my lungs with just enough oxygen so I wouldn't die, then once the morning came my air supply would be turned back up to full.

This feeling of loneliness was a vicious cycle that hit me *every single* night. It got to the place that I hated to see the sun go down, afraid what the darkness had in store. It was a feeling that I'd never experienced before. Maybe I was stressed from trying to overachieve. Maybe I just needed someone to talk to, but I talked to Jeannette all the time. Who was I fooling? I was a woman and needed the comforts of a man. That's right a *woman!* In a few short months I went from a scared young girl to a woman who was definitely handling her business. Striving for a better life for me and my baby girls.

Someone special to hold me gently, and talk sweet and soft in my ear was what I needed. Someone to tell me I was beautiful. A man who would listen and be my strength when I had a hard day, and share my joy when the day was good. As the kids slept, and I was all alone, I'd lay on my couch in the dark, listening to the quiet storm slow jams on the radio, pretending.

"Oh, baby, I wanna do you right girl, inside and out," the song would say. Closing my eyes, I'd call up the image of some brown, honey man who was about to make love to me. To his touches, my body would respond. Sometimes the feeling was so real that my flesh would scream. Sliding my hands down feeling the softness of my warm thighs, we would become one.

As the music played, we'd gyrate to its rhythm, my imaginary man and me. Climaxin'! Climaxin'! Then Silence. The thump, the thump, the thump of a single heart beat- mine. Reality. Music refocusing around me in the dark, with no after glow- empty, sad, and alone.

Barely Getting By

The long miserable winter was finally over. Snow, ice and bitter cold weren't my cup of tea. But now that it was spring, the rain and wind were just as bad. Every weekend, I had been cooped up in this little apartment, watching that broken down TV, going stir crazy. The only places I'd been besides school were either to mom's house, Jeannette's, or on occasions with mom to church. My bus pass was only good for weekdays.

Taking advantage of the warmer air outside, Jeannette treated me and the girls to the movies. We all had a ball. It was the first time I had taken Kiara and Tianna with me to the movies. I thought they'd act up, but they didn't. I guess they were just as glad to be out as I was.

Now that it was nice out, I had a major problem, my spring clothes were shabby. It's been over two years since I had any new clothes, besides maternity clothes. All of my street wear were from before I got pregnant with Kiara. Looking through the bag that I had stored my summer clothes in, I realized the stuff was played out, and Kiara needed new clothes too. Tianna was the only lucky one. All of Kiara's clothes from last year would fit her perfectly.

As usual, I was at Jeannette's using her phone. She was walking around her apartment searching for her orange Home Depot apron so she could leave for work. I called my mother to see if she would let me use her credit card to buy some clothes for me and Kiara. "Ma, can I use your Sears card to buy me and Kiara some summer clothes? All the stuff I have is old, and Kiara outgrew all of her clothes from last year."

"Tammy, I don't mind helping you out when you need something, after all, that's what me and your father are here for, but we just bought you and the kids some things not so long ago. What you doing with the money you gettin' from downtown?"

"Ma, the stuff you bought for us was for winter. We need summer clothes."

"What you doin' with the money you get on the first? You don't have to spend no money on food. You got stamps."

"Ma, I have bills, you know. I'm not blowing my money up." I clenched my teeth.

"Well you ain't doing somethin' right. You need to start budgetin' your money so you won't have to depend on your father and me to pick up your slack. Have you thought of maybe gettin' a part time job to make some extra money?"

That's when my attitude kicked in. "Ma, how am I gonna find the time to get a part-time job? I'm in school all day and by the time I get home, I barely have enough time to spend with my kids." I sucked my teeth. "Look, if you can't help me, forget it. I'll talk to you later." I hung up the phone, and gave Jeannette a look that told how pissed off I was. "I don't believe her. She told me to get a damn job, can you dig that? How is she gonna come off telling me to get a job. I'm doing the best I can, trying to finish high school so I can get a real job. She just shot me down. I'm never gonna do that to my children. When they grow up, as long as I see them trying to make it, I'm going to be there for them, 150 percent."

"Girl, your mom's a trip," Jeannette said laughing.

"That lady is truly workin' on my black nerve now."

"Oh no, not the black one."

"Yes chile, the black one. That means she done ran through all the other ones and the black one's the only one left."

The weekend after our conversation, mom picked the girls up. When she brought them home to me on Sunday evening, she handed me a bag filled with new clothes for them. They were set for the summer, but there was nothing inside for me. After I thanked her, I had to listen as she told me how I should be handling my business. She was right, I did need to budget my money and try to be more responsible, I guess, but I wasn't blowing my money. By the time I finished paying for my bus pass, rent, utilities, buying laundry products for the month and diapers and other personal things, my money was gone. Mom acted like the welfare department gave me an unlimited cash flow. She didn't understand how hard it was. Before she left, she gave me twenty dollars. Like, what was twenty dollars going to do for me?

THE FABULOUS LIFE

Early Friday morning I stood inside the carwash staring through the glass as the white foamy soap sprayed down and the long flaps began to slap across the hood of my ride. With arms folded across my chest, the famous words of my man Don King, 'Only in America' came to mind as the corner of my top lip curled.

Only in America can a twenty-three year-old brothah like me go from drivin' a fucked up Pontiac Trans Am with the played out eagle spread across the hood to pullin' off the lot in a fifty thousand dollar Lexus. It only had three miles on the gauge, and shit, I put two of 'em on when I test drove it. Oh yeah, boy! The fabulous life.

When I was satisfied that everything was everything, that the dudes vacuumed the inside right and sprayed the cleaner on my chrome wheels, I took a seat and rested my eyes. Had a late night last night. Correction, I hadn't been to sleep yet. Stretchin' my legs, I crossed them at the ankles thinking to myself how time most definitely changes things. Just three years ago I was finishin' up my sentence at the work house servin' time in juvie. That's juvenile detention. Just before my release I was under big time pressure, wonderin' how I was gonna make it when I got out. No way was I movin' back in with my mom. She had moved from our crib in the city to a house in the township. Besides the township being too damn quiet for my taste. I was a twenty year-old man and needed my own space. So I rented a one bedroom apartment on Prospect Street in Trenton. It was chill. When mom brought herself a new living room set, she gave me her old shit. I didn't care, somethin' was better than nothin'.

A lot happened after I got out of jail. You know how niggahs be trippin' when they locked up. Be confessin their faith to Allah, a straight and narrow path for themselves and undying love for their woman. Debbie was my woman back then. She was faithful. Accepting every single collect phone call I placed, sent me everything I asked her for, and every visiting day she'd show up wearing them long skirts for my lap dance. Thought I was in love.

I knew it wasn't gonna be easy for a brothah with a drug conviction and a GED to get a job. But my mind was made up, whatever it took for me to take care of myself, I was gonna do. My days of being irresponsible were over. Three years is a lot of time to get your thinkin' on, and I vowed to myself that when I got out that I was gonna do things right.

When I was released, my parole officer had assigned me to work up at the mall doing maintenance shit. True, I said I'd do whatever it took, but this was bull. Pushin' a broom, cleanin' up some damn public toilets. Hell naw, I was better than that. And besides the mess was fuckin' embarrassing. For lasting a week, I give myself a pat on the back.

My parole officer didn't play. When the people from the mall called and told her that I had quit, she got in touch with me and said I had twenty-four hours to find another job and to give her proof of employment, or by the twenty-fifth hour she'd have my black ass back in jail for breakin' parole. And yeah, those were her exact words.

My only choice was to work for my mom's brother, my Uncle Roger. He had his own small business as a roofer. He also did handy man stuff around Trenton. I knew it was gonna be a bad idea to work for him, but I needed something quick, and anything was better than that mall shit. I didn't want to but I picked up the phone, dialed Uncle Roger and had to beg his old ass to give me a job. First thing came out his mouth was, "Now boy, you know I can't pay you much cause business kinda slow." Bull-shit, I was thinkin' to myself. He was just tight as hell and didn't want to get up off the dough. You could never catch Uncle Roger without a wad of cash in his pocket. Now he was a true hustler. Even though his main gig was his roofing business, the handy man title covered everything else. He'd cut your grass, paint your house, fix your car, anything just to make a buck.

His own son, my cousin, Sho Nuff and I were hangin'' out one night when we caught a flat tire. I ain't have no spare in the Trans Am so we called him to come out and pick us up from downtown. Uncle Roger charged us twenty dollars for making him get out of his bed. But the main reason I didn't want to work for him was because when I was young, after my father left us, my mom used to make me work for him. During the summer months, we'd take care of people's lawns. Uncle Roger had me and Sho Nuff out there in the scorching sun all day long then at the end of the week after he made his money, he'd give us fifty dollars each. And if we missed a day he'd have the nerve to try and deduct shit. Fuckin' ten dollars a day for breakin' your back and bakin' in the hot sun. I'll never for get that slave wage mess. So yup, I went to work for Unc and just like I expected he paid just enough to cover the rent and put gas in the Trans.

Might as well had moved in with my mom cause I was eatin' dinner over her house every night. Shopping from the kitchen of Judith Colbirth. All up in my mom's refrigerator and cupboards fillin' a plastic bag full of food bringin' it back to my crib. Talkin' 'bout makin' a brothah feel *less than*. At least in jail I felt like a man. Don't get me wrong, I don't ever want to be locked down *ever* again. But at least back then I had dreams of how it would be when I got out. Shit, my day to day reality was fuckin' depressin'!

Not that I needed much, but I wanted shit. Life sucked when you saw a pair of Georgio Brutini's you wanted, but your phone, cable and fuckin' public service was due. Later for the food, cause like I said I ate over mom's, but you *need* lights. A brothah ain't tryin to sit up in no dark apartment with Georgio's on his feet.

One thing I learned back then was never say things can't get no worse. Six weeks after my release, right in the midst of my fight to stay on my own and not have to move back with my mom, Debbie announced that she was pregnant. *Pregnant*! Now if I couldn't take care of myself without struggling, how in the hell was I gonna take care of a kid? "Yo, we gonna do this." I told her trying to keep it tight. Cause well, I was still on that righteous high from being locked down. You know, true to my lady and all. But when the baby entered the world, workin' for Uncle Roger just wasn't makin' it. Now I had another mouth to feed besides my own, and I wasn't about to expect my mom to feed me and my kid. That would have been weak, and I *ain't* no weak brothah. I takes care of mine.

My partner Bubby came over to my crib and we was kickin' it man-to-man. He said, "Hassan, man look at you all stressed out over bills. Now take a look at me," he said pointing to himself. "I ain't stressin' about nothin'." And he wasn't stressin'. My man was geared up in his two hundred dollar sneaks, hundred fifty dollar name brand sweat suit, drivin' a brand new Ford Bronco. And true dat, I was *tired of stressin'*!

Bubby turned me back on to a life that when I was locked down and swearin' the straight and narrow, I said I'd leave behind. The drug life. And word, just like he said, the money was plenty! After a short while, not only could I afford food, diapers, and booties for my baby's feet, I got myself a couple pairs of Brutini's.

That righteous high didn't last for too long afterwards either. Couldn't blame Debbie for not wanting to put up with my creepin'. I mean we had a beautiful son that she made her number one priority over my shit, and rightfully so. Because, honies were jockin' this jail house physique and I was all about makin' up for lost time. Wasn't even tryin' to slow my roll.

My thoughts were interrupted by the door opening and closing shut as a lady walked inside the carwash and up to the glass. She stared through as the foamy soap began to spray onto the hood of her car. Standing to my feet, I stretched then walked up front to pay the woman at the register then she handed me a receipt. As I opened the metal door and walked outside the sun had sort of a blinding affect. I walked over to the little dude wiping my ride down and handed him the register receipt. Then gave my LS 400 the once over walking all around it to make sure everything was straight. It was. Opening my sunroof, I tuned into Power 99FM and drove off.

A Man and His Ride

Friday morning, and it was time for finals at school. Shoving the last piece of toast in my mouth, I zipped up Kiara's sweater, and strapped Tianna into her stroller. We rushed out of the apartment. My bookbag and Tianna's baby bag weighed down one shoulder, one of my hands held the stroller handle, and the other held Kiara's hand. I was strapped.

As we approached the bus stop I noticed two guys watching me. One good looking brothah was sitting in this big black Lexus. The other was leaning inside talking. As we walked past them, the guy on the inside said, "Baby, you need a ride? I'll take you anywhere you wanna go."

"No thanks," I answered and kept on walking.

Why would someone as fine as that even be interested in a woman like me. He looked like one of those dudes who only dated sophisticated women, *Miss Five Thousand*, and that definitely wasn't me. The bus came, we got on, and started our day.

Much to my delight Friday flew pass. I had a good day at school and looked forward to some "me" time this weekend. When we lived with Mom, she wanted us out of the house so bad. Now that we've moved out, she comes and gets the girls *every single* weekend. "I miss my grandbabies so bad," she would say. "I'll come and get them on the weekends. This way you can have some time to yourself." Lord knows I did need the rest this week. Studying for finals and dealing with Tianna's teething all night long just wore me out. Daddy came to get them around six. Kiara and Tianna were so glad to see him. They loved their grandpop. I walked him and the girls outside to the car and saw them off.

After they left, I went over to the bench where Jeannette was sitting. We watched the fellahs play B-ball. She was drinking a brew, and had an unopened can by the side of her leg.

"You want some," she offered.

"No thanks! I told you, I don't drink."

"Good for you, but if Pee Wee don't get his ass off that court, I'm gonna drink his other beer when I'm finished this one," she said laughing, taking the can of Bud to her mouth. "You wanna get a soda, then?"

"No money," I patted my pockets.

"I'll get it for you. Come on, let's walk to the store." Jeannette had a buzz on.

The temperature was pleasant. It was hot, but there was a nice breeze in the air. We walked down to Kim's Korean Mini Market on the corner. Every time I went into this store, I'd find the Korean owners arguing with some brothah over something.

"You put dat back or you buy, you buy!"

"Fuck you, you Korean mothah fuckah! You buy it if you want somebody to buy this shit so bad!"

This went on from the time the store opened up, early in the morning, until the time it closed in the wee hours of the night.

Me, personally, I gave these merchants an A+ for bravery. They took on the baddest of the bad in this neighborhood. Makes me laugh though, I wondered if this is what they imagined when they dreamt about the American dream.

When we left the store I spotted that black Lexus I saw this morning. It was parked across the street.

"Jeannette, do you know who drives that car over there?" She knew exactly who I was talking about before I even got a chance to point out the car.

"Yeah, why?" she asked with a surprised grin on her face, "Sister Mary No Man, finally tired of living the nun life huh?" Jeannette asked, clowning around.

"Stop, girl, I just asked you if you knew him," I said trying not to seem too interested.

"His name is Hassan Colbirth, but he suppose to be all righteous now and everything. He calls himself, Hassan Ali. He's fine, but he's a *coooold blooded* MacDaddy. All the ladies be jockin that dick, and that's for real."

"What you telling me that for? I don't want to get wit 'im I just wondered who he was."

As we walked past, Hassan and his crew were coming from around the building. My stomach rolled up in knots. I could feel him staring at me from behind. Casually I turned my head over my shoulder, and sure enough, I was the center of his attention. He puckered his lips and blew a kiss to me. My heart stopped for a second. Melting, I turned back around with a frozen smile.

"Hassan's diggin' on you girl! You in the house."

Playing it cool like it wasn't a thing I said, "Yeah right. He probably wants to hit it and run, and I ain't' havin' it."

"Hey, Tammy, let's you and me go out tonight?"

"Naw, I don't go out."

"Come on, please," Jeannette begged.

"Where? And besides, I don't have any thing to wear," I said, not really wanting to go. It's been so long since I went to a party, I thought I would embarrass myself trying to dance.

"Chuck's. I can borrow my sister's car and we ain't going to no place that's all that. Just put on some jeans and a nice shirt and you in there."

Jeannette and I waited until around eleven o'clock to leave the apartment. She said she wanted to make an entrance. When we got to the club it was live. The bass was pumpin' so deep I could feel it inside my chest. Energy was high. The place was packed and everyone was having a good time.

I didn't know exactly how wild Jeannette could be. It seemed like she knew everyone in the club. She introduced me to some of her friends, and we danced so much, I thought I was going to fall out. The bar stool was calling my name so I walked over and took a seat and watched Jeannette dance. It didn't seem that she would ever get tired. Her slender dark frame was smooth as she clubbed, twisting and jamming, and never missing a beat. It was in her step, the way that she bopped - she loved it here.

"You gonna order anything?" the barmaid asked.

"No thanks, I'm fine."

"Well, honey, how you expect me to make any money if you not gonna buy something. You just gonna sit there with your sexy smile? OK then, if you need anything just yell," she said laughing. After wiping the bar in front of me, she slung the white towel over her shoulder, and walked off to wait on someone else.

Jeannette came over to me excited, "Guess who just walked in here?"

"Who?" I said equally as excited.

"Look over by the pool table."

It was Hassan and his presence was large. People were all around him talking and laughing. My heart fluttered.

"Oh my God! How do I look?" We ran into the bathroom. Jeannette fluffed my hair as I put on more lipstick in the oversized mirror, which by the way, was the only thing nice about the yucky bathroom with the tacky 1970-looking, yellow, wall paper.

"You got any perfume on you?" I asked Jeannette.

"You know I do, girl." She pulled a small bottle of 'Beautiful' out of her purse.

I got all dolled up then I started to think. "Jeannette, wait a minute. I got two kids. What is he gonna want with me?" Self-pity is a M-F.

"Look, T, don't even go there. You're pretty. You got your head on right. You got a lot to offer a man, and you should know that. Besides I know Hassan, and he ain't like that. He's a real cool dude, and if not, fuck 'im."

When we came out of the bathroom all fine and freshened up, some female was all up on Hassan. It looked like she was trying to get him to take her home and fuck her brains out. Hassan was leaning up against the cigarette machine, and she was kickin' it all up in his face. She looked hot. She had long hair, *probably a weave*, and a tight, short blue dress that showed off her thick, curvaceous body. She was all over him, and he seemed to like what he saw. Feeling let down was putting it mildly, more like someone pushed me down the stairs, was about right. Realistically, I didn't stand a snowball's chance next to her. Their bodies were close, and Hassan was looking down at her smiling. Then he whispered something in her ear, she giggled and left.

Jeannette patted me on the shoulder and went back on the dance floor. Following her, I danced for a while, but I just couldn't get myself back into the swing of things. My eyes were locked on Hassan. The guy I danced with was talking to me, but being so engrossed with following Hassan around the room, his words were just not registering. Hassan walked around the bar talking to everybody. He was leaning on the back of another girl's chair for the longest time. Hoping he would notice me, I got off the dance floor and sat down, but by then Hassan was gone.

I was tired and I guess I looked the part. The bar maid looked at me and playfully smiled. She walked over, filled a glass with ice, and placed it in front of me.

"Here, doll, I know you can use this," and she filled it with orange juice. "I don't know what your pleasure is, but everyone loves OJ. It's on the house." More play was coming my way from her tonight than from the fellahs.

Sipping on the cold juice I had to admit, yes I needed it cause dehydration was definitely setting in. My eyes started once more searching the room for Hassan. Bingo! In the corner, I spotted him talking to some dude. What was up with him, didn't he see me? Maybe not, because if he did, it sure didn't make sense that he didn't come over and say anything, after all, he acknowledged me in the street. Fed up, I motioned to

Jeannette from the bar stool to come on so we could leave. She held up her index finger, and kept on dancing. After what seemed like a lifetime of waiting, she finally dragged herself off the floor.

"You ready to go already? The place will be closed in another hour anyway, can't you wait, girl?"

"No I can't wait. You said that you would leave when I was ready, and I'm ready."

Just as we were making our way to the door, I felt someone touch my arm. Glancing back, it was Hassan.

"You leaving already? I was hoping that I could get a dance with you tonight." Speechless and frozen in my tracks, I looked at Jeannette, who in turn looked at my stunned expression and broke into laughter. Without saying a word she threw her hands in the air to the hip-hop beat and bopped all the way back to the dance floor. Turning to Hassan, I managed to say, "Sure. Let's dance."

He took my hand and lead me onto the dance floor. His hand swallowed mine. This can't be real, I thought. We partied for a while and then the DJ announced that they were going to slow the pace down because it was almost time to go. "Before y'all leave my club tonight, I want to make sure that everybody is in the mood for love." He was behind the glass enclosure with the head set pressed to his ear as he mixed in his slow jam, "Make lots of love. Increase the population y'all. 'Cause the more of us there are, the stronger we stand."

Turning away to walk off of the floor, Hassan gently caught my hand, "Where, you going? What's your rush? Come on back here and dance with me for a while."

He looked so fine wearing a white and blue nylon Nike sweat suite, blue T-shirt, and white Nike leather sneakers. Sweat was all on his beautiful black face and on his thick neck. Damn he was sexy. Engulfing me in his big, strong arms, Hassan held me real tight. My body was trembling, pressed close to his chest, and his cologne was intoxicating.

"What you shaking for? I know you ain't cold." Embarrassed, I looked away from him, with a shy smile. "You nervous, lady?" he asked sweetly.

"A little."

"There ain't no need for that. You're in good hands." Hassan smiled devilishly. His full-faced, shadow beard accented his caramel brown skin. He stood about six feet tall with a thick athletic build.

"You live around here?" Hassan asked me looking deep into my eyes.

"I moved to Domtar Courts last May. I just don't hang out too much."

"Yeah, I been checkin' you out. I be seeing you at the bus stop sometimes with two little kids."

I smiled. "You have? I never noticed," I said, lying through my teeth.

"By the way my name is Hassan Ali. What's yours?"

"Tamlyn, but I like to be called *Tammy*."

"Tammy, sexy name for a sexy lady."

The song was just about to end, Hassan ran his nose up and down my neck and then he kissed me softly behind the ear. Electric tingles surged all over my body. The lights came on in the club, and we walked off the floor.

"So Tammy, can I have your phone number?"

Composure! Composure! I ordered my excited mind, "I don't have a phone. But my address is 917 D.C., Tower A. Do you need to write that down?"

"No, baby. I'll remember that," Hassan said. "Peace, lovely."

The entire ride home, a euphoric high held me captive. All Jeannette and I did was rant about Hassan, and how *fly* he was.

For a whole week I had Hassan on the brain. Vividly I could smell his cologne, and feel the sensation of his hands on my waist. I wondered if he would *really* come by to see me or if he was just playin' with my mind. Jeannette and I were outside enjoying the weather and watching the fellahs playing B-ball underneath the setting sun. At first I didn't want to move into Domtar Courts, but I had to admit, these people knew how to have a good time. It wasn't even summertime yet and someone was having a barbecue. Someone else's boom box was sounding off by the court, and the kids were riding their bikes up and down a ramp they made from an old mattress and some boards. Feeling quite at home, I was actually having fun buggin' out with Jeannette and the gang. It was then that Hassan drove up in his Lexus. My heart quickened and I couldn't take my eyes off of him. Dressed to impress in a pair of black trousers and cool looking button down beige short sleeve shirt, he walked over to where we were sitting on the bench. As he approached me, I know I must have looked silly, because I had this big ole cheese smile plastered across my face. Tianna was in my arms and Kiara was playing with the other kids.

I wasn't dress anything like him. I had on some junk I threw together out of that summer bag. An above the knee white skirt with yellow flowers, yellow shirt and white bobo sneakers I got from the dollar store, but I worked it.

"What's up, Jeannette?"

"You money," she responded with her lips pocked out, deliberately checking him out from the top of his *just out of the barber's chair* haircut, to his gold buckle alligator-skinned belt, all the way down to his black leather sandal shoes. That girl was shameless.

He looked at me and tapped me on my crossed leg. "How you doing, gorgeous? Is this your daughter?"

"Yeah, this is Tianna and that's Kiara over there playing," I said pointing. My babies were now one and two years old.

"I see they take good looks after their mother. Can I talk to you for a minute?" he asked twirling his keys in his hand.

"I'll look after them for you," Jeannette said, taking Tianna out of my arms. I got up, and we started walking.

"So Tammy, what's up in your life. You got a man?"

"No, I'm not seeing anyone right now. I'm just trying to finish high school."

"You in high school?"

"I was suppose to graduate last year, but I dropped out when I had my daughter. I'll be finished next month," I said proudly. "And I'll be so glad."

"What you got planned after that?"

"Hopefully college." I shrugged my shoulders. "I don't know. I'm just trying to get through this last month."

Just then some dude yelled, "Yo! Yo, Hass! Yo, Hass! Come here, man!"

"Excuse me, baby, let me go see what this dude wants."

As he jogged away I drooled over how fine he looked. Much to my disappointment though, it was obvious what they were doing. Hass and the guy took a walk to his car and I could see their exchange taking place. This was a real turn-off to me so I just walked away. Call me stupid, but it had never dawned on me that Hassan was into the drug scene. After he was finished, Hassan caught up to me.

"What's your rush, Tammy?"

"No rush."

"Sorry about that. I just had to take care of some business." We continued talking about everything. The conversation was nice, but I just couldn't see myself talking to no drug dealer. Then he popped the question, "So Tammy, you gonna let me take you out?"

"Hassan, not to be funny or anything, but I'm just not about what you're about."

"Excuse me?" he asked, knowing exactly what I meant. Hassan's sunny disposition turned cloudy, "Well tell me, baby, what are you about?"

Maybe I should have been more diplomatic, cause if looks could kill. "You too good for me?" It was obvious that Hassan Ali was not used to being turned down. "You and your *college plans* too good for a homeboy like me?" With his arms gesturing his every word, his tone was on the loud side. "Sorry I wasted your time, baby. So why don't you step before I waste any more."

He *totally* misunderstood what I was trying to say, maybe I said it wrong, but he wasn't going to let me explain so I just walked away. Crunched! I mean, I really felt bad, because I wanted Hassan to be the *one*. Ever since I left Mark, there has been a void. Something inside of me *thought* that Hassan would be the one to fill it. Guess it was wishful thinking.

Grabbing Tianna from Jeannette's arms I yelled, "Kiara! Kiara you hear me! Come on!" She jumped up out of the dirt.

Jeannette stood there yelling, "What happened, T? What happened?"

Embarrassment wouldn't allow me to stay there and explain, all I wanted to do was get out of there. Ignoring her, I kept on walking. I looked back, and Jeannette and Hassan were talking.

Several minutes later there was a knock on the door. "Tammy, let me in. It's me, Jeannette." She stepped inside like she had a problem with me, "What happened out there? First y'all were getting along fine, then what happened?"

"I just got myself embarrassed out there, that's what happened. He asked me to go out with him, and I told him that I wasn't about what he was about."

"You said what?" her mouth dropped open and her eyes stretched, "No wonder he went off. How did you think he got that fuckin' black Lexus and all those clothes you think looks so good on him? Look, Tammy, just because he's out there hustling don't make him a bad person," she said with an attitude.

"What? Are trying to say that I'm wrong? Like I don't have the right to choose who I want and don't want to be with? Is that what you're saying?" I got on the defensive.

"It's mighty funny that last week you wanted him so bad and now you don't. Don't judge him for what he's out here doing. Get to know the man first, then if you don't like him that's your business. Go talk to him, Tammy."

"Shit, Jeannette. He just told me off. I'm not going out there."

"Fuck that. Do you want to get to know the brothah, or what?"

It puzzled me why Jeannette was so upset because I wouldn't jump at the chance to talk to Hassan. He was big around the hood, true, but that didn't impress me. To get her off my back I agree, as she put it, *to get to know him*.

"He's still down there. Go talk to him."

"Hell no, are you crazy?" I was going to talk to him but not this soon. Not today, and certainly not now!

"I wouldn't steer you wrong. You're my girl, and I know how he is. He wants you and his pride is hurt. If you go out there you can make things right."

"If I go out there and he dogs me again, I'ma kick your butt."

"Go ahead, find out for yourself," Jeannette coaxed.

"Don't rush me," I said playfully, rolling my eyes at her.

The pounding of my heart echoed in my ears as I walked sweaty palmed over to where he was standing talking to one dude. "Peace man, I'll catch you later." They did a soul shake and the guy left. Hassan eyed me down, with his arms folded. "What's on your mind, Miss?"

"I been talking to Jeannette and she said I read you all wrong."

Before I could finish what I was saying, Hassan cut me off. "Read me wrong? You didn't read me at all. You don't even know me, and you talking about, *you ain't about what I'm about*. How you know what I'm about?"

"Look Hassan, you gonna let me finish? What I'm trying to say is, I want a chance to read you alright?"

Hassan looked at me and slowly nodded his head and softly said, "Yeah."

"Hassan."

"What, baby?"

"Why did you go off on me like that earlier? The only thing I was trying to say was..."

"Squash It," he interrupted me again.

"What do you mean squash it? That shit was messed up."

"Look I said squash it, and I mean squash it. What happened earlier today don't have nothin' to do with right now so just drop the subject like it never even happened." Hassan pulled me close to his body. He wrapped his arms around me and said, "Do you think you can do that?"

All I could think was that this brothah is full of shit. But he was *so* fine.

"You look so good, Tammy." He asked, "Can I kiss you?" Not uttering a single word, I closed my eyes and leaned into him. Hassan's embrace became stronger and his kiss was wet, soft, and so right. As his big hands caressed my back, I lost myself and gave him all those lonely months of pain, all the times when I needed a man's understanding and there was none for me, and definitely- all the times when I had to touch myself in that apartment in the freaking dark. After I gave him my pain, I took the good feeling he was giving- soft lips encompassed around mine, the feel of my head against his hard shoulder, his tongue sucking on mine, *I took it all.*

"You taste good baby," he said and followed up with a luscious peck on the lips.

Hassan made me feel like dynamite - I was about to *blow up*! He stared down at me in my *real* after glow, smiling, "You want to take a ride? I have to go down on the East Side and pick someone up at nine."

"I can't. Jeannette's with the girls, and I told her that I was coming right back."

"Jeannette won't mind, just run up and tell her you're goin' with me."

As I entered the apartment Jeannette was watching my old beat up TV. She looked at me, and I couldn't hold back my big ole grin. I was so excited and I think I lit up the whole room. Jeannette yelled, "See, see I told you that he was down. What happened? Y'all alright now?"

"Yes. Thank you, Jesus! We are alright now." My arms were stretched up in the air. Quickly, I gave her a run down of what happened. "Jeannette I have a big favor to ask you, and I'll owe you one, big time. Can you watch the girls for me? Hass asked me to take a ride with him."

"You know I'll watch them, girl. Just don't do nothin' that I won't do," she said opening her legs wide and laughing.

"You don't have to worry about that. It's that time of the month," I said still laughing.

"I'm gonna take Kiara and Tianna over to my house so I can get relaxed and watch a real TV. I'll see you when you get back." She laughed.

Hassan was waiting by his car. I was apprehensive as he opened the door for me. Messin' around with a drug dealer wasn't right. This went against everything I believed in. I see the females around here dragging their kids all times of night going to buy drugs. Not to mention the fellahs who done sold their souls for a crack pipe. When you look into their eyes- no one's home, just an abandoned body wondering after its next hit. I always wondered what kind of pig did it take to do that to people.

"Is everything alright with Jeannette and your kids?" Hassan asked, breaking my train of thought.

"Yeah, she didn't mind."

"Jeannette knows you're running with good company, that's why."

Getting in the car, Hassan closed the door behind me and I thought I was in another world- the planet luxurious. Oh my goodness! Hassan's Lexus was even nicer on the inside than it was on the out, and the outside was laid! It had black soft leather seats, pitch clear CD stereo system, a nice smell of incense, dark tinted windows, and sunroof. It was strictly first class, all the way. Jeannette had warned me with a stern, "When you get in that car don't you act goofy. Act like you're used to it. Just sit back and relax."

And that's just what I did. "You have a nice car, Hassan."

"Yeah thanks. I've had it about six months." Hassan had on an old Prince CD, *The Beautiful Ones*.

"I haven't heard this song in a long time. I love Prince."

"Yeah, Prince is the Man. I got all of his music from way back. I don't care too much for his movies though."

"Well what kind of movies do you like?" As we were talking, I drank in every word he said, watching his mouth, the way his muscles moved in his jaw and the way he talked with his hands when he was deep in conversation.

We talked a little about family. He told me that he had a three-year-old son named Erkell. We talked a little about our past relationships. He told me that he wasn't involved with anyone right now but, that the only woman he saw regularly was his son's mother. They agreed to have a civil relationship because of their son. He assured me that it was strictly platonic, that she had a man. When I talked, he listened to me as if I were saying the most interesting stuff. Every now and then he would say that I was so pretty. I would blush.

We came to the corner of Market and Broad, where there was a guy standing, waiting. Hassan pulled up next to him, the automatic locks popped, and this dude got into the back seat.

He looked at me. "How you doing!" Then to Hassan. "Right on time, man."

"Don't I always take care of you?" Hassan stuck his hand back and the guy slapped it. "Yo, this is my girl, Tamlyn. Tammy this is Chief. That's short for Chief Rocker." They laughed, and I was smiling. I loved to hear *man talk*. Leaning toward Hassan, with my legs crossed, now I felt like *Miss Five Thousand*.

"So, Chief, you take care of that?" Hassan asked with one eye on the road and the other on my thighs.

"Yeah, I called Sho Nuff, and he supposed to meet us there in an hour," answered

Chief.

I was just checking out their *fly* names: Chief Rocker and Sho Nuff. We drove over to a house and Hassan parked the car. "I'll be right back." He left the car running and they both got out. Resting my chin on my knuckles, I was thinking over the events of the day. It all was so crazy; it was literally tripping me out. First, Hassan and I were cursing each other out, now I was chillin' in his ride. And I wonder what he meant when he told Chief that I was his girl?

The evening was exciting. It felt a little dangerous and mysterious. What they were talking about had to have something to do with drugs, and I wondered what they were doing in that house. *What am I doing*?! What if we got pulled over by the cops? But...damn he was so fine! And I really loved his car, and the attention he gave me. No, this ain't right. But...I could get used to this.

To watch Hassan was entrancing, just the way he carried himself. He exuded self-confidence like he actually believed he was invincible. Hassan and Chief looked powerful together. They returned to the car, and we were off again.

Hassan drove me back to Domtar Courts. He leaned over and kiss me on the lips. "I'll catch up to you later."

Chief took my place in the front seat. "Peace, my dear."

"Good night," I said back, feeling a bit starry-eyed. And indeed it was a good night. The sky was pitch black, but there wasn't a sad or lonely cell in my entire body.

Hassan waited until I entered the lobby then pulled off.

A New Life

I took the girls to day care, came back home and jumped back into bed. It was a school day, but I didn't feel like going. Being mommy and student had me burnt out. For the rest of the day, staying in bed watching talk shows and catching up on the soaps were the only thing on my agenda.

Someone knocked on the door. Grimacing at the clock, it was just past eight. Jeannette was my girl and all, but this was my time. Hearing her gossip was not on my list of to do's I grumbled to myself. Grabbing my robe off the bottom of the bed, I slipped it on over my panties and bras and walked to the door prepared to send her away. A second knock.

"Just a minute."

The peep hole was cemented closed, so I couldn't see who it was until I opened the door. "Hassan." Standing there with my mouth open, I couldn't believe that he actually came to see me. Feeling naked, I knew he could see through my thin robe. "Hey, come on in." Boy I was sure glad I cleaned up last night.

He walked in and his eyes definitely saw through my robe. "Hey girl, you always answer your door lookin' like that?"

"I thought you were Jeannette."

"I hope you don't mind me dropping by."

"No I don't mind. How you know I was home? I'm usually in school at this time," I asked smiling.

"I got my ways."

Feeling a bit exposed, I thought it would be a good idea to get dressed. "Excuse me for a minute, I'm gonna go and put some clothes on."

"No don't do that. You look so good right now. Don't spoil it."

As I walked toward my room to change, he gently grabbed my arm, pulling me into his. Looking me in the eyes he kissed me deep, untying the belt on my robe. Hassan's big strong hands caressed my bare sides, and the small of my back. Cupping my behind, he started to grind. It felt good. I can't lie, but he was moving too fast. My hands went up to his chest as I backed away. Catching my breath, I retied my robe and got back into his arms.

He kissed me smiling, "You something else."

Hassan had beautiful dark eyes, and the way he used them to stare at me was unnerving. "What?"

"You know what." And I did! We sat on the couch and talked. Hassan and I clicked. Our conversation was so easy it felt like we knew each other for a long time instead of just a couple weeks. And he tripped me out being all relaxed in my apartment for the first time. One leg on my coffee table, while his head leaned against my shoulder as we laugh at some crazy thing he said. Clear out of the blue he said, "Baby, I'm starvin'. I been out all night. Do you think you could fix me some breakfast?"

Breakfast, I thought? Pushing him up so he would look at me, I said, "You're assuming that I have food in the fridge, which I do, but what if I didn't?"

"Well then, I'd have to take you put to breakfast," he said confidently.

"Good answer." Damn, there was something about *Hassan* that made me want to jump in his lap and call him daddy. Breakfast, no problem. I'd been cooking ever since I was ten, and in the kitchen I could *throw down*! I made cheesy grits, eggs, sausage, toast and orange juice. Would have made him some coffee too, but there was none in the cupboard. Hassan doesn't eat pork, I learned when he asked me what kind of sausages was on the plate. He told me I shouldn't eat it either. How fast can you say *history*. After breakfast he asked if I would mind him chilling out and watching television, while I cleaned up my kitchen. Embarrassed I told him sure, but he would have to unplug the TV and wheel it into the living room. Hassan went into the bedroom, alright, but he didn't come back out.

It only took me fifteen minutes to clean up the dishes, but when I walked into my room, Hassan was stretched across my bed on his back sleeping. Standing in the doorway with my arms folded, I admired how gorgeous that black man looked on my, let me repeat, my bed. Simply put, he was beautiful. A chuckle slipped through my lips as I thought about the movie Misery. Relating to the character, I too could have shackled Hassan to that bed so he would never leave.

Ummm, I was getting so moist staring at the lump between his open legs. Those cotton sweat pants weren't hiding a thing. I wanted to feel him inside of me, I thought as my entire body grew hot! No, this is too soon. Yes! No! Yes! As my body and mind went to war, my robe dropped on the floor. Slowly I unsnapped my bras, then stepped out of my panties, whispering, "Please don't break my heart, 'cause I could really fall for a brothah like you." I crawled between Hassan's legs and placed my naked body down on him and my lips on his juicy full mouth. He must have been real tired, 'cause he was snoring. Then gently I kissed him again. Hassan opened up his eyes startled and he realized what I was about to give him.

He rolled me over getting on top covering my mouth with his soft warm lips. Hassan then stood up with this intense look on his face. His eyes were locked into mine as he took off his clothes. As he stood there bare, all I could think of was I was right, he is beautiful. My thoughts must have slipped out cause he started stroking himself and said, "Wait til you feel me." Hassan laid all of his two-hundred and ten pound sexy body on top of mine. "Tamlyn..." He called deeply in my ear, but he didn't say anything else.

My finger tips traced his body like a blind man reading braille. The hardness of his cut muscles were wrapped in baby smooth skin and a light covering of hair laid across his bulging pecks. Hassan cupped my face and we began to kiss like we were lost lovers reunited. Taking his time, he crept down my neck, to my breasts, sucking and circling around my nipples with his tongue. With eyes closed I meditated on the sensual feeling flowing through my body. Slowing my breath to control my racing heart, I didn't ever want that feeling to end. Leaving a trail of kisses down my belly, Hassan's warm breath rippled between my legs. Automatically my knees bent until my feet were flat on the sheets. Hassan's mouth encompassed me and his hot tongue went places were only my dream man has gone before. At that delicious feeling, tears streamed out of my eyes. "Ooo Hass..an" soft and easy I repeated over and over. He was making me high, out of my mind. His tongue was rubbing up against the most sensitive parts of my walls, and just as I was floating on his cloud he switched the gears and started nursing my pearl. The intensity was too much. With heels now dug into the sheet, I straightened my knees separating myself from him.

Hassan looked up smiling this quizzical smile, "Nobody ever ate you before?" I shook my head no.

"Let me teach you." Sliding back down onto the bed, Hassan continued where he left off. The contrast was like night and day...like soft and hard. Then I quickly remembered that he was an experienced man, not some high school boy. Shamelessly, I yelled, panted and moaned. Passion was so explosive in my little room that I imagined all of Domtar Courts heard me and was cheering me on. After I was completely satisfied, Hassan moved up on me hard as steel. He was sweating, and had this serious I'm ready look on his face. "You protected?" he asked catching his breath.

"Yeah...I'm on the pill." After I had Tianna, I got on the pill. Even though I didn't have a man and wasn't having sex, being on the pill in a strange kinda way it made me feel better. I did think about getting on the pill after Mark and I became sexually involved, but I was so afraid of my mother finding it, that I didn't. "You got protection?" I asked him.

"Yeah, but I wanna feel you." I wanted to feel him too. Laying between my brown thighs, he pushed, but my zone wouldn't open up for him. Driven by blind passion, Hassan persisted and persisted until we were one. As I held him tight around his cobra shaped back, I didn't remember it hurting when Mark and I did it, but when Hassan penetrated me, boy, did it hurt. I felt like a virgin all over again. In his arms we kissed slow as he long-stroked. He made sure I felt every bit of his thickness. He'd pull back almost to the point of withdrawal, then resubmerging deep to the bottom right into my spot! Delirious, I never had it this good. My juices poured as I started to cum again. After Hassan said, "Oh girl, you got some good pussy," I knew he was there too. "Damn, baby, this shit is good." He said deeply in my ear as he feverishly pumped his body into mine.

While he came I opened up my eyes to watch his expression, listening to the husky groans he made. I felt connected to him as he wrapped his arms tight around me. Hassan's cum felt warm, wet, and so very nasty. I loved it! I was strung over his lovin'.

We laid there in each other's arms, fingers intertwined, talking, kissing, and fondling for almost another hour. We couldn't get enough of each other. When the spell somewhat lifted, it was well into the noon day hour. Pulling ourselves out of my sweat soaked bed to take a shower, my throbbing middle quickly reminded me that I hadn't used it in awhile. Out of the clear blue sky as we got dressed Hassan asked, "You wanna ride up to Philly with me? I wanna get some shoes to match this suit I just brought."

My eyes lit up in disbelief, "I have to be back here by five."

"I'll have you back by five."

Excited, I slid on my jeans and a shirt, and we were off. Although I have lived in Trenton, New Jersey, sandwiched between two major cities, New York and Philadelphia, I had never been to either and always wanted to. Finally I'd be going to see Philadelphia, and with Hassan of all people!

During the ride Hassan asked me so many questions. He wasn't satisfied with just any quick answers. He wanted to know why I felt the way I did about everything.

Hassan handled the road so masterfully. He weaved in and out of the lanes, passing everything in his way. It seemed like forever since I had been on a highway going anywhere. The last long trip I'd been on was down South to grandma's house about eight years ago.

When we arrived in Philadelphia, I was amazed at how large the city looked with all of its tall buildings. We drove past City Hall and Hassan even showed me where Rocky ran up the museum stairs. I was just awed. Hassan parked downtown and we got out and walked around Center City.

Holding hands, we acted like lovers. And Mr. Cool himself was just a clown. Hassan kept me laughing, saying the darndest things at the darndest time. Never in a million years would I have guessed that, the notorious Hassan Ali had such a shot out humorous side to him.

Did he show this side of himself to everyone- I doubted it. So why me? Did he slip up? Did I sneak inside of him, like he snuck inside of me? There was no way in the world that I thought it possible for me to be so infatuated with a drug dealer. Did I get into his soul in a way that he hadn't expected? I wanted to ask him, 'What do you see when you look at me?' but I didn't, cause he probably wouldn't know. So many questions. He pulled me into a boutique and bought me a genuine Gucci bag that I had admired through the window. Wow!

The weather was picture perfect out, and after a lot of walking we finally reached the men's shoe store. Hassan picked out these funky burgundy alligator skin shoes that cost almost three hundred dollars and brought a matching belt. He was spending money like it was *no thang*. I can't lie, I was also in awe with this brothah's money knot. Going through the financial hardships of living in the projects and being on welfare was a *hard* thing! To smell poverty...the urine in the hallways, to taste poverty...the packaged instant noodles and kool aid that the girls and I ate from around the twentieth of the month until the end when the food stamps arrive on the first. Something in me didn't feel that it was right for Hassan to have all of that money and spend it so freely, but a bigger part of me craved to have some of it spent on me.

To top off our Philadelphia atmosphere, on our way back to the car we stopped and got hot dogs and soda from a street vendor. By then, it was almost four o'clock. During the ride home I was on cloud nine. Hassan was steady talking about everything that came to his mind. I was just hanging on his every word. In front of my building he dropped me off. Said he had somewhere else to go. Kissing my lips, he asked, "Did you have a nice time?"

"Yes, a very nice time! Can't you tell?"

"Good. I'll catch you later on then."

There were a lot of people outside. Fellahs on the court and females sitting on the benches talking, kids playing. Looking around, it seemed like everyone was watching me step out of that Lexus. It felt good!

Just four days after the trip to Philly, I went to Hassan's apartment. The girls were at day care, and I had finished my exams early that morning. I had talked to him on the phone once since I saw him last. I was so nervous because I didn't want him to treat me like a one-night-stand. He didn't.

Before I left school, I called Hassan on the pay phone and asked him if he felt up to having company. He welcomed my call and the suggestion. The entire bus ride to Hassan's I had butterflies dancing around in my stomach. When I arrived, he opened up the door looking so too fine. I just had to smile in anticipation. Hassan had on a pair of blue jeans and a sleeveless T-shirt. "Come on in. I was just making some breakfast. You want some?"

"You cook?" What a pleasant surprised.

"I gotta eat, don't I?"

"Sure, I'll have some." Hassan was breaking a lot of stereotypical images I had of a hustler, like his humorous side, he liked to have fun. But I couldn't picture, Mr. Mac Daddy, rough neck, Mr. Testosterone himself, in a kitchen cooking, and I sure couldn't picture him at the laundromat adding softener to the rinse cycle.

He lived in a house apartment. It was so masculine looking. The walls were beige with brown trim, bamboo shades to the windows, and hardwood floors, In the center of the room there was a big black throw rug, and on top of it was a coffee table made of round smoked glass with antique brass legs. There was a black leather sectional and two black leather director's chairs. His place had this rough exterior. Over on one side of the wall was a huge wooden entertainment unit with a large TV and impressive stereo system inside. He also had some wooden African sculptures around the room. And through the smell of breakfast cooking, I picked up the scent of incense burning.

I threw my bookbag on the couch, and followed him in the kitchen. There was a pot of grits bubbling on the stove and biscuits in the oven.

"I hope you like turkey sausage 'cause I told you already, I don't mess with the pig." He turned the sausages over with a fork.

"I never ate them, but I'm not choosey."

"You'll like 'em. They're just as good as any other."

Hassan scrambled perfect, yellow fluffy eggs that melted in my mouth. Whether it was his cooking or if it was my hunger, I couldn't tell you but damn, that food was good.

Hassan took off his shirt and walked around the apartment with his massive bare chest exposed. His jeans hung low around his contoured hips, and his hairline headed south, right into his pants, where I wanted to be.

Gladly, I washed the dishes for him, letting my mind explore the idea of how it would be, if I lived here with him and washed his dishes every day. Hassan walked up behind me and started to kiss my neck.

"Come on, baby. Why don't you do that later?"

"Don't you want me to finish these dishes?"

"I want something else from you."

Hassan rubbed himself up against my behind, and I knew exactly what he wanted. Turning around, we got busy. He cupped my face in his big hands and put his tongue in my mouth. I was weak.

"You wanna see my room?"

"Your room? What kind of girl do you think I am?" My hands flung to my hips and I looked at him through the corner of my eyes.

"Why don't you show me what kind of girl you are," he replied, looking seductively in my eyes rubbing his hand across his own nipples. What in the world did I do so good to deserve this. Drying my hands I followed Hassan into his room.

It was cozy. There wasn't much furniture, just his bed, a chair, and a cherry wood highboy. The box spring and mattress were on the floor. It was covered with a nice, dark blue and maroon down comforter and matching sheets. The floor was covered with wall-to-wall carpeting. Hassan said he couldn't stand the coldness of putting his bare feet on the floor in the morning.

Hassan flopped down on the bed, unzipping his jeans. Stepping out of my clothes piece by piece, I twirled them around, prancing. Hassan's eyes were hungry as I teased him. He grabbed his 'man size' and stroked it firmly. It turned me on to see him this hot.

"Come on to daddy, baby. Come on and ride this big horse."

I climbed on and rode him right into the sunset.

Collecting My Props

June had come, and it was the day I had anticipated for so long. Finally, I was graduating. My parents were very proud that I had finished high school. They hoped I'd attend the community college in the fall.

Mom drove some of us in her car, dad piled some in his, Tim drove his own car, and Jimmy, his wife, Sharon and their girls met us at the high school. It was wonderful having them all there for me. Kiesha took the girls as I joined my class in the center of the football field. It was decorated with hundreds of flowers. It wasn't long before the commencement ceremony began. Our principal Mr. Jones began his speech about us entering the real world - what a laugh, I was already in it.

Two week prior to that night, Mrs. Palmer called me into her office and gave me a pleasant surprise. She informed me that she wanted to give me an award. Blown away, I gladly accepted, but didn't tell my parents about the award. I wanted them to be surprised. Mrs. Palmer approached the podium.

"This award is entitled Academic Achievement While Overcoming Unsurmountable Odds. It was founded for students who do not have the ideal surrounding conducive for their studies. In today's society a lot of our youth fall through the cracks, and some of them are lost to us forever. And then we have some shining stars who, regardless of their situations, somehow excel. This year I have chosen a special young lady to present this award to. She, at the tender age of seventeen, dropped out of school to become a full-time mother of two children. Although she admits that keeping her studies up was difficult, she didn't give up. Instead, with the support of her family, faculty and friends, was not only able to come back to school, but she is graduating today within the top ten percentile of the graduating class. This special young lady, serves as a role model for many of today's youth to prove that hard times don't mean the end of the road, but that hard times mean we have to be that much tougher in our convictions toward excellence. This year

I am proud to present this award to Tamlyn Blake for a job well done."

Standing up from my seat, I paused before continuing my journey to the podium. My heels were digging into the turf and I was praying I didn't lose a shoe on the way there. Thunderous applause from my classmates, and the crowd hushed to a single shout of 'Go Tammy!' that sounded like Tim's big mouth. I laughed. Mrs. Palmer had tears in her eyes. My mind went back to the day that I walked into her office with my babies, not knowing if I would ever see this day. An overwhelming feeling of emotion took over me. Falling into the cushioned embrace of Mrs. Palmer, we held each other tightly and the crowd applauded once more.

"Thank you," I said to her.

"You deserve it Tamlyn. You really do." She handed me a plaque that I raised high toward my parents' seat, and they waved proudly. The graduation lasted two hours. Tamlyn A. Blake, a high school graduate. Yeah! I like the sound of that. To celebrate the whole family drove to PJ's Southern Styles, an all you can eat restaurant. We took up an entire section by ourselves.

That Saturday night, I went over to Jeannette's house. I had left a note on my door to let Hassan know where to find me. When he showed up, he had four tickets for a party boat in Philly. He asked Bull and Jeannette to hang out with us to help me celebrate my graduation and nineteenth birthday since it was tomorrow.

CLOSER TO YOU

Summertime! It was hot as heck up in my apartment. The fan was in my window blowing full speed, but the only thing coming out was a blast of hot air. I had on a pair of shorts and a tank top, but I wished I could have been butt naked. Jumping off of the couch I answered the knock at the door.

"Tammy, Hassan's on the phone for you."

My face lit up like a diamond in the sky.

"Hi Aunt Jeanie."

"Hey Kiara mama. Give Aunt Jeannette a kiss."

In one second flat, I was in Jeannette's apartment grabbing the phone, "Hi, Hassan." That man melted me in my shoes.

"Hey baby girl, how you doin'?"

"I'm fine babe, and you?"

"Good wit you all up in my ear. Listen, I gotta go get my son and take 'im for a hair cut. I was thinkin' bout brining him by to meet you later on tonight. You want me to get you anything on the way?"

"All I need is you Hass."

"Well you got me baby. I'll be seeing you later on. Tammy, who thinks you're the finest female in Trenton?"

Covering my mouth, I laughed. He was so silly. "You do."

"And what's my name?"

"Ha-ssan," I said in my most sexy voice.

"Sho you right. I'm outy."

Floating back into my apartment, I fell on the couch next to Jeannette.

"Ahhh ha ha ha!!!" I was showing all thirty two of my teeth.

"What? What did he say, girl? Come on dish it." She said grinning.

"He's going to bring his son over here to meet me."

"Oh Tammy, that's so deep. Now, he wouldn't be doin' all that if he wasn't serious about you."

"I know! I know! Woo, let me calm myself down before I go completely insane. You know Jeannette, I don't know when I've felt this high. My graduation..." I pointed to my diploma on top of my table, "My man...oh God, my man!" As I kicked my feet up in the air, my fist banged against the couch, "Girl, I feel so good I could burst!"

"That's the way it should be. It's about time. You need to loosen up and have some fun every now and then. Speaking of fun, you wanna take the girls to the park. I have a couple hours before I have to be at work."

"Yeah sure, I'm wit it."

We spent a nice afternoon at the park. On the way home we waited with Jeannette until her bus came, then we walked the rest of the way ourselves. Once at the apartment, I gave the girls a bath and put them on a fresh set of clothes. Jumping into the shower myself, I also changed clothes. It was coming up on six o'clock and I was starvin' like Marvin. Home made fried chicken hadn't graced my pots in a while so that's what I decided to make.

When Tianna started walking two months ago, the girl was nonstop. Everything had to be moved from her reach. She was a late walker-fifteen months, and boy was she trying to make up for lost time. She and Kiara were in their room. It looked like one big toy box. Toys were everywhere.

Turning the fire down on the stove so my chicken wouldn't burn, I rushed to answer the door. My face lit up as Hassan planted a big juicy kiss on my lips. I looked down and there was his son. He was adorable. The same caramel brown completion as Hassan's. His hair was cut very low and brought out the roundness of his little head. His ears stuck out on each side, but when he looked up at me, it was like looking at Hassan. They had the same eyes, the same nose, and the same shaped mouth.

"Oh my goodness Hassan, he looks exactly like you." I laughed 'cause their resemblance was so cute. "Hi Erkell. It's nice meeting you. Your dad talks about you all the time," I said rubbing the top of his smooth head.

"Hi Ms. Tammy. My daddy said that I can play with Tahara and Kiara. Where are they?"

"They're in their room playing. Would you like to meet them?"

Erkell looked up at Hassan.

"Go head li'l man."

Erkell followed me into the room and he fell right into the toys. The girls took to him instantly. In the kitchen I took my chicken off of the stove then joined Hassan. He was sitting in my single chair and summonsed me to sit on his lap.

"Are you hungry? I cooked enough if you want to stay?"

"Only if I can put you on a plate."

Hassan and I got into a heated kissing session on that chair.

"Hassan, we better stop before one of them come out of that room."

"Girl, you tastes *so* damn good! But you're right, I better stop. I have to get Erkell home so I won't have to hear his mama's mouth. Erkell, come on!"

Erkell ran out of the room and so did Kiara and Tianna.

"We leaving Daddy?"

Hassan's son spoke so properly. He wasn't at all the little hood I'd expected.

"Yeah man, tell everybody bye." Hassan said palming his little round head. Watching the two of them together, it was plain to see the love they shared.

"Where he goin?" Kiara asked Hassan.

"I'm takin' him home."

"He goin' home, oh. Where he live at?"

"Kiara, stop asking so many questions, just say bye. Erkell, you come back and visit me again. Okay?"

"Okay."

"I might stop back by later on tonight. I'll call you if I can't make it."

Shaking my head I laughed, "Unless you know something I don't. I don't think Jeannette is going to run out of her bed in the middle of the night and tell me that you're on the phone."

"Damn, I keep forgetting that you don't have a phone. When you gonna get it turned on?"

"Excuse me, but I just can't afford it right now."

Hassan lead me in the kitchen away from the kids. He pulled out a crispy one hundred dollar bill and handed it to me, "Well you get that taken care of tomorrow." Staring in disbelief, I didn't know whether to take the money or refuse.

"Take it." Hassan insisted.

"Hassan, are you sure? That's a lot of money."

"You want your phone on or what?"

"Yeah, but I..."

"But nothing! Take the money and go handle your business." He gave me a kiss then they left.

Chocolate Girl

Digging through my mom's old albums I was singin' in some funky ass high tune. *"Chocolate giiirrrl, oh Chocolate girl, come play in myy ice cream."* I think those were the words to that *Whispers* song.

Damn, if I didn't know any better I would think Tammy done put a root on me. Got me wrapped up in some voodoo shit cause it wasn't my plan to get all caught up in Tammy's life. To me she wasn't nothin' but some more draws to get into. An easy pull, I knew she would be. Young, single mom, no man around, fucked up self-esteem. What was so hard about getting next to that? Nothin'! Like taking candy from a baby. And when she came off talking that smack 'bout not being about what I was about...shit, it was on. In my mind I was gonna show her that 'You don't fuck with Hassan!' But I was gonna get the panties first.

That first morning I went over to her apartment. I seen her as she came back from taking her kids to the day care. I had some business to take care of in her building, but after I was through, I figured I'd make a house call and start collecting on this vendetta. And sure enough, just like I had expected, getting her to give it up was, *no problem*. But something was different.

Fuckin' was nothing new to me. I've had it fast. I've had it slow, but I ain't never felt like I was makin' love before. Not until her. Not until that morning.

Maybe it was Tammy's big brown dreamy eyes that made me forget my reason for being there. Or the precious tears she cried when I was inside of her. Whatever it was, I had Tammy on the brain.

"Ooh Ooh Chocolate giiirl." I crooned the last words of the song, still hunting for that *Whispers* album. I was gonna get it, take it home, and play it until I got enough. "Mom where is it?" I asked, searching through her unorganized collection.

"Keep on looking Hassan, It's right down there. What you all keyed up over that old song for anyway?" She asked, walking out of the kitchen wiping her hands on a towel.

Looking up at her and still in my crooning mood, I blew her a verse of an even older Jackson Five tune. *"Mama, I think I've found a girl. Yeah yeah, Mama I think I found a Chocolate girl."* I finished it up my way. "Oo, here it go." I pulled the album out of the stack.

She looked at me laughing, "Oh yeah, and who is Miss Lucky?"

"Her name is Tammy. She's this pretty little chocolate thang." I stood to my feet gesturing an hour glass figure with my hands and laughed 'cause I knew she wasn't interested in *all that.*

Mom looked at me from the corner of her eyes, "So what's so special about this Tammy person? What does she do?"

"She's a student right now, but...ahh."

"But what? Why you stuttering boy?"

I know I didn't have no noble ass job, but damn. To explain Tammy's life to someone, made her sound slack, even though I knew she wasn't. Looking at mom, I paused, "Okay here it is. She's nineteen, has two daughters, lives in Domtar Courts, and just graduated high school last month." Mom looked at me like I was crazy. She didn't say a word, just turned her back and started to walk away pitifully shaking her head. "Mom, hold up!" And what surprised me was, I was taking the shit personal.

With a smirk on her face, she faced me, "Sounds like quite a girl, son."

"Ma, she good people, though. Yeah she sounds all effed, but she ain't. She's special." Her glare cut me some slack, giving me a chance to explain. "Tammy's on welfare, the whole nine, but she's strivin'. She'll be starting college next month. She's a good mother, and she *love* herself some Hassan." I said smoothin' my beard with my hand. Mom cracked up when I said that.

With a smile she said, "Look Hassan, I raised you. I know that you are capable of doing way more with your life." She was referring to my hustlin'. "But honey, don't just completely sell yourself short and settle for just anybody."

Smiling I picked up the album from the table, walked over and gave her a squeeze, "Thanks for the record." Kissing her on the cheek, I said, "I'm gonna bring her over so you can see for yourself, and I bet you gonna love her." I smirked playfully.

Mom laughed, "Yeah, you just make sure you bring my *Whispers* back here without me having to remind you."

At home that night, I must have listened to that song at least fifteen times.

A Quiet Place

It was every bit of 3:45 in the morning when I started banging on Tammy's door. I knew she had to be sound asleep in her bed, but I needed a place to settle down. I was keyed up like a mug after beatin' some punk down. I gave him three grand worth of rock, then he sent one of his boys to me with twenty-five hundred. Tryin' to beat me for five hundred dollars? Four things you don't *ever* fuck with of mine are my son, my mom, my woman, or my money. What made me extra mad was I had planned on chillin' with Tammy, since I ain't seen her all week. But instead, I had to go hunt some dude down for my money!

Spent all day long playing detective, driving around puttin' the word out that I was looking for that fool. Caught up with him at some after hour joint, where he gonna look me square in my face and tell me *I* only gave *him* twenty-five hundred in rock. I gave his ass a five hundred dollar beat down, a fuckin' broken jaw, and told him to keep the change.

Tammy answered the door lookin' like who did it. Red sleepy eyes, night rag falling off her head, but through all that she was still fine. Storming in the apartment, I was hyped! "I don't believe this shit! I hate when muthah fuckah's try to test me!"

"Hassan, what happened to you? Look at your hand, it's bleeding!" The knuckles on my right hook were all tore up.

"I just got finished bustin' this niggah up for tryin' to cheat me out of my shit! He gonna act like 'He the Man', so I served him like one."

"Come here, Hassan, let me take care of your hand," she said, holding her hand out.

"Fuck that shit! He must think I'm some kind of punk muthah fuckah, that I ain't gonna know my shit." I was zoned out. "When I see him, I should sneak his bitch ass again." Tammy walked over and closed the girls' bedroom door.

As I walked around from one side of the room to the next she stood there looking at me. "Hassan, baby, you got to calm down. I know you all worked up and everything, but that fight is over," she said, wiping the sleep out of her eyes.

"But..."

"But nothing. Come over here and sit down! You're gonna give yourself a heart attack."

Taking my good hand, Tammy led me to the couch. "At this time in the morning, I am not up to all that loud talking and trying to keep up with you as you roam around this room. Sit right here and don't move, alright?" She kissed me on the lips.

"But, Tammy...!" I was still racin'.

"And don't say a word." She kissed me again, this time with a little tongue. "I'll be right back,"

She went in the bathroom and stayed a few minutes. I was quiet with my head leaned back on the couch replaying that mess over and over in my head. I knew I had a reputation, but contrary to popular belief, I didn't like to fight. But I did when I had to. The thing I hated most about fighting was it took me so long to come down from that adrenaline high. When she came back into the living room she asked, "Are you feeling any better?"

"Naw, baby," I said, with serious stress written all over my face.
Tammy got on her knees and started to untied my sneakers. I started to take off my shirt, then she said. "No, you relax. Let me undress you."

Damn, she caught me off guard. *I can take off my own shirt.* I was about to say. But there was something in her eyes. I just looked at her not knowing what she had planned, but being down with it.

"Hold your arms up," Pulling my shirt up over my chest, she said, "You're my baby tonight. Now stand up." Resting her knuckles on my bare flesh, she slid my pants and boxers down to the floor.

I stepped out, and she led me toward the bathroom. When Tammy opened the door it was completely steamed over inside. She closed the door behind us. Only the night light was on so it was dim, and the tub was filled with bubbles. My mind was blown. "Aw, baby, this is right on time," I said looking at her in disbelief.

I stepped into the tub submerging myself in the hot, scented water. I was a shower kinda man, so that tub action was a different pace. Tammy knelt on the floor besides me and with her hands I ran the hot water under my neck and over my chest. With my head tilted back on the tiles I closed my eyes and could literally feel myself defusing.

My stiff shoulders dropped, and my breath became long and drawn out. "Girl, you make me feel like a king."

"That's what I'm here for baby, whenever you need me." Tenderly she kissed me above my brow. Tammy got up, went into her medicine cabinet and took out some peroxide and bandages. Then fixed my hand up.

With a bar of soap and her bare hands, she washed my whole body. The sensations of her fingers felt good as she was teasin' me. Kissin' me, givin' me some tongue then backin off. She thought it was funny. I had a hard on. Taking her hand I wrapped it tightly around my erection, guiding it up and down until she could groove it by herself. Behind the neck I held her as our kissin' became deep. "I need you baby, I need you." My voice husky.

"You need me, love?" she asked, standing to her feet. Our eyes never broke gaze. Tammy reached under her night gown removing her panties, and stepped into the tub. With her gown still on, she sat as I navigated myself inside her. Clear through the break of dawn, Tammy pacified me. That was the first night I ever told *any* woman I loved her. Tammy was my first.

PENETRATING HIS WORLD

Hassan told me over the phone earlier that day that some of the fellahs were over his place last night watching the fights on Pay-Per-View. He said he was still cleaning up the mess they left behind. When I asked him how bad a mess it was, Hassan sprang for a cab so I could see for myself. The girls and I were at his place in no time, and he *was not* exaggerating. His apartment was in bad shape. Potato chips smashed into the carpet, beer cans behind the couch, dirty plates on the coffee table, and an ashtray had overturned on his leather sofa. It was a mess!

Hassan was usually dressed to kill, but today he was dressed to clean, wearing grey cut-off cotton sweat pants, a sleeveless T-shirt and old brown house shoes. He still looked good to me.

While I was helping him clean, the door bell rang.

"Babe, can you get that?" Hassan yelled from the kitchen, where he was hard at work washing a ton of dirty dishes.

Putting down the trash bag, I opened the door and my heart sank. It was a woman! She was attractive, on the plump side, dressed real nice. Her yellow sundress was either silk or rayon, with an African print that matched her headband. Long black and blond extension braids hung all the way down her back. Her fingernails were seriously gaudy, at least three inches long, painted candy apple red. And on top of that, she wore gold rings on every finger, even her thumbs. I could picture Hassan walking' down the street with this type of woman. Even though shades covered her eyes, I could see from her raised brows, that she was as surprised to see me as I was to see her.

"Where's Hassan?"

Before I could answer, he came up behind me. "Come on in, Debbie."

"I didn't know you had *company*," she commented sarcastically as she passed him. He ignored her.

"Tammy this is Debbie, my son's mother. Debbie, this is Tammy."

We both said our shallow hellos, then I went into Hassan's bedroom where the girls were looking at TV. Moments later, Hassan popped in the room and flopped down on the bed.

"I'm hungry. Y'all want to go get something to eat?"

"What did *she* want?"

"Somebody's jealous..."

"No, I'm not, I'm just curious." And I was *just curious.*

"I owed her some money for Erkell, and she just came over to pick it up. Okay, baby?" Hassan held his hands up like he was surrendering.

"Stop it. I'm not jealous," I said with a smile.

"So what about that food. I have a taste for some fish, myself."

Tianna grabbed Hassan by the back of his Tee shirt to pull herself up. Hassan scooped her up onto his lap. It was then that Kiara announced that she was hungry, also, "I wanna eat too, da dee."

Daddy?! Oh man, I thought I would die. I hoped Hassan didn't think I put her up to saying that. "No Kiara, you say Hassan."

"No, mommy. I wanna call him da deeeee!" Kiara tapped her little index finger insistently on Hassan's leg.

"Babe, it's alright. She just hear Erkell call me daddy, that's all. You ready to eat, little fox?"

"Um hum." Kiara's long plats flapped back and forth as she nodded her head.

"What do you want to eat? Do you want to take a ride over to Hermitage Ave. and get a couple of dinners from Miss Dolly's Restaurant."

"That's the place where...what does her signs say?" Hassan and I said in unison, "If the food had any more soul, you'd have to go to heaven to eat it." We started cracking' up.

"Yeah babe, that's why I want to go there cause I want to take you to heaven." Hassan had this playful smile on his face while trying to look serious.

"Oh,...so my baby wants to take me to heaven, huh?" I teased.

"Damn straight!" He winked his eye at me. "So you wit it?"

"Sounds good to me. I'll get the roast beef."

After we picked up the dinners, and returned to Hassan's place, he turned up the music so we could jam to Mary J. Blige on his mega system. We were eating and bugging out at the same time. Kiara was in the middle of the floor gyrating her heart out.

"That girl watches too much Soul Train." Hassan was laughing.

"She gets that from my sister Nichole. That's all her and her friends be up in their rooms doing is listenin' to that rap crap, tryin' to dance."

"Work it, mommy." Hassan yelled clapping his hands to the beat. I thought Kiara was going to throw her little back out. The house was still a mess, but we were too busy eating all that delicious food and having too much fun to even care about cleaning right now. Kiara would eat a spoonful off my plate, and go right back in the middle of the floor to dance .

"Damn baby, this fish is good. Miss Dolly be cookin' her ass off." Hassan's jaws were stuffed. "You ever have a taste for something, and you want it real bad but you just didn't have the time to get it? Well, that's how I feel about this fish, I been wantin' some all week. Here taste it." He put some in my mouth with his fingers.

"Ooh this is good." I didn't know which tasted better, the fish which was seasoned to perfection, or his fingers.

"Da dee, looka me," Kiara said.

"Ahhh shake it, mommy!" Hassan got up from the couch and started dancing with Kiara. He was grinning from ear-to-ear took Tianna out of my arms and put her on the floor with Kiara. Her little hard white shoes were buzzing. It was good to see that Hassan was great with my kids. That was a real concern of mine, being a single mother. Cause if a man couldn't love my kids, then he definitely couldn't *love* me.

As the weeks rolled on, I was moving into Hassan's world, going places with him, meeting his crew and being recognized and respected for who I was: *his lady*. All of Hassan's boys were cool. They were business men. No dummies. It was Hassan, Chief, Fletch, Sho Nuff and Bubby, Their tag was the 'Furious Five'. I asked if they named themselves after the rap group and he looked at me like I was crazy. At their meeting they would discuss current events of the streets, and pool their money together to buy large amounts of dope, which they called product.

They had under age gophers to transport the drugs from New York, dealers on consignment selling the drugs, lookouts to spot cops and warn the dealers so they wouldn't get caught in a transaction with customers, and recruiters to round up more dealers. As corrupt as the whole thing was, it was amazing how organized and business-like their operation was run. And it was also mind blowing to see the money they generated--tens of thousands.

Hassan explained to me once about how they saved. The Furious Five couldn't go to a bank and deposit all this money without being questioned and caught. So they handled that part of the business through Sho Nuff's father, Hassan's Uncle Roger who owned his own handyman/roofing business.

Uncle Roger would take the money and invest it with his company's money. When they needed money, he would write it off as a company expense. Hassan and Sho Nuff were even listed on his payroll if they ever needed to prove that they were employed. If only these brothers could put this ingenuity into something legal.

Good Lookin' Out

The summer was winding down to an end. It had definitely been an exciting summer for me. But I was glad that it was almost over because Tamlyn Annita Blake was a college girl!

The West Windsor, Mercer County College campus was beautiful. Even though it was a junior college the only thing missing were dormitories. It looked just as elite as any Ivy League establishment. Even though a lot of junior colleges had a bad rap, I for one was overwhelmed with pride to be a student at MCCC. So far all of my classes and professors have lived up to, if not surpassed, what I had imagined.

Pulling a full schedule of college level studies, I was right back to the same rugged routine, riding the bus to the day care center, then to school. From school, I would catch the bus back to the day care, then home again day after day. Quite frankly, I was tired of this. Determined not to spend another freezing cold winter with my children standing at the freakin' bus stop. I saved up five hundred dollars to get me a car. Not knowing the first thing about automobiles I talked about it with Hassan and he offered to help me find a good used one.

One afternoon after my classes were finished Hass picked me up from the college, and we drove around to several lots. Up until now my driver's license had never been used for anything more than identification. But I was determined to get a car *tonight* and change all of that.

At Kramer's, which was at one time a gas station, now turned into a greasy old automotive shop and used car lot, I fell in love with a burgundy compact Subaru. Fifteen hundred dollars. A thousand more than I had. Hassan test drove and liked the ride, but wanted his mechanic to take a look at it. Only problem, it was a stick. I didn't know how to drive a stick. Hassan told me not to worry that he'd teach me. He did all the talking and dealing. By the time Hassan was through, he got ole' Kramer to drop the sales tax and put on four new tires. Gladly I gave Kramer my five hundred dollars, and Hassan took care of the rest.

The next day, I couldn't wait to pick up my car. Kramer had washed it down, polished it up and outfitted it with the four new tires he promised. The car had standard bucket seats which were also cranberry to match the exterior. But the color of the seats were starting to fade from the sun. The car had a pop-up sunroof and a radio, but best of all, *it was all mine*! Hassan spent the next two weeks teaching me how to drive a stick. My man was so good to me!

You, Me and She

Looking at the calendar hangin' on Tammy's kitchen wall, I couldn't believe that it was March. My girl was in her second semester in college already. She truly amazed me how she just seemed to have it so together. Being a good mother, an honor student, and a good woman to her man. Whatever I asked or needed from her, I knew she'd come through. Here it was almost ten o'clock at night and she was still hitting the books. I was checking her out from the couch where I was reading some ole crazy ass story from Tammy's English Literature class about this dude living up in the attic of some castle in England and nobody knew he was there. As I finished the short story, I was thinking, 'What's the point?' and slung the book onto the other side of the couch. My twenty minutes would have been much better spent reading about a real revolution rather than some asshole who locks himself up because he thinks the world was so fuckin' unkind.

"I'm so glad I'm finished this chapter. All this work is kickin' my butt." Packing her books in her bag, Tammy threw them into the closet, "Now I can snuggle up under my baby," she said doing just that.

"Tell me something." I asked sarcastically, "You like reading this shit?"

Tammy picked up the book giggling cause she knew which story I was talking about. "Yeah, it's pretty deep."

"Deep? What's so deep about it?"

"Because the reader is not suppose to be focused on the man, Benson's situation. But instead on what the situation symbolizes."

"Symbolizes? You have a man who hides out in someone's attic, who's afraid to come out and only survives off of what he steals out of the kitchen when no one's home. Am I right?"

Tammy looked at me amused and nodded her head. After letting out a big sigh, I asked her, "So what's so symbolic about that?"

"The story symbolizes true freedom. Benson looked around and finds society so undesirable that he drops out and makes his own kind of freedom."

"His ass ain't free. He's locked up in somebody elses crib stealin' their shit to live off of. And if he got caught would probably get his ass whooped. Free?"

"Think about it. He's probably just as free if not more so than we are. Take this apartment for instance. Every first of the month I pay my rent to say it's my place, to feel like it belongs to me. I have all of my things here, but actually it's all a lie. It's false security. I can't bring a washing machine in here if I wanted to. No one can move in here unless I ask management, then they would make me pay extra. And speaking of paying...let me decide that I didn't want to pay them their rent for a couple of months. My ass would be out on the street. When Benson realized that freedom's price was too high, he decided to go somewhere where he could be truly free and make his own rules."

I laughed, "I don't care what you say, it sounds like bullshit to me." Tammy started laughing. "The brothah finds *true freedom* by locking his dumb ass up in an attic? Girl, get out of here." Playfully I pushed her away from me.

"Think about it Hassan." She said hitting me in my arm, "He's living by his own rules."

"Sounds like some ole intellectual shit. Like showing some fool a plain white card with three black dots and they suppose to see a fuckin' pink sky or blue dog." I had Tammy rolling. "Bring that same card in the hood and we gonna tell ya it's three black dots on a white card." Grabbing her in my arms I started biting her on the neck, and she was laughing up a storm. I loved her laugh, her smile. Everything about Tammy I loved. "How long you got to go before you get your degree?"

"Well, next year, I'll have my associates degree. But after I'm finished with Mercer, I want to go to a four-year college and get a BA in business."

Our eyes made contact with a roach crawling across the wall. "I'm not going to be here long. This is just a temporary stop on my way to bigger things," she said jumping up and squashing it with a shoe.

"Oh, is that so!" I said knowing where she was coming from. Even though I've never been inside of her parent's house, I've driven her by there on several occasions. From the neat as a pin look of the outside, I know the inside must have been nice as well. Tammy definitely wasn't use to living like this.

"Yeah, when I'm in class, my instructors, they talk about how it is in the corporate world, all that wheelin' and dealin', the big cash to be made, that's what I want to do.

I want to have a job in one of those fancy buildings downtown, and wear expensive suits and carry a brief case. Then my girls will be proud of me, and my parents will see that I didn't screw up my life."

"I'm proud of you already." I told her and I was being straight up.

"You are Hassan, really?"

"Yeah, babe, I am. You ain't sittin' on your ass, givin' up because some brothah left you hangin' with two kids. One of the things I noticed first about you, before I even knew your name, was that you knew you weren't suppose to be here."

"What do you mean?"

"Anyone with eyes could see it. When I first saw you at the bus stop that morning, I fell in love with you. You were loaded down, girl, carryin' all those bags, and they looked heavy as hell. I watched you get on the bus. You had to put all those bags down on the ground and take Tianna out of her stroller. Fold that damn thing up and put the kids on the bus. *Then* come back and get your bags off the street."

"Oh don't remind me. I hated those mornings." Tammy buried her face in my arm.

"No baby, that's the stuff you ain't never supposed to forget." Lifting her chin, I look her straight in the eyes. "You reminded me of the little ant that could."

Laughing, she corrected me, "That's the little engine that could."

"Yeah, him too. But that morning, this skeez named Lynn came out of the same building you came out of. She got three boys and don't give a damn about them. Probably don't even know who their damn daddies are. She was going to the corner store with a rag tired around her head, but came over to me bummed a cigarette, then went on her merry way. Do you see what I'm gettin' at?"

"Kind of, but not quite."

"What I'm saying to you is, she belongs here, but I know this is just a temporary stop for you. I know you're determined to get out of here and off welfare, and I believe you're gonna get that job downtown. And I knew that about you the very first time I saw you."

"Thank you, Hassan. That means alot to me," she said giving me some of them juicy lips.

"Word baby. You my star." I kissed her back.

Kiara came out of the bedroom crying with the front of her pajamas soaked. Tammy got up and took her into the bathroom. Right behind her I leaned my head in the door, "Babe, I'm getting ready to roll. I'll talk with you tomorrow." She had Kiara stripped and standing in the tub.

"Daddy, I bad. I pee pee on myself," She said crying

"You daddy's big girl. You just had an accident, that's all. Daddy love you okay?"

"Kay," she said sniffling.

Tammy bent over into the doorway and gave me a kiss, then I was out.

Sho Nuff and I were gonna meet up together at Chuck's Lounge tonight and have a couple of drinks. I wanted to go home, jump in the shower and change first 'cause I been in these clothes all day. My shit had to be fresh when I went out, and who cares if it was only a club in town. On my way out the door the phone rang.

"Hass here."

"Hassan, Erkell's sick. I'm gonna take him to Mercer's ER. Can you meet me there?

"ER, what's wrong with him?"

"He's burnin' up. I been tryin' to break his fever for the last four hours, but it ain't breakin'. He says his stomach and head hurt. Look..." she said impatiently, "...I'm leavin' now. Are you gonna meet me there?"

"Yeah, I'm on my way." Hanging up the phone, I went for my keys. It was well after eleven o'clock. Something serious must be wrong with my son, 'cause Debbie don't call me at this time of night for nothin'.

By the time Debbie walked through the automatic entrance door of the hospital, I was already waiting for her in the E.R. "How is he?"

"'Bout the same." She sounded worried. Debbie wore a sharp blue rain coat, over a yellow blouse and blue jeans. She was one for fashion. She looked like L.L.Cool J's version of an *around-the-way girl.*

It was cold outside, but damn, she had my son dressed like it was zero below. He was wearing a thick winter coat, hat, gloves, scarf, the whole fucking nine yards, everything except his boots. No wonder he was burning up. Taking Erkell from Debbie's arms, I went and sat down while she rushed over to give the nurse Erkell's information. His cheeks were red hot and his lips were parched. "Daddy, it hurts, daddy."

"What hurts, little man?"

"My eyes, my stomach, and my head," he said, moving his hand to each part he described.

"Your mom brought you here so the doctor can check you out. They'll give you some medicine, and you'll feel better. OK?"

Erkell nodded his head. He covered his mouth with his hands after coughing, curled into my arms, then fell quickly asleep. Debbie came and sat down next to me. She took Erkell out of my arms and cuddled him into her lap.

"I'm going outside for a cigarette. This place gives me the creeps." There was an old white couple a few seats away. He was babbling on about shit that made no sense to me. He kept rocking back and forth, and he had these damn ugly, red patches on his arms. He kept scratching 'em. "I'll be back. I just have to get out of here."

Fifteen minutes later, they were still sittin' there. Erkell was sleeping, but soon awoke and began to cry. We sat there for what seemed like hours. Back outside, I had another smoke, but when I returned and they were *still* sittin' there I was big time pissed off. "They ain't call him yet?"

"No, we been waitin' almost forty-five minutes. I hate this damn hospital. Mothah fuckah gotta be half dead before they take you right in."

Erkell started heavin' and threw up all over the floor. I was insane now. Debbie quickly moved Erkell away from her clothes, but he still got her coat messed up.

"Nurse, can my son get some help over here!" we yelled in unison.

Over to the nurses' counter I charged and looked square into her face. If she didn't get up off of her ass quick, I was gonna hurt somebody. "We been sittin' here all this damn time and my boy's burnin' up. Now you gonna get a doctor out here, or do I gotta go back there and get one myself?" My nostrils flared! She looked at me and jumped her narrow ass up out of her chair and ran to help Debbie with Erkell. They took him right in. My son meant everything to me. Erkell was the one perfect thing I've ever accomplished in my entire life.

Along the dark, almost empty highway, I followed Debbie to her place in Levittown, Pennsylvania. It's a twenty minute ride outside of Trenton. She lived in a nice apartment complex. Clean and quiet. Nothin' like the city. There was more white people out there than black folk. Debbie said she liked it, because it was a good environment for Erkell. She's right I guess, cause ain't much trouble for young kids to find themselves in around there.

That time of night, all of the drug stores were closed, so they doped Erkell's little butt up before we left the hospital. Debbie bathed him, put on his motorcycle pajamas, then tucked him into bed. Every now and then, we'd hear him cough.

Debbie went into the kitchen and poured herself a taste. "Hassan, you want a shot?"

"What you got?"

"Baccardi and Coke."

"Yeah, hook me up, straight."

She walked out of the kitchen, handed me my glass, then went into her bedroom. From where I sat, I could see her getting undressed. Debbie pulled her shirt off, unzipped her pants, and bent over with her ass high up in the air. Damn, what a nice view. She tried to act like she didn't know I was watching, I couldn't take my eyes off of her. My dick was swelling. Debbie's skin was bright as the sun, and she was just the right type of plump. She was wearing these panties with a little strap that disappeared between the crack of her round ass. I envied that strap. Debbie walked over to her closet, put on her robe, and slipped her bare feet into her slippers.

She came into the living room, grabbed her glass and sat at the opposite end of the couch from me. Kicking off her slippers, she propped her feet up on the coffee table. Beautiful, soft looking feet, and perfect little toes.

"Hassan, thanks for meeting me at the hospital tonight. No matter how many times Erkell gets sick, I never get used to it. I can never keep myself calm, you know? If anything ever happened to him, I don't know what I'd do," she said taking a long slow drink from her glass.

"Ain't I always here for my son?"

"Yes, you are Hassan. I got to give it to you, you're a good man and a good father." She took another sip and brushed her long braids out of her face with her manicured fingernail. "The doctor said for me to keep Erkell home from school for a few days. I done used up all of my sick time at work. If I stay home, I'll get docked and I can't afford it." She sucked her teeth and held the glass tightly in her hands. "Maybe I can call Sandy and see if she can come over and babysit Kell until I get off during the day, at least until Thursday."

Reaching inside my pocket to pull out my knot. I opened it up, thumbing through the bills and shelled off two hundred dollars. "Here," I placed the money on the table. "Erkell needs his mama to stay home and take care of him. If you need anything else, you let me know."

Debbie reached for the money. Her robe opened exposing her large, full breasts pushed tightly together in a white lace bra. The dark circles around her erect nipples were showing through. Grabbing the cash, she leaned back, crossed her legs and began to count the money. Across her thick thighs, Debbie's robe flowed open to her crotch. My mouth watered for her. *She knew what she was doing to me.*

"Where's Nate?"

"I don't mess with him no more."

"Tell me about it."

"Ain't nothing to tell. Just say he wasn't man enough to handle all this," she said fanning herself with the cash.

"Come here."

Debbie looked at me to confirm the meaning of my summons. I answered her with lust-filled eyes. She put the money in a candy dish on the end table, got up and opened her robe. Her hips swayed gently as she walked around the coffee table to me.

Pulling Debbie onto my lap, I gave her a deep throat kiss, running my hands across her shoulders until her robe fell to the floor. From back-in-the-day, I knew Debbie was an aggressive lover. You had to be up on it, cause she wasn't about to fake her satisfaction. You had to deliver, and that night I was the postman. No sleet, nor rain, snow, wind *or* ice was gonna stop me from cumin'. And just like UPS, my shit was guaranteed! I guess that's one reason why I always come back for more. Her sex was mad!

WORDS OF WARNING

In the family room at my mom's house, I was hanging with my sisters, my girls, and my brother Tim. We were all watching television, bugging out, laughing and having fun when mom walked in with a basketful of clean clothes. She sat down next to me and started folding so I pitched in and helped. Mom looked at me strange and said, "This sure is nice," reaching over to feel my twenty-four inch gold rope necklace. She inspected me further. "And I see you got earrings to match?"

"Hassan gave it to me," I boasted proudly.

"Um hum." She continued folding the towels. Plain as day, I could see the wheels turning. "You know, you been dressing kind of nice, lately. Do you mind tellin' me where you gettin' all this money from?"

"I get a check," I blurted out defensively.

"Yeah you do, but we both know that money ain't buying you all those clothes either, don't we?"

Tim and Keisha were enjoying seeing me sweat. "Hassan been buying' me some things."

"Oh yeah, so how can he afford to keep you in such fine threads? What kind of job does he have?"

"Dag mom, why you askin' me all these questions? You act like I'm not suppose to have nice things." I was fuming.

"I never told you that you shouldn't have nice things Tamlyn, but if he's givin' you all these things, what's he gettin' from you? I hope you takin' care of yourself. Don't be no fool!"

Enough! I got up took my kids in hand and went home. She's trippin' like this over my clothes. That's exactly why I didn't tell her how I got my car. Seems like anything Hassan does for me or my girls, she has a problem with it. Like the other day Hassan brought Kiara and Tianna two beautiful hand made black dolls. One had a pretty yellow dress and the other a purple dress. Kiara told her, "Look at what my daddy brought me." Instead of saying that the doll was nice, she jumped down my throat about how I shouldn't allow my kids to call *that man*, as she put it, daddy.

At least once a week Hassan would ask me if I needed anything. Sometimes I'd say yes, and sometimes I'd say no, but he always offers. There are times when he just shows up at my door with things for me.

Once when Hassan was at my place, this dude showed up with a microwave--no box, no nothin'; straight off someone's kitchen counter.

"This got to be worth fifty dollar, Hassan man, what you say, are we square now, man?"

"Babe, you want a microwave?"

Microwave? I stuck my head out into the hallway to see what he was talking about. It was a big Magic Chef with a turn table. Good enough! Hassan brought it in, I cleaned it up and put it on *my* counter. Thanks to Hassan, I don't have to struggle and be without the sweet things in life.

Debbie's Cookin'

Early Saturday morning, I went over to Debbie's to pick up Erkell for the weekend. Even though it was early April, and still cold out, Tammy wanted us to take the kids to the Philadelphia Zoo. Hey, I was down with it. Every once in a while, it was good to skip all the fast paced madness and take time with the munchkins. Debbie was dressed already which struck me as odd. Whenever she had a weekend off from the nursing home, where she worked as a nursing assistant, she would always be loungin' in her pj's when I came over the get Erkell this early. "You going somewhere?"

"Yeah, I was just waiting for you. Me and Sandy, we're going out to Englishtown. I want to get some nick knacks from the flea market."

"Is Erkell ready?"

"Yeah, he's ready. I just want to talk to you for a minute, before he comes out his room."

"So what's up?"

"Now Hassan, don't go getting all mad and shit, cause I ain't made my mind up one way or the other about this."

"Just say what's on your mind." I hated fuckin' guessing games.

"I missed my period this month. I done been to the doctor, and I'm pregnant." She said clearing off the couch with her back toward me.

I stood there with my arms folded, watching her, "Is it mine?"

Debbie spun around with a few pieces of clothes and some of Erkell's toys in her arms, "Hassan don't even try that shit. Yes, it's your damn baby." She grimaced.

"Umm...So what you gonna do about that?"

She stood there looking at me then spoke softly, "I really don't know, I been thinking about it a lot. Erkell's getting all big and shit, you know. It would be nice if he had a little brother or sister to grow up with. What you think, Hass?"

"Damn, Debbie, you ain't askin' me if you can buy a damn puppy. You talkin' about a baby? I don't know."

Erkell ran out of his room.

"Hey, dad. We still going to the zoo today?"

Erkell's face was all lit up. My boy had the roundest head in the world, and his ears stuck straight out on each side. Picking him up, I gave him a kiss. "Yeah man, we still goin' to the zoo. And while we're there, I'm gonna put you in the lion's cage and let him eat you up for dinner," I said tickling him.

"No, daddy. Don't let him eat me up," he said, laughing.

I grabbed Erkell's over night bag. "Yo, Debbie." She gave me her attention. "We'll talk later."

That made the third time I got her pregnant. The second time was a year after she had Erkell, and I told her then that she couldn't have it. We weren't ready for that kind of responsibility. Erkell was still in diapers, I had some bullshit job, and she was still living home with her mom. The timing just wasn't right. Her announcement was heavy on my mind all that day. Tammy kept askin' me what was wrong. Erkell was getting big, I reasoned. And I *didn't* want him growing up lonely, like I did. There was a lot that I missed out on by not having a brother or sister. After my parents split up, my pops had several other kids by different women. But the way I saw it, if they didn't come from my mom, I wasn't claimin 'em. I wasn't down with the idea of me and Debbie havin' another kid, but I wasn't against it either.

TIDES TURN

I was awakened by mom's phone call. She wanted to know if the girls and I would attend church with her this morning. Every July they had a special Women's Day program. After I spoke with her I felt sick to my stomach, and started getting hot. The fact that it was a steamy July morning didn't help. Pushing the sheets from off of my legs, I got out of bed, turned up the window fan and stood there allowing the air to blow in my face. Even though my body cooled down, the sickness in my stomach was rising rapidly. Hurriedly, I fled into the bathroom, dropping my face in the toilet, heaving up what little I did have inside.

With liquids pouring from my eyes, nose, and mouth, on all fours I stayed there holding on. Reaching in back of me, I felt for the floor before lowering myself to sit down. My head was swirling and all I could do was just sit there until I regained my bearings. The first thing I thought of was, 'God, no. I can't be pregnant!'

Grabbing the sink I pulled myself up slowly. Turning on the cold water, I splashed some on my face. From my cupped hands I drank some then went back into the bedroom. 'I can't believe this.' I thought reaching to get my purse out of the closet. Rambling through it, I came to my pocket calendar where I kept track of my period and counted in intervals of twenty eights. When I finished, I counted over again. According to this, I was safe. My period came last month, and in fact, I wasn't due to come on until two weeks. *Damn, was I relieved*! Must be a virus.

Calling my mom back, I told her that I had to pass on church this Sunday 'cause I was sick. I jumped into bed, turned over, and went back to sleep.

All week long I was sick...violently sick! I didn't have much of an appetite, but when I did try to eat, whether it came out from the front or the back, it was coming out. I couldn't keep anything down. Hassan came over to my apartment on Thursday afternoon to spend some time with me. I hadn't seen him in about a week. Over the phone I told him that I had a virus and wasn't feeling well at all.

We were watching television, and I'm usually talkative and happy-go-lucky, but today I laid limp across his lap as he sat on the couch. He lit a blunt and I started to heave then ran to the bathroom and threw up all over the place.

"Tammy, you pregnant?" he asked sharply, helping me to my bed as I fell across it.

"No, Hassan, I'm not pregnant. My period came last month, and it's not due to come on for about another week," I explained.

"You sure, because I don't want to hear nothing about no baby." He was being real serious. "You better get yourself checked out to find out why you sick like that."

Hassan left and I just stayed in bed.

The next morning after I dropped the girls off at daycare, I went to our neighborhood clinic as a walk-in patient. Spent half the morning waiting then they finally called me in to be examined. The female doctor wrote on her chart as she talked to me. "Well, Tamlyn, you don't have a fever, and I can't find anything visibly wrong with you." She had asked me if I thought I could be pregnant. Quickly pulling out my pocket calendar, I showed her the dates of my last periods. After she noted the dates on my chart as she said, "I'm going to order some blood work to see if we can determine what's making you feel not so well. Okay?" To help with the dizziness and nausea she wrote me a persciption for motion sickness. "Now these will make you sleepy, but it will help to ease your symptoms so at least you'll be able to function during the day." As she prepared the needle, I held out my arm so she could draw my blood. After I left her office I filled my prescription at the clinic's pharmacy.

Just like she instructed I waited three days to call for my results. As the phone rang, I said a little prayer that everything was alright. Those pills she gave me must have be designed for a horse, because I took one before bedtime and I was out like a light *immediately* after it hit my system. That was the first and last pill I took. I threw that bottle on my nightstand and didn't look back.

The doctor said, "Hello Tamlyn. I want you to come back to the clinic this morning if possible."

After being sick for almost the entire week, all I wanted was some medicine so I could get better. But the concern in her voice scared me. "Why? What's wrong?"

"Tamlyn, you're pregnant. I want you to come in today to have an ultrasound so we can determine how far along you are."

At the sounds of his words I felt all of my blood drain out of my body. "No I can't be pregnant. My period came my period last month." Feeling as if I were having a nightmare, I thought about what Hassan said and about what my family would say. *I was scared*! Tears rolled down my face, and I took long, deep breaths to make sure I didn't hyperventilate.

A bundle of nerves, I got myself dressed and rushed right over to her office. During the ultra sound I could see my little baby's heart quickly beating. Overcome by the unbelievable reality of it all, I just cried.

The nurse tried to console me by talking about alternative choices that I could consider. How could I think about killing my child after I just saw its heart beating? "*Oh my God,* what am I going to tell Hassan." He already made it clear that he didn't want to hear about me being pregnant. After I got dressed I walked home in tears.

Needing someone to talk to, I started to knock on Jeannette's door, but remembered she was at work. So I went in my apartment and cried myself to sleep. When I woke up it was time to pick up the girls from day-care. I definitely couldn't get up the energy to get off the couch. All the shades were pulled down in the apartment. In desperation, I paged Hassan, and he called me right back.

"What's up baby?"

"Hass, can you get Kiara and Tianna for me? I have to talk to you when you get here," I said in a sleepy depressed tone.

"Sure, babe. We'll be right there."

Half an hour later Hassan opened the door and Kiara ran over toward me. "Hi, mommy!"

Bending down, I let her hug my neck with her little arms. Tianna was in Hassan's arms half asleep. Hassan gave me a kiss, and I took Tianna from him.

"Hi, sweetie." I kissed her on the face. "And how are you doing today?"

"Hi, mommy," said Tianna, half-heartedly as she burrowed up against my chest. On the couch next to Kiara I sat her down where they watched Nickelodeon.

"You look bad, girl" Hassan said looking worried, feeling my forehead for fever.

"I feel bad."

"You want me to take you to the hospital?"

"Come in the bedroom. We have to talk."

Lord how I dreaded having to tell him that I was pregnant. As we entered the bedroom, I asked Hassan to close the door. With my head hung low, I sat on the bed.

My fingers fumbled to dig the yellow napkin out of my pocket. Tears were starting again. Hassan leaned silently against the dresser, which stood directly in front of me.

"What? Why are you crying? What do you have to tell me?"

"I went back to the doctor's today, and...and..." I couldn't bring myself to tell him.

"What is it baby? Did they find something serious?" he asked sympathetically.

Keeping my head down, I shook it. "Well, what then?" he asked impatiently, then it hit him like lightning. "Damn, Tammy you pregnant, ain't' you?" He looked piercingly through me.

"Yeah."

"How the hell you let this happen! You told me that you were on the pill." His voice came from the depths of his gut and he slammed his hand down on the dresser.

"It's not my fault, Hassan. I didn't want this to happen!"

He looked like he wanted to strangle me. I had never seen this side of him directed at me. Afraid of getting hit, I got up and moved across the room.

"Damn! How can this shit happen to me?" There was a moment of silence. "Well, you know what you gotta do!"

These were just the words that I did not want to hear. Sure, I knew people who had abortions, but I couldn't make that choice. I could have made that same decision with my girls, but I chose not to. Taking my own child's life was not an option. Frantically I shook my head because the words weren't coming out fast enough, or in any fashion that made much sense. It seemed like I was reliving the moment when I told Mark that I was pregnant with Tianna.

"The heartbeat! Hassan it was beating! I saw the heart beating today, Hassan!" I was hysterical.

"What the fuck we gonna do with another baby, Tammy? You ain't thinkin' straight. You already got two kids and I got...Shit!" He said putting his hands over his face, not finishing his sentence. "You can't do this Tammy. Between clenched teeth, he repeated, "YOU-CAN'T-DO-THIS-TO-ME."

"I'm two months pregnant Hassan. The baby already has a heart. I saw it beating today. I can't kill it! Please! I need you. Please, don't make me do this." With all my might I pleaded. Tears fell from my eyes down my face and under my neck. What did he mean 'do this to him'? Religiously I took my birth control pill, I never missed...except for that time me, Hassan, Sho Nuff and his girlfriend Cynthia drove up to Maryland, and instead of coming home that night we wound up staying...*oh no*. We wound up staying the entire weekend. That was two months ago. I told him that I didn't have my pills cause we were suppose to be coming back home the same night. He told me don't worry cause he'd pull out. All of that must have slipped his mind, just like it slipped mine.

Hassan paced my room like a caged, wild animal. The more I begged, the more he paced.

"Call the fuckin' doctor Tammy. You know what you gotta do."

Without even thinking, I just blurted out, "No, I'm keeping my baby. I'm not calling for no abortion!"

He looked at me with the furry of hell in his face. "Oh, you already made your mind up, and I ain't got no say so in this matter then. Right, Tammy? Well maybe you can raise the bastard on your own too, then!" He rushed the door, yanking it open so hard, I thought it would come off its hinges.

Running behind him I cried, "You gonna leave me now Hassan?! You gonna leave me like Mark did?" *Don't leave me, I can't do this without you,* I wanted to say, but the door slammed in my face before the words had a chance to form on my quivering lips. Hassan just stormed right out of my life.

Standing there with my face pressed against the door, I cried. My two little daughters were at my sides holding me, scared for me, not knowing why but crying with me.

For making me choose between my unborn child or him, I resented Hassan. For leaving me to carry this burden alone, I resented him. Then I began to blame myself for getting back into this same old situation. Bending down I took them both in my arms holding them tight, as I tried to compose myself.

After Jeannette came home from work and received the thousand urgent messages I left on her answering machine, she came right over. By now it was totally dark inside of my apartment. My babies were in their room sleeping. "Tammy, what's wrong with you girl?" she asked, turning on a lamp.

"Jeannette, I'm pregnant again. I went to the doctor today, and I'm two months pregnant," I said sniffling, still in my house coat, hair smooshed down, with my eyes red and puffy.

"Oh shit...what you gonna do, you gonna keep it?"

"I want to keep my baby. This is Hassan's baby, and you know how much I love him. I can't kill something that we made out of love."

"Does he know?"

"Yeah, but he wants me to get rid of it. He doesn't want me to have our baby," I said really starting to cry. Jeannette put her arms around me as I sunk my face into her shoulder and let it all out. Gathering myself, I raised up and wiped my face with the end of my blue robe.

"My family is going to freak when they find out I'm pregnant again."

"Screw them. You're a grown woman now, and if you want to keep your child, then you keep your child. And as for Hassan, Tammy that man is crazy in love with you. Now, right now, he might not be interested in having another baby, but he'll come around." Jeannette comforted me with her hand on my arm.

Desperate out of my mind, I picked up the phone.

"Who you callin', Tee?"

"I'm calling Hassan. Maybe if I explain to him how I feel, he..."

"Tee, let him cool down and give him a chance to think without you whining and making matters worse." Jeannette guided the phone back to its cradle.

"Jeannette, I got a feeling that he's not gonna come back."

"Oh he'll be back, just give him time to think."

She stayed up half the night holding my hand as I cried. All I could think of was Mark leaving me to raise two girls alone. I couldn't imagine my life without Hassan. I *loved* him. He stepped in and became my daughters' father, my lover and my friend. How could he leave me now that I was carrying *his* child? Just didn't make sense.

JOHN COLBIRTH

With fingertips clawed to the hardwood floor and my body stretched out straight as an arrow, I continued push-up after push-up. Not counting but clearly over a hundred done, sweat was pouring off of me creating little puddles. The apartment was dimly lit, incense burning and smooth jazz played in the background. My think music. *I was fired up!* Cursin' Tammy out. Just didn't want shit to do with her! Hell, she was already set-up in her own place, getting money from welfare. She was makin' it. If I jetted, she wouldn't be no more damn worse for wear.

Positioning myself for sit-ups, I clasped my hands around the back of my head and started crunching my abs. Yeah, that's what I'm gonna do. If she can't listen, then she on her own. That was her call, not mine. Crunchin' harder cause I wasn't feeling a muscle burn that matched the rage inside of me, I closed my eyes as the picture show in my mind began. *"No! No, John! Don't do this!" "Shut up woman! This is my mothah fuckin house! And if I can't be the man in my own goddamned house then I'll get the fuck out!" "I never said you couldn't be the man in this house. I just said that you have to respect this house. You get off from work at four o'clock in the evening. Why you got to come home after midnight? John I know what you be doing out there. Is respecting your home, your family too much to ask of you?!" "Well I got me a new damn family. And guess what, she way younger and finer way than you. Her pussy tighter and she don't tell me no!" "John! Watch your damn mouth! Hassan's in the other room!" "No, you watch my mouth Judy, I'm leavin you!" "What am I suppose to tell Hassan. The boy is thirteen years old, goin' through changes. Now is the time he needs his fatttthhhheeerrr!" "Tell him I went out for a loaf of bread! Girl, I don't give a fuck what you tell 'im. Tell him this was your fault...." "My fault!"*

"I am- not- like- my- father! I am-not-like-my-father! I-AM-NOT-LIKE-MY-FATHER!" Enraged I grabbed the brass leg of my smoked glass coffee table I was seated next to and flipped it over. Glass went flying everywhere. The ills of my father's ghost were eating me alive. *"Hassan, baby. Where you going?" "I'm goin' to get him! He can't talk to you like that!" "You don't know where he is. Just let it be." "No mom, I'm gonna find him and hurt 'im. I hate 'im! I hate im!" "Hassan. Hassan! Don't hate him, he's your father. Love him, always love him for showing you what type of man NOT to be. Promise me you won't be like him. Son, promise me."*

Standing there in front of the broken glass, I felt like I needed to get out and get some air quick before my entire house got tore up. Grabbing a towel out of the closet I dried myself off, got my keys and was out the door.

July and night time were always my favorite combination. Especially night time. Have you ever had on a pair of shades and it felt like nobody could recognize you? Like you were masked away from the rest of the world, and only you knew who you were? That's why I liked the night, because I didn't have to pretend for a dark place to hide- darkness was all around me.

Driving through Trenton, I was just taking in the sights. First down Olden Avenue's business district with all its brightness, then down Dr. Martin Luther King Blvd, with all its darkness. Stopped at the red light, I peered down Southard Street watching the folks sitting on their porches and walking around. As I continued down MLK I drove by the neighborhood I grew up on, passed the little store front church my mother use to drag my ass in, and across the street to the bar my dad use to drag my ass in. Had to laugh. Then I passed our old row house. Looked way better back in the day, I'll tell you that. Driving across the bridge into Pennsylvania, my mind drifted to Debbie, who was now four months along. She understood me. She knew that I'd take care of the baby and be a good father to it just like I am with my son. Debbie didn't have no expectations other than that cause she knew Tammy's my girl. But Tammy's where things got complicated. I always prided myself for not having kids spread all over the place. Might sound dumb, but it wasn't. Simply put, I loved women! The way they smelled, the way they looked, dark skinned sistahs, light skinned sistahs, short hair, long hair, big boned or a bag of bones didn't much matter to me. I loved them, and if they were down I was wit it. But two things kept playin' in my mind. One, Tammy wasn't just any woman. My feelings ran deep for her, and two- if she keeps this baby then that means I slipped. I fucked up. At the age of thirteen when my pops walked out on me, I knew what it was like not to have a father. The pain that went along with that...to always feel like something was missing. The term broken home was my life because one important piece wasn't around to make it complete. Even his fuckin'

ranting and raving when he was home was better than not having him there. The home
that my mother and I occupied became the house where we stayed. She tried, but she
could not show me how to be a man. She couldn't control me like a father controls his
son. Tammy was my love, but I wasn't sure if I love her enough for her to be my wife,
and that was the qualifications for me to have a baby with any other woman. Why?
'Cause say this shit doesn't work out between me and Tammy, and I hook up with
someone else and this same thing happens again. That's the snowball effect, and next
thing you know you got kids spread all over the fuckin' place.

Pulling into the Seven-Eleven I brought myself a pack of cigarette then headed
back toward the bridge to Jersey. Sho Nuff called me on the cell phone and asked me
to pick him up from out East Trenton from over Cynt's house. Now his ass was a
classic example of kids all over the place.

He was standing outside when I pulled up to Cynthia's crib on Walnut Avenue.
I waved at her. Sho Nuff jumped in my ride and closed the door, loud talkin' as usual.
Since way back, he was one of the happiest mothah fuckah's I knew. My mom said
he's like that cause he don't have sense enough to worry about things. He looked at me
and read me instantly, "Yo man, what's wrong with you? You lookin' all stressed, and
don't say it's nothin' either."

"When last you seen Sade?" I asked Sho Nuff about his eight year-old and eldest
daughter.

"Seen her yesterday. Carolyn came and got her from my place. Said she had some
business to take care of so she asked me to pick Sade up from school." He sighed,
"Stuck up *be-ah-ch*. Man, she always got some drama goin' on. Know what I'm
sayin'?"

Everybody knows my ride and as we were crusin around the city, people were
sendin' me all kinds of shout outs. Checkin' them out through my blacked-out tinted
windows, that made the inside look more like a space ship than a car, I'd tooted the
horn and kept on rollin'.

"Drama?" I asked Sho Nuff

"Yeah, drama. Just 'cause she work in some old high rise and wear suits and stuff
she thinks she some kinda high rent bitch." He smirked. "Man she straight from the
projects. Matter of fact, her mom, and her damn grandma still live there." We started
cracking up. He continued, "And if she didn't marry that bourgie niggah, her ass would
still be there too. She talkin' bout she wants to put Sade in some private school, and get
this...she wants me to give her *more money* so she can pay for it." He looked at me with

this jive grin on his face. I laughed at his crazy ass, "So what did you tell her?"

"I told her public school served me well, and the shit is free. If she wanted Sade to go to some private school, let Bourgie pay for it, cause I wasn't payin' for a damn thang."

"You sick man."

He smirked, "Well I just gotta be. If I send Sade to private school, then Lisa or Cynthia find out, then they gonna be pushin' up on me to send they kids to private school too. Man, ain't that much money in the world." Sho Nuff shook his head.

"Ain't you forgetting about someone?" I always liked to pull his chain about Stephany.

He started crackin'up, "Oh there you go. Man I told you 'bout that."

"No, dawg, cause if you gonna count 'em, count 'em all."

"Man, I know all my kids."

"And it takes two hands to count them too." I laughed.

"One, muthah fuckah!"

I looked at Sho Nuff like he done lost his mind, "One...try two."

"Aw man, go head with that noise." He began to count them out extending a finger with each name, "Sade, Tra (Roger the third), Brea, Isaiah, and Mustafa. Muthah fucka, now, that's five."

We were laughin' 'cause we had this same conversation before. Then I started counting them off on my fingers. "You had Sade from Carolyn, Craig from Stephany..."

"Aw, no, no, no. You know that boy ain't mine. Me and Brucie Knight was hittin' that ass at the same time. That's Brucie's kid!" Sho Nuff was so animated I thought he was gonna jump out the ride.

I continued to count "...From Lisa you got Tra and Brea, and Cynt got Isaiah and Mustafa. That's six punk." Playfully I jabbed him in the side with my fist. Then he got me back in the shoulder.

"What you so worried about my kids for? You ain't feedin' 'em," he said boisterously.

My shoulder was leaned up against the driver's side window, and I was steering the wheel with my right wrist draped across the top. Looking at Sho Nuff, my thought went distant. He's the one who should have been John Colbirth's son. They were so much alike. They both had a laundry list of kids they didn't care two shits about. Staring out into the night with my mind reelin', all I could think about was first Debbie now Tammy, *both* pregnant and I was the daddy. Guess I was my father's son afterall.

After a week, I was still sweeping up glass out of my living room. I had to order another smoked glass top to replace the one I broke. Tammy was heavy on my mind, and I was missing her real bad. But I missed what we had, and was not looking forward to what we were headed for. If I could only make her understand that an abortion was the only sane thing to do, then we could get back on track.

It had been two long weeks since I walked out on her, but these demons kept eating me up. I never wanted to be the type of man John Colbirth was. My anger toward Tammy was clouding my head. My moms was the only one who I felt could put this into perspective for me so I went to see her. Sitting at her kitchen table, I told her the entire story. She already knew about Debbie's pregnancy, almost from day one. She and Debbie talked, *a lot.*

"Hassan, It's too easy for you to be mad at Tammy and give up on her. She didn't make that baby by herself. You both enjoyed making that child, and you are both, *equally* responsible."

"Ma, but this ain't right. You talk about equally. So ain't it equally our choice if she should keep the pregnancy or not? Don't I have a choice in the matter?"

Mom looked at me with her eyebrow raised, "You don't want her to have this baby? You want Tammy to have an abortion, is that what you're saying?"

"That's right," I said, *Damn straight!* Is what I wanted to say.

"Well how selfish of you to try and deprive the world of God's creation. That child that's in Tammy's womb could be the next Dr. King, or Garrett Morgan, the man who invented the traffic light, or John Strandard, the inventor of the refrigerator. Don't you know how unique and special that child is?" Her eyes had this power in them as she spoke to me. "Hassan, your father gave up on us." she said taking my hand, "The only thing that would make you like him is if you give up on yours. It's not so much his leaving that hurt, but that he left and just gave up on *you*." She cupped her hands around my face, "Don't give up on your child. I'm not saying that it's going to be easy, cause you have spun yourself into a mess. But be a man and handle this.

Where The Rubber Meets The Road

To say that it was hard for me not to pick up the phone and call Hassan was an understatement. I called his apartment once just to hear him say, *Hass here*. Even if it was for just a second, then I'd hang up. It had been twelve of the most miserable days I ever had.

In my night clothes sitting in the dark, listening to the show *The Quiet Storm* on the radio, I was thinking about how much I missed my man and desperately needed to see him. It was then that I heard a key turn in the lock. When he came in, I ran over to embrace him. He felt so good in my arms. Hassan and I stood in the doorway and held each other as the slow jams in the background intensified our mood.

Looking up at Hassan, he looked down at me and our mouths met. Our kiss was slow and deep. Tears of relief ran down my closed eyes as he picked me up in his strong arms and carried me into my bedroom and laid me down on the bed.

"I thought you would be sleeping by now," he said in a low voice.

"I haven't been sleeping well lately."

"How you been feeling?"

"Okay I guess. I still get sick but not as bad. Hassan, I missed you so much. I didn't think you would come back."

"I love you, baby girl. I just can't get used to us having a kid, you know? I just don't think that's the right thing to be doing right now."

Rejecting his comment, I turned my back to him and hugged my pillow. Hassan put his hand on my shoulder. "Turn around, don't turn your back on me. Listen, we should really talk about this."

"Hassan, please. I'm not up to this. I don't want to argue with you," I said, looking into his eyes.

"Tammy, how you gonna raise three kids? You tryin' to go to school and get your education. You say you want to get off welfare. Tammy ain't none of that stuff gonna happen if you have this baby."

"Hassan, I don't know about all that stuff. All I know is that this child inside of me is alive, and it's not something that I can just wish away. I'm not going to kill it because it wasn't planned. Can't you see Hassan. I love it. I love this baby just like I love Kiara and Tianna. Just like you love Erkell. I love this baby. I can't have an abortion. I just can't. Hassan, can you understand what I'm saying?"

"I understand." Hassan's voice was so low I could hardly hear him. "Look, I'm gonna tell you straight, I think that you're making a big mistake, but I'm here for you, and I ain't gonna be like Mark. I takes care of mine." Into his arms I snuggled and we fell asleep holding each other.

Entering my second trimester, the morning sickness had gone and I decided to do some long overdue cleaning. Gathering up all of the dirty clothes, I carried them down to the laundry room. While I was there, loading the washer, I overheard two ladies whispering about something, trying not to look obvious. At first I didn't pay them any mind, but I overheard one say to the other "Damn, he got both of them pregnant!" An alarm went off in me. Could they be talking about me? I was pregnant, but I didn't think it was that noticeable. Who else did *he* get pregnant? There wasn't anyone else there but the three of us. Quickly I looked up and both of them were staring right at me, then they turned their heads.

"Excuse me. Are you talking about me?" I asked with some attitude.

Then one of them said, "No, we are not," with her hands on her hips.

Rolling my eyes away from them, I finished loading my clothes into the washer, and went up stairs to my apartment. What they said rang in my head like gigantic church bells. They had to be talking about me.

Although I could no longer hide the fact that I was pregnant, I still hadn't told any of my family. To tell the truth, I was still trying to come to terms with it *myself*. In a couple of months big changes were going to happen in my life, and I wasn't through thinking yet. Hassan was there for me, but he had become so distracted ever since he found out about the baby. He definitely was not talking marriage or anything, so that meant I was still on my own in this world. And instead of two children plus myself to make a life for, now there were three children involved. The baby was due to be born in February which meant that I could finish out this semester, apply for a light schedule the second semester and go to school during the summer and still be somewhat on target for receiving my degree. That was just one of the many plans that rolled through my mind on a daily basis. All I knew was I wanted to be strong enough to stand on my own two feet before I had to defend myself to my family.

Tim came over and was just hanging around on a Saturday morning playing with the girls. At first, I had my thick house coat on, but then I changed into street clothes and gave Tim the shock of his life. I don't know why I decided to let Tim in on my secret, but I guess I was tired of hiding. Besides, Tim was my favorite brother and I thought I could trust him. His eye bugged out of his head, his forehead wrinkled, and his mouth fell open. "Naw, Tammy, don't tell me you pregnant again!" He said not caring how it came out. Ignoring him I went on in the kitchen to fix some breakfast. I was too hungry. Tim got up and followed behind me. "You let that niggah get you pregnant?"

"It just happened" The words softly departed my lips.

He put his hand on my stomach. "Damn, how many months are you?" His eyes were still bugged out.

"Let's see..it's September so that now makes me four months. And don't tell Ma, okay?"

The shock was starting to wear off, and Tim started laughing. "Damn, Tammy, you was just over our house last week and you didn't look like this."

"I kept my coat on, that's why you didn't notice," I said smiling. Even though it was still warm outside it just happened to be pouring that day. Daddy was suppose to bring the girls home, but he and Mr. Will from down their street had gone out. Mom called me to come and get Kiara and Tianna. At first I panicked until I realized that with the coat on my pregnancy wasn't noticeable.

"So, is the father proud?" he asked sarcastically.

"He's alright with it." I lied.

"It is Hassan's baby, right?"

"Yeah, dummy," I replied. As I poured the pancake mix into the bowl I felt sad. This was my third pregnancy and not once did I ever receive a hug or a card which read, *congratulations on the expectant arrival.* Not even from the fathers. Being that I signed papers to have my tubes tied after I deliver this child, I guess I'll never know that type of joy.

Asking Tim not to mention my being pregnant was really too much to ask of him. The very next day Jimmy called me on the phone and gave me the third degree.

"I heard some news today about you that I just don't even want to believe." Jimmy sighed in disgust. "You pregnant again, Tammy?"

"Yes." By the condescending tone in his voice, I knew this was going to be a stressful conversation.

"What in the world were you thinking about?" He said sharply, "You were just getting to the point where your life was getting back in order and you were makin' things happen for yourself. I don't understand for the life of me how you can even consider having another baby."

"Jimmy, what do you mean *even consider* having another baby. Exactly, what are you saying?"

"I'm saying you're only twenty years old, you're not married, you're on welfare, you're gonna have three kids, and you don't have a pot to piss in. You're bringing these kids into the world with no consideration for their well being. You're being selfish, and if you were smart, you should have handled this situation when you first found out you were pregnant."

"You know what, Jimmy, with all due respect, you got a damn nerve callin' my fuckin' house tellin' me that I should get an abortion, and kill my child because *you* don't think I have anything to offer it. Well, let me ask you something, when Sharon got pregnant for the third time and y'all was on the verge of being evicted, did I call your damn house and tell you to kill your child? No, in fact, everyone stuck by y'all and helped you out, didn't we? So don't play high and mighty with me, because I knew you when."

"Look, I'm just telling you how I see things. You're the one who has to live like that."

"Yeah, you're right, this is my life. And by the way, my children come into this world very wealthy. Very wealthy with my love." CLICK!

My anger was consuming me. How the hell could Jimmy come off talking to me like he's my damn daddy. *I have a plan for my life*! But it seems like this invisible thing that no one can see but me. I'm still the same Tamlyn Annita Blake, honor student. And I *know* that I am able to make my good grades work for me. I truly believe in my vision and will make good on my life's promises. Those promises are to graduate from college with a degree in business management. Have a prosperous career. And buy a house for me and my children like the one I grew up in. Hassan is definitely a part of my dream. We'll be married and raise our family together. Whether the marriage part comes true or not, my plans are still in motion.

Reverend Brown, the minister from our church always talks about moving mountains, *And if you can't move the mountain, go around it, if you can't go around it blast through it. God will help you.* Those words started to take on a whole new meaning for me. As the tears formed, I wiped my eyes thinking about my mountain, and it wasn't my baby. This child was loved and I couldn't wait to hold what Hassan and I had created in my arms. And I will sing to this baby the same love song that I sing to Kiara and Tianna when I rock them to sleep, *Always And Forever* by Heat Wave. That's my declaration to them, to love, protect, educate, and always, always be there for them. No, my mountain wasn't my child, but putting up with the negative attitudes of others was the mountain, cause you see...I have a plan.

After I pulled myself together, I spent the rest of my afternoon washing, greasing, and cornrowing Kiara and Tianna's hair. Both of them have thick long hair and I was at it almost five hours. The only thing I was thinking was Lord, please let this be a boy so I can take him to the barber shop and get *all* of his hair *cut off.* My fingers were numb, and I couldn't even imagine having a third head to do.

Not being in the mood to be doing any major cooking, I went in the kitchen and opened up a big can of Spaghettios. Then someone knocked on the door.

It was my sister Kiesha and I wasn't in the mood for any more shit. She bopped her self-righteous self inside, and I knew what she was there for. I loved my sister and everything, but we didn't always see eye-to-eye.

"I just had to came over here to see you for myself."

"Kiki, I'm not in the mood for you right now. I spoke with Jimmy earlier today, and I'm gonna tell you the same thing I told him. Mind your own damn business." Kiesha was in her first year at Rutgers University doing great, living the life that you're suppose to be at the age of eighteen, and I was very proud of her. But that didn't give her any rights to down me.

"I just can't believe that you are gonna keep that baby. Where the hell y'all gonna sleep in this little ass match box? And you know you can't do any better. Y'all gonna be living like fuckin' refugees, fifty to a house," she said looking amused. "This really don't make no sense. This is plain stupid, Tammy."

"Thank you for your insight." Opening the door I said, "You better leave right now, before I show you just how stupid I can get."

"I'm only concerned for your well being. Don't you even care about Kiara and Tianna? You know this is not fair to them. Did you think about that?"

"Kiesha, who in the hell are you to stand here and try to act more concerned about my kids than I am. I'm their mother, not you. If you want to play the concerned mother, have your own damn kids. Now get out of my house."

As the days went on, this overwhelming depression set in and I couldn't shake it. Seemed like shit just got harder and harder to deal with. I was in my second year at Mercer County Community College, and I was finding it hard to concentrate on my studies. Needless to say, my mind was not on my schooling. Last year I aced, but now I was having trouble just keeping up with the class. The morning sickness was so violent that I missed too much of the information being taught.

If that wasn't bad enough, Hassan even slowed down on coming around. He would drop in maybe twice a week on a mercy call. And I couldn't leave my apartment without someone approaching me, feeling it was their appointed duty to tell me that they had seen Hassan out somewhere messing around. Mostly it was those crabby females who live around here trying to act all sincere like they actually gave a damn about me. I knew Hassan was a popular person, and he had a lot of friends, both male *and* female so I wasn't *really* feeding into their trashy conversations. But several times I did break down and ask Hassan about the rumors. He always denied them. Then he'd throw the ball back in my court by asking, who I was going to believe, him or the people in the streets. 'Seeing is believing Tammy,' he'd say, 'And you ain't never seen me cheating on you cause it ain't nothing to see'. That was good enough for me.

The afternoon sun casted a beautiful orange glow through my living room window. Kiara and Tianna were both sitting on the floor playing in a mess of toys, and the sounds of the television playing came from my bedroom. As usual I had been feeling nauseous all day long. With this pregnancy, I didn't get morning sickness. Some days,

I just stayed sick around the clock. In the kitchen I reached into my cupboard and retrieved the box of Alka Seltzer, plopped it into the water and chugged it down. As I washed out my glass I heard the dead bolt turn on my door and Hassan stepped through. A smile warmed my entire body as he looked at me, and I looked back at him. Even though we talked on the phone, I hadn't seen him in almost a week. The girls ran over to him and he scooped them up giving them both kisses. "Hey," he said to me kinda sober-like, then sat in my single chair.

"So you decided to pay me a visit today." I said sarcastically. "I'm honored."

"Tammy come on. Let's not do this okay,"

Throwing up the palm of my hand, I grimaced, "What ever Hassan!" Leaning up against the kitchen counter top in my night shirt, I folded my arms around my protruding belly looking away from him.

"Tammy, come here." He said sounding as emotionally drained as I was, but my feet wouldn't move. I just lifted my eyes to him and watched. "Babe, come here." He said again.

"Mommy, daddy wa youuuuuu!" Tianna's little mouth yelled.

A smile cracked across my lips and I looked at her sideways like, who was talking to you. Hassan also got a kick out of it and said to them, "Y'all go on over there and bring Mommy to me."

They both jumped up and ran over to me. I held out my hands so each could take one and they pulled me over to where Hassan was seated.

"Now!" He smirked at me and stuck his tongue out and I cracked up. Hassan reached out his arms and sat me on his lap. Tianna grabbed his shirt pulling him to the side of the chair and gave him a big juicy kiss, before she ran back to her toys and Kiara did the same.

"Luv you daddy." She added. While the girls played, I leaned back into Hassan and caressed one of his big strong hands.

"Did you go to class today?"

"Couldn't. I was throwing up all morning."

He slipped the other hand up under my night shirt and gently stroked my belly. And as his warm hands rubbed me, my baby thumped inside for the very first time, and we both felt it together. "Hassan did you feel that...!"

"Baby, what was that...?" Our words came out at the same time. "Was it the baby...?" He asked. "It was the baby..." Our words continued to excitedly leap-frog over each others, then in unison we both said. "The baby kicked!"

And we both laughed.

"Shhh, shhhh let's see if he'll do it again." Hassan said with his hand on my stomach slowly moving it around and around. Nothing happened for awhile then, *thump*! As Hassan and I laughed, I was so glad that he was here to share this moment with me. Feeling as if they were missing out on all of the excitement, Kiara and Tianna came over to me wanting to feel the baby as well. Before I knew it I had four hands up under my shirt waiting for the chance to be thumped by the baby. It was truly a Kodak moment. Sitting between Hassan's legs resting my back against his chest, everything felt so right. His arms were wrapped around me as we talked and laughed like in our better days, while the girls continued to play.

A heavy knock on the door shattered the serenity in the room. Hassan and I glared at each other wondering who it was, on the other side of the door, that done lost their mind. "Who is it?" I enquired.

"It's your mother!" Since everyone else in the family knew that I was pregnant, mom had to know too. If I didn't go over there, I knew eventually she would come to me. My face drained of its color. Hassan shook his head as if to say, he'd rather be anywhere but there. When I got up and opened the door, mom stormed into the apartment, and she was not one to hold her tongue no matter who was in the room. "Did you think that I wasn't going to find out about this?" She glared at my stomach, not acknowledging Hassan's presence. He just sat back in the chair with his hands across his chest watching like he was at a show.

My mom continued, "And this is how I have to find out. By overhearing that you are pregnant with some drug dealer's baby." She directed her attention toward Hassan. He sat up on the edge of the chair ready to pounce, as he struggled not to say anything. His words were written all over his livid face. I was crushed and embarrassed. She didn't even have enough courtesy to tell my girls to go into the other room as they looked on wide eyed and confused. "I don't know what's wrong with you. You the only one of my kids who's just plain stupid! It's like you don't have no pride in yourself, and you just wanna be a nobody!"

Her words hit me over the head like a shovel. Hurt and humiliated, my body trembled as tears ran down my face.

My mother kept on, "Do you honestly think that this punk is gonna stay around and help you raise your kids?" She had one hand on her hip and the other fist poised at Hassan.

"Ma, you don't have no right talkin' like that." I spoke on Hassan's defense, though afraid that she would slap me.

Hassan rose up out of his chair with his jaws tight. "I'm out!"

"Hassan, where you going?" Touching his arm as he passed me, I just felt like screaming.

"She's fuckin' buggin'. I'll catch you later." He closed the door behind him.

Furious, I started to holler back at her. I don't even remember what I said. Marching into my room, I slammed the door, turning the TV up full-blast and stayed there until I was convinced that she was gone. It was understandable the hurt she must have felt, but I didn't understand how she could justify yelling at me in front of Hassan and my daughters. Mom had laid it out. She said I was setting a bad example for the girls and if I kept up the way I was going, I'd have a baby from every man in town. I was acting like a whore and letting everyone down.

After mom left I couldn't stop crying. I had cried more within the last two and a half months, than I had in two years. Picking up the phone I dialed my parents' house. Tim was going to get told off because he had no right to tell them I was pregnant when I asked him not to. When I felt the time was right, *I* would have announced it.

"Hello"

It was daddy and he was just as good a person to tell off as anyone. "How could you let her come over here and talk to me like that?" I blasted him.

"Tammy, what are you talking about?" He was baffled.

"Mom, she came over here and called me a whore, and said that I was a bad mother and, and..." I couldn't finish my sentence because it just hurt too much. Why couldn't she be like Hassan's mother, Mrs. Colbirth, who called me and simply said, 'Whatever you need Tammy, I want you to know that I'm here for you'. Even a damn dog deserved respect. Mom didn't have to be happy, but I didn't deserve her cruel treatment.

"Baby, stop crying now. You know how your mother gets when she's upset. I'm quite sure she didn't mean it." He went on to comfort me in a way that only daddy could. About an hour later, daddy came over to my apartment. He gave me a hug and rubbed my stomach and chuckled. "I sure can't see how you fooled all us for so long."

Through puffy, tear-stained eyes, I smiled. Daddy grabbed my hand and led me to the couch. We sat down and he put his arm around me. My eyes were red from crying. Daddy and I talked for hours about everything. He told me that I was a wonderful mother and that he was very proud of me. Just as daddy was leaving, Hassan returned. They shook hands and daddy met the father of his grandchild for the first time.

It took me another month before I could bring myself to go to my mom's house. It was October nineteenth, daddy's birthday. After all that stuff she said to me, I couldn't forget. I just prayed that one day I'd be able to forgive her for it.

The girls had been at mom's since Friday night. By the time I got there everyone had arrived except Jimmy, Sharon, and their daughters. Walking in I pulled off my coat, and hung it up on one of the wooden coat hooks by the door. This baby must have felt the tension, because it was balled up tight in my belly. I said hello to everyone and headed for daddy and gave him a big birthday hug and kiss.

Mom and the rest of the family were celebrating with a family get-together, like we do every year. She cooked a big dinner as usual, roast beef, collard greens, candied yams, macaroni and cheese, shrimp salad, and wild rice.

My stomach grew big over the last couple of weeks. Even though I was only five months, I looked at least six. Mom was over in the corner placing the hot casserole dishes onto the table. Out of respect, I headed over to speak to her. She saw me from the corner of her eye and gave me a deadly look, then rolled her eyes away. That turned the knife that she had already placed there. Instead, I turned back and sat down on the couch.

Finally Jimmy and his family showed up. He walked as if on egg shells around me, trying to say all the right things, being overly polite. He knew he had hurt me.

As the evening progressed, Sharon and I found ourselves off in a corner alone. She said that Jimmy felt bad about what he had said to me. He had been upset for me. Here I was making such great progress with my college studies, with the apartment, and with the girls, he just hated that my life would have to be put on hold again. Sharon and I hugged. I thanked her for caring enough to tell me.

All evening long, mom bulldozed around the house with her face balled up like she smelled somethin' *stank*. She would not talk to me. She would not even look my way. This hurt me terribly. Everyone knew how she felt about me being pregnant. Everyone knew about our argument. After daddy made his wish and blew out the candles, I wrapped up three pieces of cake *to go*.

I loved my brother Tim with all my heart. Out of all of our siblings, we have always been each other's favorite. But lately, we've been fighting like cats and dogs. He called me back when he got home from his job. Jimmy was able to pull some strings and get Tim a job with him. The company that Jimmy works for, Powell Electronics, paid for all of Tim's computer training. He's been working there for about a year now.

Earlier that day, I left word with my little sister, Nichole, that I wanted to speak with him and clear the air. She was the only one of my sibling that wasn't treating me like I was something on the bottom of their shoes. She was a sweet girl and her kindness was definitely appreciated. When Tim finally did call me, the conversation quickly turned toward Hassan. We began to argue. Next thing I knew I was listening to a dial tone. Tim had hung up the phone on me! My head began to throb. How could my own family just turn their back on me. I loved my children with all of my heart, and no matter if they grew up to be successful millionaires or flipping burgers at McDonald's, my love for them would never change. Sure, everyone has certain expectations that they want to see their children achieve, but aren't they still worthy of love *no matter what*?! I never murdered anyone. I'm still the same Tamlyn Annita Blake that I've always been. I'm still me, a human being deserving of respect. Determined to claim mine, I loaded the girls into the car and headed over to my mother's house for a face-to-face with Tim. This way he couldn't hang up on me.

When I got there he wasn't home, so I waited. Tim walked into the kitchen and slung his keys onto the table acting like I wasn't even there. "Tim why did you hang up the phone on me?"

"I don't even want to get into nothin' with you." He threw up his hands, "What's the point?"

I got up, walked over and stood in front of him with my hands on my hips, "Do you know how much this hurts me to have y'all treating me like this." My words started sticking in my throat. I needed my brother to put his arms around me and to tell me that everything was gonna be alright.

"You the one hurtin' yourself, messin' around with that punk ass chump. Don't nobody feel sorry for you Tammy! You brought all this shit on yourself." Tim used his hand like a paint brush to gesturing across my belly. And my tears, *once again*, just started flowing.

"So if I wasn't pregnant, or if I didn't have Kiara or Tianna and went to college, then I would be *down* in your eyes? Is that it, tell me cause I'm missing it here. You think you better than me? Tim with all them ho's you be with, tell me, how many abortions you done paid for?" I knew for a fact that Tim got this Puerto Rican girl, Carmen, that he use to go with pregnant and talked her into getting an abortion. But he went to great lengths to keep that from my parents. Right in the middle of my sentence he showed me the palm of his hand and walked out of the kitchen. I didn't want to fight, but *damn it*, he was going to talk to me. Right behind him I stayed as he made his way up the stairs and entered his bedroom.

"I don't get you, girl. I told you to leave him alone. That niggah ain't shit! You know what he's into."

"Look Tim, I don't need this from you. I'm grown, and I know all about Hassan. It's cool with me, alright?" I had made up my mind to ignore Tim's personal vendetta with Hassan. Whatever problem he had with Hassan in my opinion was just plain tired. I wanted to concentrate on why all of a sudden Tim and I couldn't stand the sight of each other. There was something specific going on in his head, and I wanted to know what it was so we could just get past it. But he kept harping on Hassan.

"Oh, so you know *all about* Hassan, and it's cool with you?" He repeated sarcastically.

"Yeah." Forget it, I thought. I'll play his stupid game.

"So it's cool he's out there selling drugs to his own people, huh?"

"Yeah, whatever."

"And it's cool he's out here mackin' every woman he sees?"

"Yeah, that's cool too, alright. Look Tim, what do you want from me?" I threw up my hands ready to walk away from him. He wasn't about to tell me what was bugging him. Or so I thought. Just as I did an about face he took out his big gun and blew me away.

"And it's cool with you that Hassan got his son's mother pregnant, too?" He shouted.

My heart dropped then I remembered what those ladies in the laundry room had said.

"So, she's pregnant. That don't mean it's his!" I shouted in utter denial.

"You so stupid! I told you to leave that mothah fuckah alone. Now he done stuck both y'all."

"Fuck you, Tim!"

Into my parents' bedroom I stormed and closed the door. Hassan never told me that Debbie was pregnant. Why didn't he tell me?! Shaking like a leaf, I feverishly dialed his number, and on the first ring he picked it up.

"Yo, babe, what's up?" He asked sweetly.

I was crying, upset and couldn't hide it.

"Hassan, a couple months ago I was in the laundry room washing clothes and these two women were talking about me. The only thing I heard was somethin' about someone getting both of them pregnant, but I didn't pay it no mind. And today, Tim just told me that Debbie's pregnant by you. What's up with that?"

"Look, Tammy, I don't know what you're talking about." He was stalling. I could hear it in his voice.

"Is she or is she not pregnant?!" I asked in a steadily increasing tone.

"She's pregnant but it ain't mine." I didn't know whether or not to believe him. "Baby, I swear to you on my son's life. I didn't get her pregnant. Please believe me, Tammy. Babe, do you believe me, Tammy?"

"I don't know what to believe."

"Tammy."

"What?"

"I love you. Do you love me?"

"Yeah Hassan, I love you." I was skeptical. Could everyone else be wrong?

"Where you at, I'm coming right now. Tammy, you home?" Hassan sounded upset and scared.

"I'm over my mom's."

"I'm coming to get you."

"I drove over here."

"I don't want you driving like this. Be lookin' out. I'm coming now."

Walking out of my parents' room, I went into the bathroom to dry my face. In the mirror, I saw someone mighty stupid looking back at me. Everything started to fit. Even though I felt betrayed by Hassan, I still wanted to believe what my man was telling me. Gathering up the girls, I got them dressed and we waited in the doorway until I saw Hassan's car pull up in front of the house. No good-byes to anyone, I just removed my unwanted self from that house. Once the girls were in Hassan's back seat, I got in the front. When I looked at him, my emotions spilled over. My hands covered my face and I cried like someone had beaten me. Everything around me faded into blackness, and I was aware only of my own pain and helplessness.

The baby was balled tight in the bottom of my womb and wouldn't relax. It was painful, and I had a low tolerance for pain.

No Way Out

I was busted, but I couldn't fess up to getting Debbie pregnant now.

"What wrong wit my mommy, daddy?"

"She's just feeling a little sad, Tianna. Daddy's gonna make her feel better," I said, taking off her little pink and grey coat. Then I felt a tap on my back pocket.

"Daddy, I know who made my mommy cry."

"Who, babe?"

"Uncle Tim. Mommy told him, 'fuck you, Tim' then she started crying."

"Hey Kiara, I don't want to hear you saying bad words. You understand me?"

"I tell you what mommy say, daddy."

"Yeah, but you heard what I said."

"'Kay."

"Y'all ate over your grandmom's house?"

"No" Tianna closed her eyes, flapping her beaded braids from side to side.

Kiara corrected her, "We had some cookies."

"That ain't no food." Lookin' through Tammy's kitchen cabinets, I wanted to find something quick. She had all kinds of food in this place. Opening up a can of Ravioli, I heated it on the stove, and gave them each a bowl full. While they ate, I went to check on Tammy. She appeared to be asleep, but she wasn't. I could see her eyes blinkin' fast from tryin' to keep them shut. 'Cause I wasn't ready for her yet. I just let her be, and sat on the couch while Kiara and Tianna ate. My beeper went off, and when I called the number back it was some kid talkin' nothing but problems. I called up Chief and asked him to handle it. My mind wasn't focused on no street business tonight. Then I put on their night clothes and put them to bed. Instead of going in to see about Tammy, I just stayed out on the couch thinkin'. Eventually, the truth was gonna come out, but for some reason, I couldn't bring myself to tell it to her.

Falling

A notice came from the community college stating that I had flunked out for the semester because of poor attendance. A dull pain flickered inside of me as I stood in the cold courtyard at the mail box reading the letter. The sun had gone down in my life and I felt so void, like I was lost and didn't know where to find myself. True it had been a month since I attended class, but this paper was just so definite, so tangible. It was the undisputed truth that I had once again fallen. In my soul some where my plan still existed. I knew all of this would work itself out and my little family would be alright. But for now, I felt like I was standing screaming my head off and no one could hear me.

The days that followed were dismal. Not having a reason to leave, all I did was stay in my apartment. School was no longer a factor, my mom's house was no place I desired to be, and I didn't even want to be bothered with Hassan.

All cried out, the only emotion left was anger. Justified or not, I was so angry that I began to yell and take that anger out on my daughters. The other day, I was in the kitchen trying to make lunch for us and Kiara kept whining about wanting some juice. Over and over again I kept telling her to have a seat, but she wouldn't. Before I realized what I had done, I had slapped Kiara right in the face. When I looked at her the red outline of my hand was across her cheek. I grabbed her in my arms and we both cried together. I *hated* myself for that. Never had I struck my girls out of anger. Because of my rattled nerves, even my hair started to fall out. My mother and I hadn't spoken to each other ever since her angry visit. I couldn't eat or sleep. I was just a mess.

❖

The weather man predicted the first snow fall of the season, and I was depressed as hell. I couldn't seem to get a grip on my situation. After she got off of her night shift, Jeannette came over to see me.

"Girl you alright?" she asked, looking worried.

"No, I'm not alright. Everyone keeps telling me that Hassan and Debbie are screwing around and that she's pregnant with his baby. When I asked him about it, he denied it. I just need to find out for myself."

"Tammy, I don't think you want to know that for sure. With all the pressure you got on you right now. I don't know. I don't think that's the thing to do."

I got upset because I felt that she knew something and didn't want to let me in on it. "How are you gonna tell me what's right? You're not feeling my pain." I raised my hands up to my head. "I feel like I'm going out of my mind. I *have to know*, Jeannette. I need the truth. Besides it can't hurt any more than it already does. Ride over to Debbie's house with me."

"Tammy I don't think..."

"Whatever, Jeannette!" I snapped, "Either you ride with me, or I'll go by my damn self, but I'm going." I yanked mine and the girls' coats out of the closet.

Jeannette looked at me and shook her head. "Wait up Tee!" She reluctantly said, "Let me go and get my coat and I'll go with you."

After I dressed the girls, we were off.

Driving around that night looking to see if I could catch Hassan doing something that he didn't have any business doing made me sick. First we drove by Debbie's house, but he wasn't there. Then we drove around to his usual hang outs, still no sign of him. Having an uncomfortable feeling that *something* was going to happen tonight, I told Jeannette to go back around to Debbie's. Sure enough, there they were in the parking lot, standing around with a couple of other people. Erkell was with them too and, she was as big as a house. It felt like a thousand hot pins were going through me. They were laughing and playing around. Hassan had grabbed her from behind and was kissing her on the neck. Even the blind could see by the way he was all up on her, the child inside of her body was his seed.

"No! No!" I cried. "How can he do this to me?"

Hysterically, I jumped out the car and stormed over to them. "Ain't your damn baby? Right, Hass? You ain't shit! What the hell you doing over here if it ain't your damn baby? You ain't shit." So badly I wanted to hurt him like I was hurting inside. Cursing and swinging, I clawed at him. Debbie jumped out of the way and everyone was watching. I was in a blind rage. And even though Erkell was crying and my two babies were calling for me from the car, I couldn't stop.

Jeannette ran over to me. I was hysterical. "I hate you! I hate you for doin' me like this!"

"Jeannette, what the fuck you bring her around here for?" Hassan yelled. I had scratched him in the face.

"I hate you! I hate you, you muthah fuckah!" I said, but translation of the heart was, *I love you more than I love myself. Way down in the core of me there's you. So deep down inside til I am you, you are me, and we are each other. Seeing you with her was so repulsive, so opposite of the truth it would have made more sense to have the earth spin backwards than to accept that you could hurt me this way. So here I stand yelling and belittling myself by allowing primitive reactions to convey what intellect can not.*

I continued to yell then Hassan grabbed me in a bear hug from behind and pushed me toward Jeannette. As he pushed me away, I *needed* him to hold me in his arms and hush my screaming soul.

"I hate you too, bitch! Take her ass the fuck home!" Hassan ordered Jeannette. He missed my SOS.

"He don't want your ass anyway, so why don't you leave him the fuck alone, you stupid bitch!" Debbie yelled.

"Forget her!" Hassan said to Debbie holding her arm as if he were protecting *her*.

Hassan's words ripped the rug of sanity out from under my feet. I *died* right there on the spot. Jeannette guided me back to the car and from that point on, the night became a shadowy haze. When Jeannette opened the car door all I heard was, "Mommy, Mommy." Kiara and Tianna were both scared for me. Jeannette didn't know what to say except, "I should have talked you out of this, Tee."

Sitting there as if in a trance, I was in a calm hysteria. "How can he do me like this?" I whispered. "How can he do me like this, Jeannette?" Tianna and Kiara were in my arms the entire trip home. The pain I felt was unbearable. Never had I felt such torment.

Walking into the lobby, Jeannette kept asking the same questions over and over, "Tee, you gonna be alright? You want me to come in with you? Do you wanna stay at my house tonight?" Deeply distraught, I didn't answer her. Instead I just walked out of the elevator, into my apartment, and closed the door on her.

The night was eery. Feeling more like an observer than a participant, I was going through the motions, but I was not there. Immediately I put the girls to bed then started pacing around the house. My mind began to race over the events of the past month, the stories, the whispers, my brother and his warning. It was like a runaway train, the memories just ran on and on. With my arms around my head I couldn't make them stop. I wanted to cry, but I was all cried out. I wanted to scream, but when I opened my mouth...a moan. I wanted to run, but I fell to my knees. Dazed and confused, I longed to be comforted wishing that Hassan would come over and beg for my forgiveness. Then I painfully remembered how he held Debbie and rubbed her stomach with their child inside. "You're so stupid." I kept hearing, "You're just a nobody. He's gonna leave you, just like Mark did." The voices had no mercy. Gasping for air like a fish out of water, I stumbled in the darkness of my room, reaching for the bottle of pills from the night stand. Sleep! I wanted to sleep so I wouldn't feel the pain. As I twisted down hard on the cap, the bottle fell and the pills scattered all over the floor. They spoke to me. *Come here baby, relax your mind. Grab hold and take a ride. Lay back and open wide and feel my magic carpet ride. So high we'll fly, but when we land you'll be far away from the problems at hand. Hey girl, don't hesitate, lay your burdens on me. In another land, you'll be free. Let me bridge that gap from here to there. It won't hurt. You'll just float on air. Free, free, free!* I remember being on all fours, my belly hanging low, putting the pills, one after the other, into my mouth. All I wanted was to stop the pain.

THIS AIN'T HAPPENIN'

Glancing in Debbie's bathroom mirror, I saw how Tammy had clawed my damn face up. My feelings were all fucked up. Really, I felt bad about having Tammy find out the truth about me and Debbie havin' another baby, but damn. She didn't have to take it to this extreme. I didn't want to hurt her but shit, how the fuck she gonna come over here dissin' me like that. She knew better than that shit. Then Debbie started soundin'off in my ear, talkin' 'bout how I better put Tammy in check cause if she wasn't pregnant, what she would have done. And I wasn't tryin' to hear her shit either.

It was one thirty in the morning when my pager started blowin' up with Tammy's number. No intentions did I have of even callin' her ass back. I was pissed and wanted to be left the hell alone. If I went over there, I was bound to hurt that girl. Zipping up my pants, I flushed the toilet and came out of the bathroom.

Debbie was in her night clothes sitting in front of the TV drinking a diet coke soda. Grabbing my coat I headed toward the door when my pager went off again. Lookin' down I didn't recognize the number.

"Why don't you answer that shit, or turn it off?" Debbie snapped.

Glaring down at her, I snatched the phone and began to dial the number having this strange feeling that it was Tammy. Even though the number wasn't hers, she could have been using someone else's phone. "Hassan here. Who dis?"

"Hassan, it's Jeannette..."

"What?!" I cut her off quick and hostile. Just the sound of her voice incensed me.

"Tammy swallowed a bottle of pills. She's at Mercer Hospital. I don't know if she's gonna make it." She said then the phone line went dead. "Wha...?" *If she's gonna make it...If she's gonna make it...Tammy swallowed a bottle of pills. I don't know if she's gonna make it. If she's gonna make it.* I rewound the tape over and over in my head to digest that shit and see if she really said what I thought she said. But it wasn't registering. It was like my brain suddenly locked up. Slammin' the phone down I yelled,

"What kind of fucked up game are they playin'?" My system kicked into overdrive as part of me knew it was not a game.

"What happened *now* Hassan?" Debbie grimaced.

Running out of her crib to my car, I had no time for explanations. Flying down the highway I sped all the way to the hospital. In the hospital's parking lot I didn't recognize any cars that might have been there for Tammy. As my pulse raced, I prayed that this shit *was* a joke. Some mess that Tammy and Jeannette cooked up to *pay a brothah back.* Maybe they were somewhere clockin' me and laughing their asses off cause they knew I would be getting to the hospital 'bout now. Rushing through the emergency room doors, the hard force of reality slammed into my mind when I saw Jeannette and all of Tammy's family sitting around. Everything came to a screeching halt...then the sound of my pounding heart filled my ears.

As I walked over to where everyone was sitting I felt like I was about to get sick, "How's Tammy?" Standing in front of her parents nobody opened their mouths to say a word. They just gave me this fucked up look like I was to blame for all of this. That fat fuck, Mrs. Blake, got up turned her back to me and walked away.

Mr. Blake stood to his feet with attitude, "What happened between you and my daughter tonight?" He asked, ignoring my question.

Before I got a chance to say my piece, Tammy's mom started goin' off. "If you were so damned interested in her well-being, you wouldn't have gotten her pregnant in the first place!" She blasted. "You ain't no good. You just got her pregnant and left her there to fend for herself. You ain't even man enough to face your responsibilities!"

"Ain't man enough...You gonna talk that shit to me?" I didn't like that bitch one bit and now sure wasn't the time to test me, "You the one went over to Tammy's place spoutin' off at the mouth, callin' her names, sayin' she ain't shit. You did that!" I snarled in her direction.

Then punk ass Tim grew some balls and jumped up in my face, and there we were standing chest to chest *after all these years.* Tim and I had some history that went way back to when we were in high school together. Even though I never graduated, I got my GED in Juvenile Detention. In the eleventh grade I got arrested, pulled out of history class by school security, *and* the city police. They had this targeted locker search and in mine, they found ten rolled up joints and a bag of weed. I had a nice little business goin' on. If you wanted some smoke, you'd put five dollars in your note book, pass it over to me and when I went to the locker during the change of class while I was getting my books for my next period I'd put a nickle bag inside their book. Everything-was-everything. The shit was smooth, and I was making 'bout two-fifty, three hundred dollars a week. Enough to keep me looking fly, and my pockets jinglin'. That is until, one day Tim saw me talking to this female he was trying to talk to. We was just kickin' it when he walked over, and I knew he wanted to say something to me but he didn't. Instead the two of them started arguing. I wasn't about the drama so I stepped. The next fuckin day I got arrested. To this day, I know that punk had something to do with it. But it damn sure is a small world cause at first I had no idea that he and Tammy were related.

"That's my mother, muthah fuckah!" Tim spouted in my face.

Before I got a word in the security guard ran over toward me. Mr. Blake, Tim, and Tammy's oldest brother were all standing around me, and I was ready to pounce. "Enough! This is not the time for this!" Mr. Blake blasted. "Son, you are making matters worse by being here. I think you should go!"

"That's my girl, and my baby in there and I ain't goin' a damn place!" As the security guard stood next to the Blakes, a nurse dashed over and persuaded me to take a walk with her outside to get some air and calm down. Yes! I needed it 'cause my fight or flight mode was stuck on *fight*. My head was a mess from all the shit that happened earlier, not knowing what was up with Tammy and the baby, and dealin' with her crazy ass family. The nurse went back inside a minute later, but I stayed outside smoking three cigarettes, back-to-back. It was cold as shit outside.

After what seemed like an eternity, a doctor came into the waiting room and up to the family. When I saw him I rushed over. I had been sitting on the other side of the waiting room. The doc looked wiped out, like he'd been in hand-to-hand combat. We all gathered around him. He shook his head, then placed one hand on the back of his neck to squeeze out the tension. Mrs. Blake held on tight to her husband's arm, and for a second I felt for her. We all were feeling the same thing - *scared*.

"It was touch and go there for a while. We almost lost her. We got as much of the medication out as possible without harming the baby, but there is no way to be sure if we got enough out of her system. Tamlyn has still not regained consciousness. We're still very concerned about that." It seemed just as hard for him to tell us as it was for us to hear it. "The next forty eight hours will be crucial."

"What about the baby?" Tammy's sister, Nichole asked and I was all ears.

"The baby is alive, but he's weak. We ran an ultrasound and an amnio to determine the extent of damage, if any. The little fellah is a fighter.

"It's a boy?" she asked with a half smile. Tammy always talked about how if she had a boy that it would be the first boy born into their family since Tim.

"I see I let the cat out of the bag. Yes, it's a boy." He nodded in confirmation.

"Another son." Shaking my head in disbelief I sighed then started walking toward the exit door. Tammy was alright. I mean, even though she wasn't awake yet, the doctor didn't say she was gonna die or anything.

"Hassan!" Jeannette called out running to catch up with me outside. "Aren't you gonna wait and go see Tammy?" I just looked at her somewhat dazed, still pissed because she brought Tammy to Debbie's house in the first damn place. Throwing my hands up, I kept stepping then replied, "Yo, J. This ain't my scene right now. There ain't nothing I can do here." My temper started to rise. I didn't even want to go there with her. Pulling my collar up around my neck I asked, "Where's the girls?" Wondering where in the hell they were when all of this was going down.

"They're at Mrs. Evette's place across the hall," Jeannette answered, shivering and rubbing her hands together as we stood in the dark besides my car.

It was freezing cold outside. I got in my ride, popped the locks for her to get in, and started the car up turning on the heat. Taking a deep breath, I put my hands over my face and looked at her with my head leaned back on the headrest, "What the fuck happened, man?" Gesturing my words, I slammed my hands down on the stirring wheel.

"I don't know. It still don't seem real to me. Me and Bull were sleepin' and I heard Kiara and Tianna screamin' and cryin'. I ran out the apartment and banged on the door." She paused. "Bull knocked the door down and..."Jeannette shook her head as the tears rolled down her face, "Man, she looked dead."

I could picture my baby in all that pain...needing her man. Instead of being there for her like I should have been, I let my pride keep me away. Was it pride that kept my father from coming back home, from being a man to his family? But I had deserted Tammy and our child, just like he did me. So what kind of man did that make me? Bitting my bottom lip, tears started to roll down my eyes, but I wasn't giving up my mad dog glare. "This shit is all my fault. My girl and my baby are lying up there half dead, and it's all my fault," I confessed out loud.

"It ain't all your fault, Hassan," Jeannette tried to consoled me, but I felt guilty all the same.

"Yeah, it is. If I didn't fuck up her head, she wouldn't be in there, just like her mom said." I looked at her. "She ain't like us, Jeannette. She's strong in some ways, but a lot weaker than us, you know?" I spoke slowly, as the thought of shedding Tim's blood started to occupy my mind. Jeannette's voice became a faint sound in my ear.

"You played a part, her mom played a part, I played a part. We all did in some way. We were dumping all this shit on her, and we didn't realize how much pressure she was under. And last night she went over the edge."

Through gritted teeth I blurted out, "I'm a *fuck* Tim's ass up when I see him."

"If you start fighting with Tim, that ain't gonna help Tammy none," Jeannette snapped angrily.

"There's more than one way to do things." I grimaced.

"What you mean by that?" she asked, raising an eyebrow. "Look, Hassan, don't start up with Tim! Think about Tammy, okay?" She tried to reason, but I didn't answer. My mind was set and Tim was gonna get his.

"Are you gonna come back and see her? Even though she's hurting, I know that she wants to know that you care enough to be there for her and the baby," she said.

"Yeah, the baby...Tammy's having a boy." I smiled slightly. "I hope she ain't hurt my son," my semi-smile turned upside down. "Look, Jeannette, I gotta go cool out for a while. I'll wait till they leave, and I'll be back later on."

"You take it easy, Hassan."

"Yeah, babe. You got my number. Beep me if anything comes up."

She went back into the hospital and I drove off.

It was around four o'clock in the morning and I drove past my apartment and went to my mom's house. Needing something to numb my feelings, I went into the kitchen and poured myself a tall glass of mom's vodka and added a drop of O.J., then sank into the couch. At 6:15 a.m. mom came downstairs. She was getting ready for work.

"Hassan, Hassan," she said gently, waking me. "Are you alright? What are you doing here, boy?" She walked over to the window, pulling up the shade then looked back at me. The sun hadn't even come up yet.

"I couldn't go back to my place." raising up to a sitting position, I rubbed my hands over my heavy eyes. "Ma, Tammy is in the hospital. She OD'd last night."

"What?!"

"She ain't dead," I blurted out to calm her down. "She took a bottle of pills, but they got to her in time. I was up at the hospital until late." Walking over toward the couch mom stared down at me looking deeply troubled. "Tell me, son, what would make her do something like that?" She knew I played a part in it. She just wanted to hear me say it. "It was all messed up, Mom." Covering my face, I could hardly believe it myself. "Tammy and one of her girlfriends came over Debbie's house."

When I said that, my mother closed her eyes tight shaking her head, "Is the child alright?"

"It's a boy. The doctor said he was tough. Tammy's in the ICU. She was still in a coma when I left."

Mom looked disturbed. "Go in there and call up to the hospital and find out what's going on," she ordered.

I'm the man no one talked down to in the streets. I gave the orders, and when I did, people jumped. But around mom, gentle as she is, I had no choice. When I was young, I'd watch as mom worked her ass off trying to keep the house going, me in clothes and food on the table. Many times I heard her on the phone with my father, when she could catch up with his ass, and how she'd be crying for him to send us some money, which he rarely did, or to come visit me, which he never did. For all she's done, I respected my mom.

She made us breakfast before she left for work. When I called the hospital, they said that Tammy had regained consciousness and was being moved to a regular room. That was good news. Until later that afternoon, I laid low chillin' at mom's house. During the day, Debbie had paged me several times, but I just couldn't handle the questions so I didn't return her call.

BABY PLEASE

When I realized where I was and what I'd done, I started to cry. Mom was sitting in the chair next to the bed. She got up and held my hand.

"Tammy, can you hear me? Baby, you're at Mercer Medical. Do you remember anything that happened last night?"

I was slow to nod.

"The girls are fine. They're home with daddy now." Mom wiped my eyes and kissed me softly. "I'm sorry, Tammy. I didn't mean to say all those things. I love you. I love you and that baby. You see this belt right here." She showed me the monitoring belt on my stomach. "This lets you know that your baby is doing fine."

Truly, I was relieved to know that I did not harm my child. My mind went back to the events of last night, and my thoughts just seemed so heavy. This might sound silly, but I was glad to be in the hospital, because at that point, I had needed to be taken care of. Just needed time, not much, just a little to get my head straight. Mom held my hand and I didn't want to let go of her hand. It was obvious she didn't want to let go of mine. Unconditional love was what I needed from her. Whether right or wrong, I needed her in my life. We hugged, and talked and cried. That was the kind of medicine *I* needed. Mom looked like heck. She must have stayed all night.

A nurse came in to check my IV and to make sure everything was alright.

"Good morning, Tamlyn. How are you feeling?"

"I'm sore."

"Well, that's to be expected." She went on to explain what happened while I was under doctor's care. She told me how the baby was and that it was a miracle that it survived, and that I was on the maternity floor.

Mom stayed till late afternoon, and I practically had to beg her to go home cause she was falling asleep in the chair. She said she would send one of my sisters to come and stay with me for the rest of the day. Needing to be alone, I told her not to.

Shortly after mom left, I was taken downstairs, where doctors ran some tests on the baby. When I got back to my room, a beautiful arrangement of flowers was there to greet me. It was signed, "I love you, Hassan."

Doctor Suri came into the room with a tall slender, white woman.

"You gave us quite a scare there, young lady. We had to work a long time on you. This is Dr. Shirmanski, our staff psychiatrist. I brought her to meet you, so maybe you can work through the problems that got you here in the first place. I'm going to leave now, but I'll come back through to see how you're doing later."

Dr. Shirmanski sat down and asked me the usual questions: my name, my age, my address. She seemed nice enough but I wasn't in the mood. The perfume she wore smelled rich and probably cost a fortune.

"Tamlyn, do you mind talking about what upset you?" Talk, sure, I just wanted to blab it all out to the world, but what was the point? "Tamlyn, I know that it's not easy talking about what brought you to the point of an attempted suicide, but maybe we can walk through this together."

Becoming angry, I started to cry just thinking about how everybody hurt me. No way did I plan to kill myself. It wasn't something I thought about, it just happened. I still don't quite understand why I did it. *It just happened.* Angry with the whole freakin' world, I let my frustration out on her since she wanted to talk so damn much, "I can talk about what happened until I'm blue in the face, but it's not going to change anything!" How dare this white lady, with her sixty-dollar perfume and probably the perfect family in a house with a white picket fence, come in here and assume that she could *help* me.

"Tamlyn, I can come back later. I'm here for you. I'm going to leave my number. We have meetings every Wednesday night at seven, right here at the hospital. You will be surprised how much talking out your problems really can help."

What was her problem, I wondered? Wishing she would just leave and take her *let's talk* with her. Ready to argue, my pain turned into words, "Talk about how I messed up my life, how I have two kids and one on the way that I can't even take care of. Or would you like to hear about my man's other pregnant girlfriend." I burst into tears. "My life ain't shit, lady, so how is talking going to help me?"

Turning my back to her, I asked her to leave my room.

"Tamlyn, please give me a call. Whenever you're ready. I will be here for you." She left a business card and a pamphlet on the night stand then left. Once again drowning in misery, I cried loudly. The nurse came in and told me to calm myself down. She said that if I stayed upset I would upset the baby. Well what about me, I wondered?

While absently staring at television, Hassan walked into the room. He was looking good as usual. At the site of him all sorts of emotions started colliding, I was embarrassed, mad, and I was so hurt. Despite all that though, there was a part of me that was glad to see him.

"Hey, Tammy," he said kissing my cheek. "How you feeling? I see you got the flowers I sent." I didn't speak to him. I didn't even look at him. "Tammy, I didn't mean to lie to you. I just didn't know how to tell you. Debbie called me over to her house one night because Erkell was sick. We drove him to the doctor's and when we brought him home, he was still sick. Debbie was upset and I was trying to be strong for her and one thing lead to another. Then next thing I know, she's tellin' me she's pregnant. Baby, it was just that one time, I swear. I don't love her. I love you."

Like I really needed to hear that. Why would I want to picture my man with somebody else? "Fuck you, Hassan. I asked you so many times if she was pregnant and you just kept on lying to me. I asked you if there was something going on between the two of you and you just kept on lying."

"There ain't nothing going on between me and Debbie. I swear, Tammy. It was just that one time."

"You know, Hassan, I don't care if it was one hundred times. My brother was right about you."

"Don't be bringin' your brother up in my face, Tammy. This is between you and me."

"There ain't nothing between you and me. Get out, Hassan. Go on to Debbie and your family."

"No, I'm not leaving you, Tammy. Erkell and this new baby, they are mine, and I'm gonna take care of them. But my place is with you, babe." Hassan took his hand and turned my face around toward him "Tammy, you're my woman. I wanted to tell you, but I was scared. I knew you believed in me girl, and I didn't want to let you down. I knew that if I told you the truth you would leave me and I can't go out like that." Hass had tears in his eyes. Never had I seen him this torn up before. It hurt me to see him like this, but I felt I had to be strong.

"Hassan, you were right. You did let me down, and we are over." We both cried. Hassan walked over to the window and stared out. Looking at him, I just wanted to put a knife through his back. "Tell me something, Hassan, how far along is she?"

He looked at me hesitantly. "Eight months."

"Eight months! Is that why you didn't want me to have my baby, because you knew that she was pregnant?" When he didn't answer me, I knew I had him pegged. "You son-of-a-bitch! What made her so damn special that it was alright for her to have her baby, but I couldn't have mine? Get the fuck out of here, Hassan!"

He came over to me, his nose glistened with moisture. "Naw, baby. I can't do that. I can't let it end like this."

"Like what? You let me go from the moment you took her side over... mine...Ahh!

My abdominal muscles cramped up and I doubled up in pain. Hassan froze looking scared. "Tammy, what is it? Is it the baby?" The pain was so intense, I couldn't respond.

Hassan ran out into the corridor. "Nurse! Nurse, my girl needs help in here!"

He came back into the room and tried to comfort me, when two nurses took over. "Excuse me!"

"Ahh!" I hollered. The pain was devastating.

"Tamlyn, can you straighten up? Tamlyn, we have to check you," the nurse said while the other looked at the chart. "These are strong contractions. I'm going to get Dr. Suri!"

Moments later Dr. Suri came in and examined me. "We have to stop these contractions. This baby's too young. This is no good."

"Ahhh!" I had another big contraction and my water broke.

"Oh my goodness," Dr. Suri said, shaking his head. "I hope that you are ready to have this baby, because it's coming."

The nurses moved at lightning speed preparing the room for the delivery.

"Ahhh! I have to push! I have to push!" The pressure was heavy, and I just wanted some relief.

"Not yet, Tamlyn. You're not ready for that yet," the nurse cautioned.

"Ahhh!"

Hassan stood still, as if in a trance, not believing that the baby was on its way.

"Okay, daddy you go up next to mommy's head and give her some support." The nurse broke Hassan's stupor. He walked over next to me and grabbed my hand. My legs were bent at the knees and spread as wide as they could go.

"When you're ready, I want you to give me a big push now, Tamlyn," Dr. Suri coached. Bending my head down into my chest, I began to push with all my might.

"Ahh!" I hollered "It hurts!"

"Close your mouth and push, Tamlyn," Dr. Suri said.

My nails dug into Hassan's hands and he took it like a trooper. As my contractions eased up, I laid back on the pillow and closed my eyes. Hardly catching my breath, I was able to relax for about thirty seconds when my hands automatically tightened around Hassan's.

"Ahhh!" It was a big one.

"I can feel the baby's head," Dr. Suri said. "Now I want you to push. Give it all you got."

Hassan had his mouth next to my ear, "Come on baby, you can do it."

Using the strength his voice gave me, I bore down and pushed.

"Here's the head, Tamlyn."

Hassan's eyes grew big as he looked down between my legs, "Wow...I can see it, baby."

"Exhale." Dr. Suri instructed, and I did. "Now push, Tamlyn!"

Once again I bore down and pushed with all my might. Dr. Suri was pulling and yanking the baby's head so hard it seemed that he might pull it off. Just then the baby's head was completely out and the shoulders appeared. Hassan was totally amazed to see his baby coming out of me. By the time the shoulders appeared the rest of the baby came right out.

"It's a boy, Tamlyn!" Dr. Suri said.

The nurses quickly wrapped up the two pound, six ounce little baby and rushed him out of the room. They didn't even give me a chance to touch his little hand or to kiss his little face. They just rushed him away from me. This alarmed Hassan, and I panicked.

"Is he alright, Doc?" Hassan asked with concern.

"He's very premature. He's only had a gestation of 26 weeks. When they're that small, we can't take any chances. So, procedure is to take him directly to the high-risk unit and examine him and administer any special care needed." Dr. Suri called the time to the nurse that the baby was born and continued to remove the afterbirth and examined me one final time. "You're fine, Tamlyn. I want you to try to take a shower. But I don't want you walking around. I want you to rest. I'm leaving and I'll check on you tomorrow. A pediatrician will be in to see you and let you know how your baby is doing."

I was exhausted. The nurse helped me out of bed and into the bathroom for a shower. While I showered the nurse stripped the bed and remade it with clean bedding. She left closing the room door behind her. Emerging from the bathroom with a big pad stuck between my legs, I had a towel wrapped around my body. Slowly I walked to the bed and sat.

"Could you look in that drawer and hand me a clean gown?" Earlier mom brought me three new gowns. Hassan chose one and handed it to me. "I want to see my baby."

"The doctor told you not to walk any place and to get some rest."

"I can't rest, if I can't see my son." Hassan knew there was no use trying to talk me out of it. "Go out there and get me a wheelchair please." My baby had been growing in my womb for six months, and now that he's in this world, I wanted...needed to look at him, feel him. I needed to let him know that I loved him and I was there. Bonding with my baby was what I needed and *no one* was going to stop me.

Hassan walked to the nurses station and came back with a wheel chair. Dressed in a gown, house coat and slippers, I eased into the wheelchair then Hassan pushed me to the high-risk nursery. There was still considerable tension between us. But neither of us wanted to acknowledge it at this point.

Over my baby's incubator, there was a blue and white card that read *Baby Boy Blake*. "Oh Hassan look at him. He's so tiny." I was so sorry for the way he had begun his life. Baby Boy Blake lay in an open incubator with IV's in both his arms, and an oxygen hood placed over his head. A gold heart-shaped monitor ran from his chest to a respiratory machine. Hassan and I were completely blown away. With tears in my eyes, I could only look at my son. Hassan stared quietly, giving my shoulders a squeeze. We were unsure of what kind of future this helpless little baby would have or if he would have one at all. He even had a bloody bandage on the heel of his foot.

"Hello, are you his parents?" a black nurse asked.

"Yeah," Hassan answered.

"Have you picked out a name for him yet?" she asked, washing her hands after tending to another premature infant.

Before I could say anything Hassan spoke. "His name is Hassan Hateem Colbirth."

"That's a strong name. And it's perfect for him, since he's a real fighter." She dried her hands then removed the old name card from the incubator and replaced it with one that read *Hassan Hateem Colbirth-Blake*. She explained that in order for us to drop the name *Blake*, we would have to fill out the proper paperwork. The nurse also explained what all the tubes and wires were for and why Hateem had to have the oxygen hood over his head. "It's actually not as bad as it looks," she assured us. She was just trying to make us feel better, because it looked real bad to me.

Standing up, I touched his tiny hands. The tip of my index finger almost covered his entire hand. His skin was loose, and his eyes looked overly large for his little face.

Stroking his legs softly, I talked to him, and he squirmed at my touch. Hassan stood beside me and stroked the baby's legs and felt his hands. "Hey, Hateem. This is daddy. You gonna be a strong boy. You fight to get better so you can get out of here and go in the nursery with the other babies. Then me and mommy gonna take you home to meet your brother and sisters. I love you, little man."

Standing there, I began to break out in a cold sweat. Grabbing hold of Hassan, he put his arm around me and helped me back into the chair. Feeling faint, I could hardly hold my head up. Immediately he wheeled me back down the hall to my room. When I got into the bed and rested for a few minutes, I felt a whole lot better. "Why you name him Hateem?" I asked curiously as Hassan smoothed the blanket around me.

"Because it's a mixture of Hassan and Tammy."

I just smiled. "I can't believe I had him," I said, taking a sip of the ice cold water which sat on the adjustable tray in front of me.

"How you feeling?" he asked brushing my hair back with his hand.

"I'm tired, but I'm alright. What time is it?"

Hassan grimaced. "Damn, it's almost nine o' clock."

"Why you say it like that? You have some place to go?"

"Yeah, I was suppose to meet up with Fletch at nine."

"Go ahead. I'm getting ready to go to sleep anyway."

He bent over me and whispered, "Baby, I know that I hurt you, but I'm gonna make it up to you, I promise. I'm gonna take care of you." He kissed me on the mouth and left. I was too tired to argue. The way I figured it, what happened already happened and there was nothing that I could do about it. After all, Hassan was there for me, and I still loved him.

Before I went to sleep I called my mom and told her that I had the baby. She couldn't believe it. Since visiting hours were over, she could not come up, but she would see me in the morning.

For three more days I stayed in the hospital to have my tubes tied. There wasn't going to be a number four coming out of this womb. But that morning was check out time. Dr. Suri came in early and told me that I could leave the hospital. As I gathered my things to take home with me, Dr. Shirmanski paid me a visit. She certainly was persistent. I had to give her that. Not being as enraged as I was four days ago when we last met, I agreed to meet with her group the following week.

By the time Mom came to pick me up, the loud sounds of the lunch carts were being pushed down the hall. All of my things were packed and waiting on the bed. Grabbing the bags, my eyes were filled with tears as I yanked on the chain turning off the light above the headboard. My heart was so heavy. On the one hand I was glad that I was leaving, but on the other I felt so empty leaving Hateem. Mom and I went to the nursery to tell my baby that I was going home, but that I would see him tomorrow. My heart ached to leave him. Mom put her hand on my shoulder and looked me in the eyes. I saw her sorrow and felt her compassion. "God has a plan for that boy's life. He ain't gonna let nothin' happen to him. You just gotta keep the faith honey. Keep the faith." She said with conviction. That was the same type of strength Mrs. Colbirth delivered when she made her daily visits with me at the hospital these past few days.

Hateem's eyes were covered with a black blindfold, as a heating lamp beamed down on him through his incubator. When I was in to see him earlier everything seemed fine, but the nurse explained to me that his body temperature had droped and the lamp was simply to keep him warm and raise his temperature back up to normal. "Lord, I'm trusting you," I silently prayed. Kissing the tip of my finger, I placed it on his little scrawny shoulder.

Once outside I felt like I could breathe. With the cold November wind and bright sun on my face I felt somewhat alive. While we were driving, it didn't take long for mom to start pushing my buttons.

"I want you to come home with me. Your dad and I have been talking and if living on your own is too much for you, then you and the kids can come back home and live with us."

After living on my own, I just knew I could not live under her roof again. Besides, she would never let Hassan come over. It would never work. Dumb idea, thanks, but no thanks. "No! I'm gonna stay in my own apartment."

"Tammy, if you stay alone, we're just gonna worry ourselves sick about you," mom insisted.

"See ma, you just don't believe in me, do you? You just think that I'm nothing. You think I can't take care of myself."

"Alright, Tammy, if you don't want to come home, that's fine." She grimaced, waiting for the traffic light to turn green.

"I have a home. *My* home."

When we arrived at Domtar Courts, my apartment was a mess. The door was busted and it could not lock from the outside. Now the only lock I had was the chair lock.

"You'd better call someone to fix that door," mom said, setting the two white plastic shopping bags that the hospital gave to me to put my clothes in on the floor. She pulled off her coat and rested her purse on my chair, then told me to rest on the couch while she straightened up.

Mom changed the sheets, put dinner on to cook, ran the clothes to the basement to wash, fixed lunch for me and cleaned the apartment. By the end of the day the apartment was its normal fresh, clean and spotless self. Even though my mother and I have our differences, we're family and loved each other deep down where it counted.

"I'm gonna keep the girls until the end of the week so you can relax. Would you like to go to church with me on Sunday? Reverend Brown has been asking about you," she said slipping her arms inside of her coat then adjusted the collar.

"Sure, I'll go with you, mom." I was tired and just wanted her to leave. I knew that she was concerned about me but I really needed to be alone.

"Dinner is already cooked, so when you get hungry, just fix your plate."

Mom grabbed her purse and stalled like she really didn't want to leave. "Thanks ma, I'll be alright, you can go."

She came to the bed and gave me a big hug. "If you need anything, just call now." As soon as she left, I fell fast asleep.

BACK WITH HASSAN

Hassan and I spent the evening at the hospital with Hateem, and I spent that night at Hassan's. It wasn't easy for either one of us to stay in the relationship. We have done so much talking in the three weeks since Hateem's birth, trying to sort all of our feelings out. Even though we both had some deep rooted issues with each other, we were going to make our relationship work. Not only did we share love, we shared a son.

Early the next morning, he left the apartment to work out at the gym. Debbie had called just before he left. Hassan told her he would call her back when he returned. Whenever she was on the phone, I kept on talking, so she would know that I was with Hassan. It was a little game we both played called "he's with me now."

Later that morning, someone knocked on his door. Grabbing Hassan's bathrobe from behind the bathroom door, I put it on then peeked out the window. It was Debbie. Clearly, I heard him tell her on the phone earlier that he was going out. "Hassan's not here," I said through the closed door.

"I know, Tammy. I came to see you," she said in a *why can't we all just get along* voice. I was real suspicious now. What did she want to talk to me about? Debbie was nine months pregnant, so I knew she didn't come for a fight. Taking the deadbolt off, I opened the door slightly while she stood on the front porch, "What do you want to talk to me about?"

Debbie stepped into the apartment, practically pushing me out of the way, and took off her coat. She hung it in Hassan's closet and sat her big ass down like she lived there. "Tammy we're both women and instead of snapping each other's head off, I thought we should talk. I was curious about you, and I guess you're curious about me, too."

She had a point. But I still didn't trust her. Closing the door, I walked into the apartment and sat in Hassan's leather director's chair which sat facing the couch were Debbie was sitting. It was a grey day outside, therefore making it dark inside. Reaching over, I turned on a light in the livingroom.

"Hassan told me that you had the baby and everything. How's he doing?" she asked adjusting herself in the chair.

"He's doing just fine. We went to see him last night," I said "we" to keep the edge.

"Uh huh," she nodded her head like she was making mental notes.

"Hassan told me that his name is Hateem. That's a nice name." I could see right through her. She was fishing around trying to see if my son had Hassan's last name, so I gave her what she wanted. "His name is Hassan Hateem Colbirth. Hassan named him."

Disappointment registered on her face, but she masked it well.

"When are you due?" I asked her.

"Any day now. I can't wait. It seems like I've been pregnant forever."

Smiling politely, I looked away from her. All kinds of things were rolling through my head that I wanted to ask. Are you and Hassan in a romantic relationship? What does he tell you about me? Then she broke the ice with, "Do you love Hassan?" Her question threw me for a second because I didn't expect it. Honestly, I thought she'd be more hostile. The room was very quiet except for the sound of the television playing in the bedroom.

"Yeah. I love Hassan. I know sometimes he does some pretty fucked up things, but yeah, I do love him. Why do you ask?" My guard started to ease because I could relate to what she was probably feeling.

"It's just something I had to know. You see, me and Hassan, we been together ever since high school. He's the only man I've ever loved. Erkell, Hassan and this baby...," she placed her hands on top of her stomach to demonstrate her point. "They are my family, and we ain't going *nowhere*."

Pissed, I shot back at her. "What are you saying? I mean, how do you want me to respond to that, Debbie?" Now I was angry because her mission was accomplished. She came to tell me in so many words that she was never going to leave Hassan. "When I met Hassan, the only person he mentioned was Erkell. He didn't say nothing about you. And he ain't say shit to me about you being pregnant." Sitting on the edge of the chair I glared at her, "As a matter of fact, when I found out that you were pregnant and asked him if he did it, he said that it wasn't his. So don't be coming around here acting like I broke y'all up."

Real cool and much too confidently Debbie began to speak, "Me and Hassan, we been on again and off again. He meets other women, but he always comes back to me because he knows that I'm not going anywhere." She drove her point home once again. Hassan was hers.

"You know what? I don't see the point in us continuing this conversation. You say you ain't gonna leave him, well neither am I. So, I guess the best thing for us to do is stay out of each other's way, because I'm definitely not interested in becoming your friend. You got it? I'll tell Hassan you came by." Standing up, I let her know that it was time for her to go.

"You do that," Debbie said. She put her coat on and left. As far as I was concerned we were back to square one, not liking each other one single bit.

Around noon Hassan came in all jolly and happy, like he didn't have a care in the world. He had on thick layers of sweat clothes, a hood on his head, a towel around his neck, and black leather gloves. He was always full of zest after he worked out. He came up to me and started shadow boxing, dancing around, shuffling his feet, ducking and diving. I couldn't help but laugh. "You so silly." Hassan grabbed me and gave me a big kiss. "I had a visitor today," I said mysteriously.

"Oh yeah, who?" he asked, pulling his clothes off.

"Debbie."

"Debbie? What was she doing over here?"

"She said she wanted to talk."

"Talk about what?" His eyebrows bunched.

"She pumped me for information about Hateem's name, and she also informed me that she wasn't going nowhere," I said checking out his face for a reaction.

"What she mean, she ain't going nowhere?"

"She ain't leaving you."

"That girl got a problem. She didn't upset you did she?" he asked, still undressing himself.

"No. I just didn't like her coming over here."

"You should have just left her ass outside," he said walking his muscular bare body into the bathroom. Expecting more of a reaction from him, I was disappointed. I wanted him to call her on the phone, curse her out and tell her that I was his only woman and that she was just wasting her time. I wanted him to tell her that the only reason he even gives her the time of day is because of Erkell and the baby that she *tricked* him into having, but he didn't. It was almost like he was just fine having us both fighting over him.

WOMEN!

The water was so hot coming out of the steamy shower that it stung my skin like crazy. Taking the bar of soap in my hands, I lathered it up working it in my face, scrubbing my scalp. With eyes closed tight, I stood under the shower head with my mind reeling. I was trying so hard to redeem myself with Tammy. Trying to prove to myself that I was a better man than my dad. My promise was that I would take care of her, and that's just what I planned to do. I don't know what point Debbie was trying to make by coming over here talking to my girl. Shaking my head, I couldn't help but think how sloppy my shit was between Tammy and Debbie. I knew I had to tighten things up. First Tammy stormed over to Debbie's now Debbie dissin' my crib all up in Tammy's face. Shit had gotten absolutely out of hand, and I was lookin' weak. Turning off the water I grabbed a towel from the rack drying myself as I walked into my bedroom.

Tammy was stretched across the bed holding my pillow looking like a sad-faced clown. She wouldn't even look at me. "What's wrong babe?"

"Hassan, you tell me!"

"Tell you what?" I sat on the bed next to her then threw the towel on the floor.

"What's up with you and Debbie? She's carrying your baby, then she's gonna stroll in here and feel that she has the right to tell me that she's not going to leave you."

"Tammy..."

"No wait. When we first started talking, you told me that she was not an issue in your life. Now she is. Everything is so complicated, Hassan."

"Tammy, I told you that I was gonna take care of you, and I'm gonna do just that. Debbie's blowin' smoke, don't even breathe it in."

"Do you love her, Hassan?"

"I'm here with you, ain't I?"

"Yeah, but do you love her?"

"Look, I love who I'm with, and who am I with?"

"Me."

"That's right baby, and don't you ever forget that. I'm gonna talk to her, and she ain't gonna bother you no more, okay?" Leaning over, I kissed her on the lips.

Tammy put on a little smile for me.

Hateem was three weeks old today, and Tammy looked as good as she did before she got pregnant. She was wearing bikini underwear and my T-shirt. Sitting there naked, my horse started to rise up.

"But you gotta take care of me first. I'm in need, babe."

"Hassan, I'm bleeding."

"On to 'Plan B' then."

Tammy got the bottle of lotion and squeezed a glob into her hand messaging me until I exploded.

Later that evening, Tammy and I went up to the hospital to see Hateem. He was making progress. They finally took that damn feeding tube out of his mouth, and Tammy was trying to breast feed him. I still thought his mouth was too small for that, but the nurses told Tammy that he would get the hang of it soon. It felt good holding him without all those wires in the way. When we left, this was the first time that Tammy didn't cry. She just looked at me.

"He's gonna be alright. I can feel it now."

"I told you that he was gonna be just fine. You should listen to me more often," I said putting my arm around her.

"Yeah, I guess I should."

"You comin' back to my house, or what?"

"No, I'm gonna go home. I need to clean up and start dinner before my mom drops the girls off."

"Now you know you don't need to be doing all that cleaning and stuff, Tammy. You just had a baby."

So she wouldn't have to cook, I brought her some take-out dinners then dropped Tammy home. I didn't stay because I had some bizz to square with Debbie. When I opened up the door, Erkell and Debbie were cuddled up on the couch watching television.

"Daddy! Hi!"

"Hey, man." I scooped Erkell up in my arms and gave him a kiss on the head. "Why don't you go in your room so that me and your mom can talk."

"Dad, can I go home with you tonight?"

"Kell, you got school in the morning. I'll get you this weekend."

"Aww, dad, please."

"You better do what I tell you, boy."

Erkell put his head down and went into his room.

"What you doing comin' over my house when I told you I wasn't gonna be home?"

"Hassan you can't blame me for wanting to talk to, *what's her name*. I knew she was over so I dropped by."

"Debbie, I ain't in no mood to be playin' games with you. Now you ain't got no business in my business, and Tammy ain't none of your goddamned business. You got that?" To stress my point, I stepped intimidatingly close to her. "You understand?" Debbie leaned away from me.

"Yeah," she said, drawing herself back. Staring her down through slanted eyes, I just wanted to slap her. "You better not ever do that shit again, and the only reason I'm not in your ass is because you pregnant."

After I left Debbie's place I got in my car and started cruising the night. On my cell phone I called Sho Nuff and told him that I'd be over in twenty. By the time I got to his junky crib on Stuyvesant Ave, Cynt was there. Her girlfriend Jackie was there too and they were all sitting around getting high. Sho Nuff was burning incense, and they were old schoolin' to the Isle Brothers on the box. It was dark inside his apartment. He had a red light on in his living room. This was just the atmosphere I needed.

Jackie was finer than a muthah fuckah. She was thirty-six, twenty-four, thirty-six, and had a *thang* for me. We met once before at Chuck's and the vibes were strong.

"Ah Salaam Alaikam, people," I said, strolling in from his tight hallway.

Cynt and Sho Nuff were sitting on his love seat, and I sat down close to Jackie on the couch. Just in time, 'cause she passed the splif and I took a hit. Passing it on to Sho Nuff, I put my arm around the back of the couch. Jackie leaned her shoulder under mine.

"I'm glad to see you here, lady," I said all up in her ear.

"I'm glad to see you here too, Hassan."

"So where you off to tonight man?" Sho Nuff asked tokin' in the smoke.

"I'm right where I want to be with this luscious thang over here." Through her sweater, I was staring down at Jackie's breasts. Sho Nuff passed me a forty.

"Yo Hass, go on and get that buzz on, man."

"Will do, good fellah, will do." I took that forty and downed it. Tammy and Debbie had been truly working my nerves. This time last year I didn't have a problem in the world. I was happy. All in love with Tammy, Debbie had her own man and wasn't jockin' me, the only baby I had was Erkell, and that's how I liked it. Now it's like I'm living somebody else's fuckin' life. I ain't about all this chaos.

Jackie was buggin' with Cynt, and I took my hand and turned her face toward mine putting my tongue down her throat.

"Dag, Hassan! Can't you wait until we finish talking!" Cynt said.

"Leave my man alone. He's about to put his thang down," Sho Nuff said, spaced out. Jackie was all in to it. She was waiting in line for me for a long time, now it was her turn, and I wasn't about to disappoint her. Grabbing her by the hand, I led Jackie into Sho Nuff's bedroom.

It was a pig sty, clothes all over the place, and the sheets looked like they needed washing. There wasn't an inch of clean space anywhere, and it smelled musty. Pushing his junk off of the bed I gave Jackie what she dreamed about.

When I opened my eyes the sun was bright in Sho Nuff's window and Jackie was asleep next to me. Coulda swore she had a smile on her face. Quietly I got up, slipped on my clothes, and was out the door. I went home, took a shower and chilled in the solace of my own domain.

No Tellin'

Hassan and I were doing alright. I still heard the usual wild things about him seeing other women, but with all his faults, Hassan was still a good father. He was almost maternal when it came to his children. Not a day passed that he didn't spend time with our son. He even introduced Erkell to his new baby brother.

When Hassan held little Hateem in his big hands it reminded me of a nut in a shell. If Hassan closed his hands, he could practically cover him up. The young nurses made such a fuss over how good Hassan was with Hateem. Even though I was jealous, *very* jealous, I tried not to act like it. They would do things like stand real close to Hassan as he held Hateem and say, *Oh you're so good at holding him. Most men are scared to hold babies this small.* One nurse bent over Hassan's shoulder, leaning her huge breasts against him, and rewrapped Hateem's blanket. "Daddy you got to keep him wrapped real good. You don't want him to catch a cold." Hassan just sat there smiling at her. I could have slapped him. Hassan was fine and he always wore those good smelling colognes. So if his sexiness drove me crazy, I could imagine what it must have done to other women.

Anyway...It was December first and I was determined to make this a new beginning. Last night daddy brought a cute six foot high Christmas tree for me. The fresh pine smell filled the apartment, and did wonders for my spirits. Kiara, Tianna and I had a ball going down into the basement storage area for our boxes of decorations. They were truly my little helpers. We baked cookies and turned up our music real loud as we dressed our tree haphazzardly with mounds of glittering tassel and ornaments, along with other things the girls made in day care. We also used spray to write Merry Christmas on the window in the middle of the taped up blinking lights. We drew pictures of Santa and snow flakes and taped them all around the apartment. It was not very neat looking, but it was certainly festive. Most importantly, it was a fun labor of love between the three of us.

IT'S ONLY MONEY, HONEY

My windshield wipers were on intermittent, clearing off the first snowfall of the season. Earlier today I collected my cash from my staff, but instead of counting it up to take to Uncle Roger for safe keeping, I figured I'd spread the joy. First I went to Debbie's and broke her off a piece to finish up Erkell's Christmas shopping, then I headed over to Tammy's place. A week ago, Tammy asked me if we could go to this Christmas Eve Cabaret that Jeannette's sister was giving. I figured it was about time that we took our minds off of the problems that we had been having. Tammy had been so stressed about everything. She was not spending enough time with the girls 'cause she was up at the hospital with the baby. She worried about our fucked-up relationship and her family. She really did need something positive to look forward to, so I figured that I would make something nice happen for her.

There was something about the snow that was getting the best of me. Didn't much feel like the Christmas season at all until then. As I pulled up into Domtar Courts, there wasn't a soul outside in the early afternoon. When I walked into Tammy's apartment she was sitting on her couch reading Ebony magazine with her feet tucked underneath her. Tianna was sitting at the kitchen table eating a sandwich Tammy had cut into squares, and Kiara was sitting on the floor combing her dolls hair. They all lit up when they saw my mug.

"Hey baby." Tammy said, resting the magazine on the couch next to her.

"I'm gonna give you an early Christmas present," I said smiling.

"You are. What is it?"

"I want to buy you a sexy dress for that cabaret next week." I leaned down real close to her pretty lips.

Tammy's big dark-brown eyes sparkled "Are you serious?"

"Yeah, I been to those cabarets, and you can't walk in there with no ordinary dress on. Those women be dressed to impress. I can't have them out shinin' my lady."

Leaning in even closer, I put my lips up to hers kissing her slow, then stood staring down at her.

She looked up at me with the most beautiful wide smile. "Well, when are we going?"

"Dress the kids, and let's go now."

Tammy was ecstatic. My girl hopped up off the couch like she just hit the lottery. I was glad to see her this way again. It had been too long.

It was December twenty-third, and Hateem was now eight weeks old. Doctors said that he still had another three to four weeks before he could come home. They want to keep an eye on him until they say what would have been his full gestation. The doctors say that they want to give Hateem the best chance of living a normal, healthy life. They explained that there's a bigger chance for premies to have birth defects, learning and development problems. Another thing that was also going on was that the Division of Youth and Family Services was also keeping an eye on the situation. They were trying to monitor Tammy's interactions with Hateem, because of the suicide attempt while she was pregnant. It was so much shit happening.

Even though we both put in our time alone with the baby at the hospital, Tammy says that it's special when we go together. Says that Hateem knows the difference. I say he don't know squat, but I'm still trying to make up for pushing her over the edge, so I go along with it.

Lying in bed, flat on my back with my hands cupped behind my head, my mind wandered. I had already went out for my morning run in all that damn slush, came home showered, and ate me some breakfast. My ass wasn't going to move from this spot until it was time for me to get Tammy so we could go and see our son.

I had dozed off then the phone woke me up. Debbie called to tell me that she was having strong pains and that she wanted me to come over to her place just in case she had to go to the hospital. Raising my wrist groggily to my eyes, I got up out of bed wondering how I could satify both Tammy and Debbie cause I told Tammy I'd be to her house by three. It was now two-fifteen.

"How far are the pains from each other?" I spoke into the receiver.

"Around thirty minutes."

"Look babe, I got to take care of some real important business. I can't miss this appointment. I'm gonna run out. I should be over your house in about two hours. If anything happens before then, beep me." I don't know shit about timing contractions except from what I've seen on t.v. and they don't get panicked until those things are five minutes apart. Right now time was on my side.

I got up and ran over to Tammy's and she wasn't ready because I was a *whole* half hour early. She was dragging around the house like she had all damned day, and I was trying to get her to move.

"Damn, Tammy would you pick up the pace!" I snapped.

"Why you coming off on me, Hassan?" She cut her eyes at me. "You told me that you were coming at three o'clock. It's only two thirty-five. Give me a break, alright?"

"Yeah, you gonna be breakin' your ass out there *walkin'* to the hospital if you don't hurry up."

We drove to the hospital, and she wouldn't say a word to me the entire time. While she was nursing Hateem, I slipped away to a pay phone. I called Debbie and told her I would see her soon.

We stayed up at the hospital for forty-five minutes. Then I took Tammy home. From there I went over to Debbie's place, where I made her comfortable for the rest of the night.

By the time the morning came Debbie wasn't having anymore contractions, so I told her that I was leaving and to give me a call if anything comes up. I went home changed my clothes then went to check on Tammy.

You should have seen her. She was beaming, talking a mile a minute. To get her hair done, I gave her fifty dollars and told her that I had a long night last night and needed to go home and get some rest for tonight. I wasn't lying cause Debbie did so much tossing and turning last night, I didn't get much sleep. Tammy was so excited she practically pushed me out the door so that she could keep her appointment.

Once at home, I fixed myself a scrambled egg sandwich and crashed. A little after noon Debbie called me. She sounded bad. Still tired, I got back up and drove back over to her place. She was in a lot of pain, so I drove her to the hospital. I had dropped Erkell off at her mom's last night. Debbie was catching big contractions but her pelvic bones weren't separating. All that time I kept looking at the clock wondering what Tammy was doing.

Debbie was hooked up to an IV to regulate her contractions. She was sweating like it was a hundred degrees in the room. I kept wiping her head with a towel, and giving her ice to comfort her. My head was racing. I was in a jam. It was coming up on six o'clock. I was suppose to pick Tammy up at eight, but I couldn't leave Debbie, and she wasn't having this baby no time soon.

By nine o'clock I felt like shit. Couldn't call Tammy to let her know I wasn't coming. What could I possibly say to make her understand? This was the night she had been looking forward to for almost two weeks, and she went out this morning and got her hair all prettied up. What could I possibly tell her that would make any difference now? *Nothing!* Not calling her was selfish on my part, but I had to spare *myself* the pain of hearing her heart break. Believe me, I was aching, too. But I damn sure wouldn't have been able to live with myself if I just up and left Debbie and my baby now. *Damn!*

Debbie had hollered so much that her voice was gone. We had been up here for almost eight hours, and she still had not dilated anymore than six centimeters. Dr. Armstrong came in and told us that they would perform a C-section. He asked me if I wanted to attend, and I flatly refused the offer.

On Debbie's hospital bed, I was sitting with my feet propped up watching TV when the nurse came in not long after.

"Excuse me, Sir. Ms. Mitchell is in recovery now. You can go and see her if you'd like."

"What did she have?"

"An eight pound ten ounce baby girl. Congratulations."

"Yeah! I got my girl." After Erkell and Hateem, I was begining to wonder if I could shoot anything besides an XY. Debbie had an ultrasound, but didn't want to know the sex of the baby. I wasn't sweatin' it either, but I'm sure glad I got my girl. "Where's the baby?"

"She's in the nursery. She's going to remain there until mom gets out of recovery."

"How's Debbie doing?"

"She's just fine. She's coming down from the anesthesia. She had a spinal tap, so she's a little drowsy right now."

Feeling pumped, I strolled on down to the nursery and saw my daughter for the first time. My little angel. She had fat cheeks, curly black hair, and a big mouth, like her mama. She was screaming her head off, and I just melted. She had me wrapped around her little finger already.

Proudly, I went to the recovery room and kissed Debbie on her dry mouth. She was half asleep, but she smiled at me.

"We got a little girl, Hassan. Did you see her?" She sounded weary.

"Yeah, I seen her babe." Punch drunk by the moment, I gazed into her eyes. She was shivering under her blanket. "Now you cold, huh?" I smiled.

"Shit, I'm freezing."

"Nurse, can you bring her another blanket?"

"Are you cold Ms. Mitchell?" The nurse verified before she went to get Debbie another blanket from the hall.

"No shit. Why does she think I need a blanket?" Debbie commented sarcastically to me after the nurse left the room. She came back and covered Debbie as I rubbed her ice cold feet.

It was eleven forty-five p.m. when they brought Debbie back into her room from Recovery. Tired as a dog, I needed some sleep *bad*. The nurse brought the baby into the room all wrapped up in her little blanket and placed her in Debbie's arms. She was just wailing away. Debbie put the baby next to her breast and placed her nipple in her mouth. You should have seen my baby girl go.

"Hassan, you like the name Jasmine?"

"I wanted to name her Noel bein' it's Christmas Eve and all."

"Can we use that as a middle name? I really got my heart set on Jasmine."

"Jasmine Noel Colbirth. That's cool."

By the time I left the hospital it was around midnight and I couldn't keep my eyes open another second. As I drove by Domtar Courts I thought about dropping in on Tammy, but I decided to just go on home. I knew if I did it would have been a lot of drama to deal with, and I wasn't up for it tonight.

All Dressed Up But Nowhere to Go

A dull white light filled the room as the sun began to wake the December 25th sky. I placed my hand under my left ear, massaging the crook out of my neck as I slowly sat up on the couch. That's where I had fallen asleep watching the late movie. Rolling my head slowly and carefully, I began to replay the disappointing events of yesterday. I had got home from the hair dresser's at three o'clock. I called Hassan, but he wasn't home. Around six, I paged him again, and he still didn't call me back. I started to become worried, but he wasn't due here til eight, so I figured I still had time. By seven thirty, I was dressed and a bundle of nerves. I called again, and he still had not answered my page. It just didn't make sense why he would stand me up. But by eleven p.m., I was taking off my new dress, peeling off my designer stockings, and putting on my old house coat. Then I flopped in front of the tube.

So use to his disappointments, my tears were constipated in their ducts. I wanted to cry. Lord knows it would have made me feel a little better, but all I had was just that dull familiar ache which resided in me. As I stood up off the couch, I wondered where he was, if he had been sleeping with Debbie last night or if he found a new bed partner to fill his needs? *Whatever* the reason, it wouldn't be good enough. I felt stupid for trusting him again.

Before I went to my mother's house to get the girls, I knew I had to brighten up. Jeannette told me about the commotion that went on in the E.R. My family had developed a real dislike for Hassan and I didn't want to give them anymore fuel to add to the fire. I took a shower, put on my clothes, and my fake grin and left. When I got to mom's, Kiara, Tianna, and Jimmy's daughters were already playing with their toys. The living room looked like Toys R Us. In front of the window, a large white artificial tree sat in a musical stand. The colorful lights blinked making the tree look like a wonderland. Mom was in the kitchen cooking a big breakfast for everyone. When she asked me how the evening went at the cabaret, I lied and told her it was wonderful.

The girls and I left mom's house around two p.m. and went to the hospital to see Hateem. After I held him for a little while I showed him his stuffed santa. A toy twice his size. According to the nurses, Hassan had not been by since our last visit together.

When I got home I called Mrs. Colbirth and wished her a merry Christmas, but mostly to see how she was and to ask if she had heard from Hassan. She told me that Debbie had a baby girl last night and went through a long labor. Debbie really meant it when she said, *I'm not going anywhere.* There were places in the world where two wives were acceptable, but this was America, damn it!

Much later that night when I was getting ready for bed, Hassan finally called to apologize and asked me to forgive him. His reason wasn't good enough for me. I didn't care who had a baby or where he was. He stood me up one too many times and all the sorries in the world couldn't make up for that. After his lame-assed apology, I didn't hear from him for another three days. I didn't even want to see him. I didn't want to talk to him. Nothing.

To burn off some negative energy, I went on an after-Christmas cleaning binge, pulling down the tree and decorations then running all that stuff back into Domtar Courts' basement storage area. By the time I reached my bedroom, I was more energized than when I first started. I changed the sheets, made my bed, polished my dresser, then opened the closet to reorganize my clothes. And there was that damned sequin dress, glittering and sparkling, looking like an oddity among my other clothes. I put the dress across my bed and thought about the evening of romance and love that I'd almost had. Somehow I knew that dress would always remind me of that night. Opening the box containing the Cinderella-slippers-looking shoes, I put one on and admired how well they looked on me. Taking them off, I threw them back in the box. *That's* when the tears dripped down my checks. Spitefully, I picked up the phone and dialed Jeannette.

"Girl you feel like taking a ride?" I asked wiping my hands across my wet eyes.

"Yeah, why not. I ain't got nothin' planned."

"Meet me in the hallway in ten minutes." In a dramatic huff, I walked out of my apartment with the dress bag thrown across my arm and in my hand the bag containing the shoes and matching purse.

"What are you up to girl?" Jeannette looked suspicious.

"You'll find out," I smirked.

We drove down to La Boutique, where I returned the merchandise for a full refund: $580.60. In exactly one point two seconds, I went from sad to sparkling! In the car I opened the bills, fanning myself happily under the chin. "Now I feel better. Fuck Hassan and Debbie too. We are going to the mall!"

I gave Jeannette a hundred dollars of the money. We laughed hard, evil, vengeful laughs, and slapped each other five.

"Yeah! This feels good!" I pushed that car as fast as it could drive up Route 1 in the snow. We tore Quaker Bridge Mall apart, from one end to the next. Jeannette brought herself a dress out of Macy's and I bought a whole laundry list of stuff: a three-quarter length leather jacket, expensive perfumes, and some Victoria Secrets silks. By the time we left, we only had money for McDonald's. We were riding high. Whoever said revenge was sweet must have felt like I did at that moment.

AMENDS

Knowing how much I let her down, I still couldn't bring myself to go and see Tammy face-to-face. Before I went over there I knew I had to plan something to make up for Christmas Eve. Fortunately, there's always something jumping on New Year's Eve. It was only a matter of deciding on which jam to attend. And I couldn't wait to see my baby looking all good in that new dress I bought her. She's probably figuring she'll never get the chance to wear it.

Only the best for my baby. Calling around I was told there was a private jam up in New York City, at this jazz club called the Brass Horn. Anita Baker was giving a performance and the tickets were a hundred dollars a pop. I got in my ride picked up Fletch and we took a spin out to the city to pick up the tickets.

"Must be love, man." He smirked. He wasn't at all impressed with the fact that Tammy had me *wide open*, as he called it. That's exactly why women wouldn't respond to him 'cause he had that ole hard-core, *ain't no love for the bitch* mentality. My man, Chief would have understood. He was so into his lady that he told me the other day, he was thinking about popping the question. Tammy's sweet, and I love her deep, but I ain't nowhere near that ball and chain shit. For now all I wanted to do was make her happy.

After we got back from the city, I went home and jumped in the shower. Took some extra time and shaped up my beard, splashed on a little Joop, Tammy's favorite, and got fly with my creased trousers, silk shirt, jacket, and leather shoes. My shit had to be tight when I saw her. Grabbing the tickets off of the coffee table I strolled out the door. Tammy's gonna love me for this.

I knew Tammy was upset, but she couldn't stay mad at her man when I showed her those tickets. As I opened up the door to Tammy's apartment, she was coming out of the bathroom. When she saw me she cut her eyes. She was playing the role, I had to give it to her. Tammy was lookin' fine in this short little mauve silk nighty that had to be new 'cause I never seen it before. But if I didn't know better, I would have thought she was expecting some company or something, lookin' all sexy like that. She sure didn't know that I was coming over, and I felt a rise comin' on.

Flip The Script

Hassan looked so good, and I could smell that Joop all the way over here. I was angry, but a part of me wanted to jump into his arms. He walked over to kiss me, but I turned my head and he got the side of my mouth.

"You lookin' good baby. Is this new?" he asked, kissing my neck. Tired of all his bull shit, I walked away, leaving him to stand by his damn self.

"You ain't talkin' to me? Come on baby, I'm sorry."

"You're sorry! You're sorry! I don't give a damn about you being sorry, Hassan. You hurt me."

"Tammy you know the situation. I couldn't help it baby. But I'm gonna make it up to you."

Waving him off, I continued, "You're always making things up to me Hassan. Unless you can turn yourself into God and can make tonight Christmas Eve again, you can't make nothin' up to me!" *It felt good*! I was letting him *have it*. How dare he think he could stroll in here and *mack* his way out of this.

"Baby, I deserve that." Hassan came and held me in his arms. Slightly I resisted, then gave in. "But I'm really sorry, Tammy. I need you girl. Don't be mad at me. I'm trying." Hassan was whispering in my ear, talking soft, "I'm trying so hard to be a good man to you." Holding me real close, he rocked me gently in his arms, then started giving me small kisses on my mouth. My defenses were down. Feeling his tongue as it parted my lips, I became weak. Breathing heavily, my juices were starting to flow. As I sank deeper and deeper into him, I could feel his nature swell against me.

"That's better." Hassan held me in his arms until all of my hostility was nothing but a distant memory, then he pulled two tickets from his inner jacket pocket. "Here, baby. I can't bring back Christmas Eve, but I *will* give you New Year's."

Taking them from his hands, my eyes saw: Anita Baker, New York City..., and oh Lord, *one hundred dollars*! He paid two hundred dollars for these tickets. Immediately,

I got hot. Hassan was all excited, talking all fast and stuff. "Yeah, baby, this party is gonna be the bomb. Check this out. A private party with Anita Baker singing, candlelight, and an intimate crowd. You can dance your heart out with me in that sexy dress. And I was thinkin', if you like, we could get a room and maybe stay in the city 'til the next day. Now you get a chance to wear that dress after all. Why don't you put it on and model it for me?"

Pulling away from him I darted into the kitchen, *to think*. What was I supposed to do now, I panicked.

"You ain't gonna model it for daddy?" Hassan asked, taking his jacket off and opened my coat closet to get a hanger. He hung his jacket up right next to my new coat. It still had the price tag on it. "Tammy, when did you get a coat?"

"I...I got it for Christmas."

"Babe, I thought you would be more excited about New Year's Eve than this." Nervously, I twirled the end of my nightie around in my fingers. "Go put your dress on for me. I want to know if it's gonna turn me on as much as I think it will."

"Not now Hassan, later."

"Yeah baby, now." Hassan walked into my bedroom and came back out. "Where's the dress and the shoes? Where are they, Tammy?" Still I didn't say anything. Hassan once again walked into my bedroom then back out.

"Beautiful, Poison, Knowing. You bought a new coat. You got on a new night gown. You sure came into a lot of money didn't you, Tammy?" He frowned at me.

"I took the dress back," I heard myself say.

Hassan started laughing and shook his head. It was not a funny kind of laugh, I just messed his head up and he didn't know how to react. Then he looked at me as his face became dark with anger. "Why you take the dress back, Tammy?" His voice came out all husky. "Why you take the dress back, huh?" Hassan walked over and grabbed me by the arm, "I brought that dress for you, Tammy. What do you want from me girl, huh? What do you want, tell me?"

From the way he walked over and grabbed me, and the way he was shaking me, I didn't know what to expect. Totally in tears, I was getting ready to go crazy if he didn't release me. "I'm sorry! I'm sorry, Hassan, I'm sorry!" was all I could say.

He grabbed the tickets and began ripping them up, then threw the pieces in the air. He walked over to the closet to get his jacket. I knew I hurt him. "Hassan, don't leave. I was mad so I took the dress back. I just wanted to get back at you."

"What was I supposed to do, Tammy?!" Hassan was irate, "I might be asking you for too much, but I need you to understand why I couldn't be with you that night! That was my baby being born, Tammy. What was I supposed to do?!"

"I can't answer that. I just don't want you to go." And I didn't have an answer. That baby didn't ask to be here, and it did need its father to welcome it into this world. But I was in love with its father and needed him too. Everything was just so very complicated.

CHICKEN WANG

Me and Bubby were sitting in his Bronco with the windows rolled down talking to two females who were standing outside- one at his door; the other at mine. Bubby and I had been bar hopping all night long and decided to check out the West Point Bar and Grill. It was this rinky dink, after-hour joint where you can get your groove and your grub on. There were a lot of people standing around the street light outside of the bar socializing when I spotted Tim's punk ass walk out.

"Hey, baby, I'ma hafta get wit you later, somethin's about to go down."

"I wish it was you on me, Hassan."

"Keep that thought," I said kissing her on the lips. Tapping Bubby, I pointed across the street to Tim.

"Show time, G." Bubby excused his lady friend, and it was on. I hadn't planned on running up on Tim, but since he was right there, wasn't no sense wastin' time. Bubby knew that Tim was a bug up my ass, so he knew what I was gonna do.

"Yo, Spoony! Come here man." I motioned for Spoony, one of my most faithful flunkies to come to the truck door.

"Yo man, I have a job for you, and it's gonna pay you real well."

"What is it Hass, man? You know I'll do anything for you, brothah."

"I need you to fix a fool for me man. But check this out, right, I don't know shit about this, you got me?"

"Yeah, no problem, how you want me to do him man permanent, or temporary. Ain't no thang but a chicken wang, know what I'm sayin'? " He said movin' his tall skinny self around like he was cold or somethin'. We all started laughing.

"Check this mothah fuckah out, *ain't no thang but a chicken wang*," I said to Bubby.

"I'm a nice guy. Temporary." Me and Bubby gave each other a pound.

"Yo man, don't fuck up. Come over to my pad later on, and I'll square things wit' cha."

"Solid." Spoony was jerkin' his body like an excited child. "So who's the fool that's gonna get it?"

"That mothah fuckah right there," I said, pointing the bull's eye on Tim's chest. There was nothing I would have liked more than to feel my fist crush against his skull. But because of Tammy, for me to fight him would have been a wrong move.

Spoony got together a couple of his boys, and they were walking toward the entrance door, when Spoony purposely walked into Tim. He pushed Tim in the chest, "Yo pussy! You just gonna walk into me like you bad! Say you sorry, mothah fuckah!"

"I'm not sayin' shit to you. Get the fuck outta my face," Tim said. Spoony hit Tim in the mouth, then they started to brawl. Three of them jumped Tim and beat him down, stomping him about the body and head. Then they ran off, leaving him on the ground bleeding. A crowd had formed, but no one jumped in.

"Oh, how sweet it is! And that goes double for your fat ass mama," I yelled, laughin', crackin' up like I was at the Def Comedy Jam. Bubby rolled away, and I was too damned satisfied. "Mess wit the five and you gonna get beat down."

"Sho you're right." Bubby said giving me a pound. He turned up his music and rolled out.

Another enemy slain.

CHANGES

Having Hateem home these past two months have been so wonderful. Kiara and Tiana are both little mommies. They want to help me do everything with the baby. So while I bathed him, I'd let one get the clothes out of the drawer, and ask the other to get the lotion and powder. They loved their brother so much. February first, the day he came home, Hateem weighted a whopping 6 pounds 7 ounces- that was two months ago. Now it was springtime, my favorite time of the year. A time of fresh starts and new beginnings. As the clock read six thirty-seven a.m., I jumped out of bed and over to my window. Could this be the sun up before me, I thought, excited about longer days beginning. I lifted Hateem's heavy butt out of his crib, smothering him with a thousand morning kisses before I took off all of his clothes.

"Kiara, Tianna, wake up!" I yelled from my room.

Startled by the loud noise, Hateem's eyes bugged as he looked at me, and I had to laugh. "Oops, I sure woke you up. Didn't I?" Laughing, I dug my fingers into his rib cage tickling him and he was cracking up.

Tianna came stumbling into my room with her eyes half closed. "Morning Mommy," she said, puckering for a kiss.

In the bathroom, I washed Hateem in the sink as Tianna bathed in the tub. "Kiara, I said get up!" I yelled again.

Thirty minutes later I walked into the girls' bedroom. *Miss* Kiara was sitting on her bed, mouth poked out, eyebrows frowned, and about to get her four year-old butt spanked if she didn't get in that bathroom. Standing in the doorway with my arms folded across my chest, I grimaced, "How many times do you expect me to call your name this morning?"

"I don't wanna go to school, ma. I wanna stay home with you and Hateem."

"Kiara, don't you want to grow up, be an intelligent young lady and get a good job?" I tried to reason *before* I yanked her by the arm and drag her to the tub.

Her little eyes looked straight into mine. "I gonna get on da welfare when I'm a young ladee." She said matter of factly. My mouth fell open. I was stunned. Her words pierced right through my heart. Did she learn that from me? Was that the image I projected to her and Tianna? I never talked about the politics of welfare with my children. Was I teaching it to be a *lifestyle choice*? Yes, they went with me when I cashed my monthly welfare check, and grocery shopped with food stamps and WIC checks, but they're still little. *What did they know?* Sure, they have even heard me bitch about *HATING* being held to the welfare system for my survival. So where did she get that idea?

"Noo, noo Kiara." I sat on the bed next to her and grabbed her two little soft hands in mine. "Baby, welfare is no kind of life for a beautiful young lady like you. God gave you a brain so that you can learn, and be anything in this world *you want to be*."

"You beautiful, mommy."

"Yes, but mommy's made some wrong choices in her life. I'm not going to be on welfare forever. Mommy's going to get a job."

"Fatima in my class said that her mommy is on da welfare and she not gonna get a job. I told her my mommy was on da welfare too, and I wasn't getting one either."

Covering my face, my eyes filled with tears. "Kiara, I am so sorry." The pain and shame I felt at that moment was for realizing what I was doing to my children yes, but it was for realizing, *for the first time*, how my mother must have felt. All that time I thought she was angry *at* me, then clearly I realized that she was hurt *for* me. But mostly, I cried for myself because Tamlyn Annita Blake had dreams of becoming a college graduate and having a career. Being my own woman! Then my case worker, Jerry DeVillo's words came to mind, *"Tamlyn, I know you must have had dreams. And with your children you can still have your dreams. You just have to be willing to work harder to get them."*

"Why you crying mommy?" She was confused.

"I'm alright Kiara," I said wipping my eyes with my hand. Swallowing hard, I looked at my child. "When you go to school today, I want you to tell Fatima that your mommy is going to get a job. And you tell her when you grow up that you are going to get one too." I lifted her little chin with my knuckle. "Is that a deal?"

"I'm gonna get a job too." Kiara, my smart, beautiful, little lady said with conviction and put her little arms around my neck.

"Now you go on in the bathroom and get washed up, because you have school today," I said, kissing her on the face before she ran out of the room.

After the girls were off to pre-school, I put Hateem in his stroller and walked down the street to the corner store to get a newspaper. My conversation with Kiara convinced me that I needed a j-o-b, n-o-w. My plan was always to go back to school after I gave birth to Hateem, but the timing just never seemed right. Something was always going on. But while I was waiting for my life to calm down before I got my act together, my daughters' lives kept right on going. Every day, they were getting older and wiser to what was going on around them. Watching *me*, wanting to be like *me*. At that moment, it wasn't about me any longer, it was about them. My children! And I knew love was more than putting a roof over their heads and food in their stomachs. I had to be someone that *I* could be proud of, so they would know how to be proud of *themselves*. I had to be their role model. And that's what I wanted them to see when they looked at me.

Sitting on the living room floor with the classifieds and a pen in my hand, I had a serious reality check. The only thing I was qualified for was to be a cashier at a department store or at a grocery market. I didn't want that. A job was a job, true but I wanted a job that would put me on track with my business career plans, and throwing food into a brown bag, and screaming 'price check' sure wasn't going to do that.

Frustrated, I slung the paper to the side. "I could always sign myself back into Mercer County's associate's degree program," I thought out loud, then shook it off, "No because that would take too long. And besides, I need something now. I promised Kiara. Who can I talk too?!" Just as the question came to mind, I thought of my former community college counselor. Picking up the phone I called and we talked for a long time about my job objectives and he suggested that I sign up at KLM Institute. A trade school that specialized in on-the-job training. Their courses were only six months, and they guaranteed on the job placement provided you carried a certain grade point average. After I hung up with my counselor, I called the Institute for an appointmet to enroll and was told that the financial aid program would pay for the whole thing!

By July, I was three months into the course. They had placed me at a warehouse in shipping and receiving. It was my job to keep an up-to-date computerized inventory list and track of each employee's work time. I stayed there until the training course was over.

I spoke the KLM instructor and told her that I was not happy working at the warehouse because they were unorganized. The place was dirty, and the men were way too vulgar. In short, I was uncomfortable there. She made some calls and managed to get me an interview at Biggron Laboratories. It was a pharmaceutical company in Princeton, New Jersey that specialized in experimental drugs for cancer cures.

GAINFULLY ME

The interview went well. The position at Biggron was on a trial basis for six months. After that it would be up to the company to hire me full time or let me go. Biggron Labs was a huge place with manicured lawns and benches. Just to come to work I would have to dress up in my Sunday best. I loved it. Two weeks later I was called back for a second interview and was hired as a temp. If everything went well, I would receive a raise in six months on top of what I already thought was a very generous check.

Driving through the October morning traffic, reporting for my first day working at Biggron Lab, my mind began to wonder. Last year this time, my world was caving in around me. Now I felt like things were finally coming together. My six months at KLM Institute dominated the warm months. I didn't really get a chance to do much with my kids over the summer. But they still did fun things with my parents and Mrs. Colbirth. I turned twenty-one in June. I believe that was the best day of my summer because, finally, my age went along with who I was. A woman with three kids, instead of the label teenaged mom.

It was hard to believe that Hateem would be a whole year old next month. I thought as my eyes caught sight of a toddler seated in a passing car. The doctors were impressed with his progress saying that his development and his motor skills were on target for his age. That was a blessing. Speaking of blessings, *I* needed one. As I pulled into the parking lot, I was a bundle of nerves. In the rear view mirror I made a final check to see if my lipstick was on properly and if my hair was in place. Taking a deep breath, I waited a few moments then got out of the car. All night I had been up trying to put my wardrobe together. I had chosen a black knee length skirt with a small split in the back and a white v-neck long sleeve blouse with matching black jacket and pumps. Dressed very business-like, I felt confident that even if I didn't know what I was doing, at least I'd look like I did. Fake it, 'til you make!

My stomach was queasy as I walked from the parking lot into the personnel office. As my eyes scanned the parking lot filled with Lexus, Acura, and Mercedes Benz vehicles. My little bit of confidence dried up and I thought to myself, 'Girl, you are way out of your league!' Even though my mind was telling me to turn around, jump into my hoopty and drive back to that filthy ass warehouse, my feet walked me right up to the personnel desk.

"Hello, my name is Tamlyn Blake. I start work today." I wasn't even sure if my voice would come out when I spoke.

"Yes, hello, we've been waiting for you." The personnel lady stuck her stubby hand out for a shake. As we walked she talked, "If you're ready, I can show you to your work station. I heard they had hired someone new when I came back. I was on disability for four weeks. Some minor surgery." I noticed pictures of the Biggron Laboratories executives on the corridor's wall. "Well here we are," she said as we approached the main lobby.

It was huge and beautiful. Large glass doors automatically opened when you walked near. The walls and the floors were made of black and grey marble. We made our way to the middle of the room, to a round sunken desk.

"Tamlyn, this is your station. You will be in charge of the executive lobby area. Visitors and clients use this entrance. All others such as service and prospective employees you don't have to worry about. The cleaners arrive at six o clock p.m. They all use the rear entrance. Just settle in and get comfortable with everything, and I'll let Brenda know that you're here."

Resting my purse on the floor by the chair, I inspected the surroundings in a glance. Everything looked so technical. The telephone looked like a switchboard and the rolodex was the largest one I had ever seen. There was a computer on my desk and dozens of reference books. Just as I began to feel overwhelmed, the personnel lady stepped around the corner with a sistah. I was impressed. She held out her hand. "Hello Tamlyn, I'm Brenda Matthews, your supervisor."

"Good luck today. If you need anything feel free to give me a call," said the woman from personnel right before she left.

Brenda Mathews then focused her attention on me and began to speak, "Your job here, Tamlyn, is very important. You are the first person that the visitors, clients, or callers will come in contact with. You must remain professional in your appearance, attitude, and your phone techniques. If you have a problem, be it professional with your work assignments or personal, I need to know about it. Although we are a big company, we try to maintain a close knit, intimate atmosphere. Do you have any questions?"

Nodding, I couldn't think of a single one.

"Don't worry, by the end of the day you'll be swimming in them." It was plain to see that Mrs. Matthews was a no nonsense lady. She was one hundred percent business. Brenda Matthews had a dark brown complexion. She wore her hair in a medium length natural. Her face was beautifully made up. Her dress was a modern business style, accented by large jewelry that made a statement of African culture. She also smelled real nice. "Here. I had this made up for you." She handed me a desk name plate that had big script writing that read *Tamlyn Blake*. It made me feel official.

"Follow me! I'm going to introduce you to some of your co-workers." Brenda introduced me to everyone that I would be directing calls to. There were eight departments in all. After my tour, we went back to the reception area when another sistah showed up.

"Hi Brenda."

"Hello Thukella. Thukella, this is Tamlyn Blake. Tamlyn this is Thukella Omowale. Thukella will be training you here for the next two weeks. There's alot to learn, but Thukella is a good teacher." For the first time Brenda smiled, parting her thick red lips, revealing white pearly teeth which housed a gap in the middle. "Good luck. I'll see you both later."

Thukella was a very petite, jet black sistah with long black wavy hair- her stuff looked real. She was stunningly beautiful. I guessed her to be around my age, and she spoke with an accent. As the day went on she proved herself to be very knowledgeable and very nice. We got along well.

During our conversation I learned that she was born in Somalia and that her family moved here when she was eight. She had been working at Biggron Labs for five years, since graduating from high school. In the course of us exchanging out *getting to know you* information, I told her that I had three children. Miss Kiara, who was five years old and so proud to be in kindergarten, Tianna who was four, and Hateem who was nearing one. Pulling my wallet out, I showed her their pictures that I carried for just such an occasion.

The morning went well. Thukella even made me laugh once or twice, and at noon we went to lunch together in Biggron Labs cafeteria. It looked like an intimate little restaurant. Around the food service areas, the floor was made of pale red sand tiles. They offered a choice of a hot or cold menu. Last night I had packed a bag lunch for myself, because I put my last bit of spare change in the gas tank.

I waited by the cashier as Thukella paid for her meal, and I mean *meal*. She had sliced roast beef, macaroni and cheese, brussel sprouts and a cinnamon dinner roll. All of a sudden, I wanted to throw my bologna and cheese sandwich in the garbage.

As we entered the dining area it was carpeted in beautiful red sand, white, and green design. Large abstract paintings of matching colors decorated the walls. And best of all, the large windows gave a blazzin' view of Biggron Laboratory's grounds. Thukella said that in the warm seasons the cafeteria offers outdoor dinning, but there were only a few people out there smoking on that day.

If she couldn't do anything else, she sure could gossip! Thukella was busy giving me the inside info on who was cool and who was not, who was doing it to whom, and all that stuff.

For such an elite company, I was pleasantly surprised to find there was a lot of different ethnic groups that worked there. Black people were well represented. Before I knew it, it was time for us to get back to work, and wouldn't you know it, after watching Thukella throw down, I was still starving. That sandwich didn't make a dent in my appetite.

The first day was real hectic. There was always something to be done. It made me wonder how I was going to manage when the two weeks of training were over.

Back at the desk working hard, Thukella said, "Straighten up," she said in reference to the sharp black Lincoln Continental which pulled up in plain view of the automatic sliding glass entrance doors, "Here come the executives!"

Four older white men, suited, carrying briefcases stepped out of the ride. As they walked through the lobby their voices echoed around them.

"Good afternoon, gentlemen," she said as they walked past.

"Good afternoon, ladies." They continued toward the elevator, leaving behind their pleasant of spearmint gum and mild cologne.

Minutes later this handsome man walked up to the desk wearing grey trousers and a dark blue suit jacket. He was smiling that kind of contagious smile, that just made you smile back. Against my will my gaze held. I didn't mean to stare as he strolled up to our workstation, but that was just what I did.

"Hey, Tom" Thukella said.

"Hello, Kell. So how are you doing today, sugar?"

Umm, his voice had this low bass, that made me want to close my eyes and ask him to repeat himself.

"You know me, it's all in a day's work. You need your mileage sheets?" she asked.

"Yes I do," he answered then looked at me. "Hi I'm Tom Lester, and you are?"

Truly taken by you, I wanted to say, but instead I just smiled. "I'm Tamlyn Blake."

He shook my hand gently. "Nice to meet you, Tamlyn. Thukella taking good care of you over here?"

"Yes, she is."

"Oh, Tom, you know you don't have to ask that. You know I always take care of business." We all laughed.

"And that you do," He winked. "You lovely ladies take care now."

"He is such a sweetheart," Thukella said as he disappeared down the hall.

"Not bad looking either." I was checking him out as he walked away. My mind mentally recording his profile, five-ten, a hundred seventy five pounds late thirties, early fortyies. He had a cool glide in his stride, like he was the man. It was strange. I felt some type of connection to that man. It was like his presence posed a question that I had to answer. Call it instant chemistry or attraction. I don't know what it was, but I knew I wanted to know more about him. And as if reading my mind, Thukella then proceeded to give me the 4-1-1 on Mr. Thomas Lester, the company's chauffeur.

One day completed. Thukella showed me how to lock up the executive lobby and how to set the alarm system. By the time I got to the car, the sun had set for the evening and I was *exhausted* in the best kind of way. My feet hurt from being in heels all day long and my mind ached from cramming all that information inside my head. But I was happy and so proud of myself! I felt so blessed to be working there. With head bowed and eyes closed, I thought to myself, 'Dear Lord, I have to stay here after these six months are over. I'll work my butt off and be the best worker Biggron's has ever seen. Please help me! This means so much to me. Thank you for listening, Lord.' I opened my eyes, cranked up my hoopty and headed for home. That was the first time since I was pregnant with Hateem that my plan was in *full* effect.

TO NEW FRIENDS

Thukella was a good teacher. By the time my training was over, I was running the reception area like a true professional. I was excited because it was Friday, but most importantly, my first payday from Biggron Laboratory! Three thirty rolled around and the time had arrived, the moment that of truth. Brenda Matthews was walking toward my desk with that wonderful little green piece of paper in her hand. Closer, closer, closer she came, then someone stopped her and they began to talk. The conversation lasted maybe two minutes, but it seemed like forever, then FINALLY!

"Here you go Tamlyn." Brenda handed me my pay. "You have certainly earned your check this week. Keep up the good work."

As I stood there filled with pride the phone rang. It was Hassan calling twenty minutes before quitting time telling me to find another ride home because my car wouldn't start. His car was in the shop being serviced so he drove mine. After I finished locking up the lobby, Tom overheard me calling information to get a number for a cab. "I'll give you a ride home if you need it."

Tom was such a sweet person. We had only known each other two weeks but in that short time he had been so nice and easy to talk to. He always came over to my station first thing in the morning to talk. One day after his opening question of, 'How are you this morning?' I told him that I was hungry because I didn't have a chance to eat breakfast. Everyday since he would show up bright and early at my work station with an apple danish and a cup of regular coffee for me. He seemed to have that effect on everyone around him and I found that appealing. "Tom, you live all the way out in Willingboro. My house is in Trenton. That's out of your way."

"I don't have anyone to rush home to. It'll be my pleasure to drive you." Tom's voice carried just the right touch of bass. Not too deep, but just enough to have a soothing quality to it.

"Thanks, Tom." I called my dad and told him my predicament, asking if he would please pick my children up from day care, then meet me at my home in an hour. Tom helped me on with my coat, I turned off the lights to my work station, and we were off.

He had a nice ride, elegant not gaudy. It was a new, beige, Buick LeSabre. He turned on the radio. It was tuned to a smooth jazz station. I didn't listen to jazz myself, but it seemed like something that I could learn to enjoy. During the forty minute ride our conversation only reinforced my opinion of his laid-back coolness that I found so very attractive. My eyes traveled across Tom's salt and pepper colored hair with the brushed in waves, and how it looked so good next to his dark brown complection. And he had this well manicured mustache that sat on a nice, full, soft looking mouth. In short, Tom was *damn* sexy.

As we pulled into Domtar Courts, I looked at him grateful for his time and his conversation. "Thanks for bringing me home, Tom."

He had this mellow look on his face. He looked at my eyes then at my lips, as if he were visualizing how it would be to kiss me. This kind of threw me cause I wasn't expecting it. He never showed that kind of interest in me before. But it wasn't threatening, something inside of me was flattered by it.

"You have a good night, Tamlyn."

"You too," I said softly then got out of his ride.

Once inside of my apartment, I took a quick, relaxing shower, got comfortable, and started dinner before dad brought the children home.

Hours later, after dinner was done and the children were in bed, I was also ready to turn in. But Hassan still had not called to tell me what was up with my car. I paged him, but he never returned my call. Then, I called his mom to see if she had heard from him.

Mrs. Colbirth, being straight up, told me that Hassan and Debbie brought Erkell and Jasmine over around five. That news flash had me seeing red. I couldn't believe he was starting that *Debbie* mess up again. For the last couple of months, it seemed like Hassan was emotionally detaching himself from me. At first I thought I was just being paranoid, but it got to the place where I just couldn't deny it. He wouldn't come by for weeks at a time. And when we did talk, it was because *I* tracked *him* down. If he did come by, he'd stay the night, then it would be another couple of weeks until I saw him again.

It was like he had me on a shelf for *his* convenience. When I started questioning him about it, that was when all the arguing started. To me, it felt like a *set up*. Like he was just looking for an excuse, *any* excuse not to come around. And it hurt like hell! His actions had me doubting myself. Was it me turning him off? Was I fussing too much? Wasn't I being sexy enough? Wasn't I being sweet enough? *Did he still love me?* Everything I thought I wasn't doing to please him, I tried to do double-time. Things that pushed his buttons I kept quiet, to keep the peace. But there *was no peace!*

Hateem was waking up as the girls were going to sleep. He had been sleeping a long time. His sweet little face had imprints from sleeping so hard and long on the sheets. "Hey baby boy," I said picking him up with my two hands. He was getting big. "How's mommy's little man." I loved him so much. Hateem was my doll baby. He looked just like Hassan. I took his clothes off because he peed right through his sleeper. I gave him a bath and put on a clean set of pajamas. He smelled so good. I still give him a warm bottle at bedtime. My mom warned me against it saying I should only give him water in his bottle when I put him to sleep. She said milk or juice could give him bottle mouth. That didn't work for Hateem, though. I tried the water at bed time but he just cried and cried so I gave in. With his warm bottle in hand, he went right back to sleep.

It was nearly eleven o' clock and still no Hassan. I paged him but he still would not return my call. As I picked up the phone to beep him again, something told me to dial Debbie's number.

"Hello," she said.

"Is Hassan there?" I was pissed off.

"Wait a minute, bitch. You don't be calling my mothah fuckin' house askin' if Hassan's here. See Tammy, you gonna play around and I'm gonna kick..." I heard her say to Hassan, "You don't be snatchin' no damn phone out my hand."

"You better go 'head with that noise!" He yelled at her.

"What?!" Hassan said all mad to me.

"You better bring my damn car home before I call the cops and tell them you stole it! And if you don't believe me, try me!" Disgusted, I slammed the phone down.

Forty-five minutes later Hassan walked through the door and I was ready to fight. "I had to catch a ride home from work and you out there joyriding your bitch in my car! What the fuck is wrong with you?" I yelled. "I ain't havin' this shit, Hassan. I done gone through too much shit with you already!"

"Look Tammy. I ain't in the mood for your shit, just go head and leave me the fuck alone!" He warned.

"What do you mean, leave *you* the fuck alone. You think you can ride your bitches in my car and I ain't supposed to say nothing to you?"

"Look Tammy, I said go 'head. I bought you that fuckin' car, and I'll drive who the fuck I want in it. Now shut the fuck up!" He said, pointing at me.

I started swinging on him. The same way he hurt me with his words, I wanted to hurt him physically. Hassan grabbed me by the arms and shoved me onto the couch.

"You better learn how to act, bitch or I might have to take it from ya!" He said standing over me. I tried to kick him in his nuts, and he slapped me real hard across my eye. I hollered then began to cried.

"Get out! Get out of here." My face was stinging something fierce.

He threw the keys at me and walked out.

Plan in Motion

April was here and it was also my six month anniversary working at Biggrons. Today would be my first review. Although I felt like I was doing a good job, I was very nervous about the outcome. This was the day where they would either tell me that they were keeping me on or letting me go, and I needed this job desperately. Besides my kids, the job gave me a reason for being, a reason to feel good about myself when it seemed that Hassan was working double time to make me feel like shit.

An hour before I was to go home, it was review time. Thukella walked up to my desk at three thirty on the nose. "Calm down Tammy, everything's going to be just fine. You know everyone likes your work around here."

"Thukella, I can't wait until this is over with. Wish me luck." I said walking from behind the sunken desk.

"Trust me now, you don't need it. But if it'll make you feel better, good luck." She smiled as I sat down in my chair, then answered the ringing phone.

Walking down the lobby to Brenda Matthews' office, I had to force myself to breathe. Lightly I knocked on her office door. The office was not large at all. Comfortable, would describe it because there was just enough room for her desk, a long file cabinet and a round conference table with four chairs. On her desk sat a graduation picture of her only child. It was obvious that she was very proud of him. In our brief conversations about our families, she had mentioned that she was also a single mother. Raising her head up from her work, Brenda asked me to come in and close the door behind me.

"Tamlyn, I'm going to go over these forms of your job description with you. Check whether you agree or disagree with my evaluations," she said getting up from her desk walking over to the conference table. She handed me my folder and we both sat down. Everything was good, except that I was running late in the mornings. My car's transmission finally blew. Since I had no way to get it fixed, I had to ride the bus to work.

"Tamlyn, I'm going to have personnel process your permanent employment papers." When she said those words I wanted to *shout!* "You have proven yourself to be the type of hard and diligent worker that will be an asset to our company. As soon as possible, go and fill out your employee benefits package for your health insurance, and your pension plan." Brenda was such a *business* person, so serious all the time. She hardly ever smiled. "And effective in your next check you will receive your raise."

I didn't even realize I was smiling, but the thought of that extra fifty dollars in my check meant that I could start savings to get my car back on the road.

When I walked back to the lobby, Tom was standing at my station talking to Thukella. "It's nice to see that beautiful smile of yours."

"Tom, do you think you can give me a ride home tonight?" I needed to get back to the city before the bank closed.

"I'll look forward to it," he said, then walked away.

Smiling, Thukella looked at me wiggling her eyebrows. "He likes you, Tamlyn."

I knew it, but I was so wrapped up with Hass that I never really gave it much thought.

SERENDIPITY

June twenty-second and my twenty-second birthday. I had no special plans. Just thankful to God for everything I did have. Can't lie though, I was trying hard not to feel let down. Haven't seen nor heard from Hassan in over two weeks. But I couldn't help from wondering if he had remembered my birthday.

Around noon a florist came into the lobby with a big arrangement of flowers with a big festive silver helium balloon that read "Happy Birthday!" I got so excited as he walked over to my station. He remembered! I knew that Hassan wouldn't forget my birthday. I felt so special.

The florist said, "Hello Ma'am. I have a delivery for Sue Stanowski. Can you sign for it?" By the time he finished his sentence, I was holding back the tears. After I signed for the flowers, I went into the ladies room, and let the tears flow. I went into Brenda's office and told her that I was sick and I had to go home.

On my way to the bus stop I saw Tom outside wiping down the car. "Where are you going, Tamlyn?"

At this point I was obviously upset and I didn't care to hide it. "Home. I just got to go home," I said, wiping my face with my hand. "Today is my birthday and nobody even cares. Do you know how that makes me feel? I signed for flowers for a lady in the purchasing department, and I got so jealous, Tom. I don't want to be like that. Not even my own mother called to say anything to me today," I said feeling sorry for myself and realizing that to him my earth shattering event may have sounded stupid. But he caught my vibe. During a conversation we once shared, Tom told me that I had an old soul. Maybe he knew there was more to my tears than a spoiled girl's pride. Maybe he knew that my cup was filled to the rim with disappointments, hurt, and so much pain that all it took was one more drop to make it overflow.

He leaned against the car, looking at me. "It's only natural for you to want to be recognized on your birthday. That's one special day that's all yours. If we can have parades for Thanksgiving, why can't you have flowers on your birthday?" Tom stood up, opening the car door for me. " Let's go for a ride."

We got in one of the company cars, a navy blue Lincoln Continental. We drove around and talked. I told him about my relationship with Hassan and the girls' father, Mark. Then Tom told me about his relationship with his ex-wife and how she cheated on him. He busted her *in their bed* with another man. They have been divorced for five years.

Tom pulled up in front of a florist, went in, and came out with a long, mint green colored box. It was tied with a white bow. He got back in the car and handed the box to me. "Happy birthday, Tamlyn."

This was by far the sweetest thing that he could have done. Untying the bow, I opened the box and inside were two dozen pink roses intertwined with baby breaths. Speechless, I just stared. I felt myself choke.

"Cheer up, Tamlyn. Your children need a strong mother in their lives. Not someone who's coming apart at the seams." Tom looked deep into my eyes and talked to me from his soul. "You're a special woman. A man should buy you roses on your birthday or for no reason at all." He gave me that look again like he wanted to kiss me. This time, I leaned over and kissed him. Closing my eyes, I opened my mouth around his and our tongues slowly swirled together. It felt so right, I wanted to crawl into his arms and have him shelter me away from the entire world.

"Let me take you to dinner this evening?" he asked softly.

Remaining quiet I stared at those beautiful pink roses, letting their fragrance work its calming magic. And as if I remembered he had spoken to me, I responded. "I would like that."

While at home, I had a slight change of heart. I called Tom at the job before he left and told him that I would like to make dinner here instead of going out, so he would be able to meet my children. I wasn't in the *going out* kind of mood. Didn't feel like being, *on*! All I wanted was to be in the comforts of my own home with the kids. He agreed and said that he would love to meet my three little ones.

It was around six o clock in the evening by the time I finished cleaning up my apartment. I cooked a nice dinner of buttered steaks, gravy, rice, cabbage and potato salad. Taking the girls to the side, I explained to them that Tom was a friend of mine and that he was going to be our guest for dinner.

Since it was my birthday I was hoping that Hassan wouldn't all of a sudden remember and show his sorry butt up over here and ruin my evening.

When I opened up the door for him, I noticed that Tom went home to get out of his uniform. He looked really casual wearing beige trousers, a black short sleeve, ribbed shirt, black belt and shoes. Although they were about the same height, his body wasn't muscular like Hassan's. Tom had a nice lean built.

"Come on up," I said smiling.

"You have a nice cozy place, Tamlyn," Tom said, looking around my apartment. But in my mind, I wondered what he *really* thought?

Kiara and Tianna were very friendly. They were comfortable around Tom, and he was comfortable around them. They showed him pictures that they made in school and they brought out one of their story books for him to read to them, and he happily read it. Hateem, on the other hand, stayed close to me the whole night and just looked at Tom. Tom was so smooth. He seemed very natural and relaxed. He was not intimidated at all by the children. After we ate dinner we all watched a bit of television. Around nine-thirty I put my kids to bed. Tom helped me clear the dishes and put the food away, then we sat on the couch and talked. He looked at me as if something were on his mind, then he spoke through an uncertain smile. "You know..." he said as the knuckle of his index finger stroked my arm, "...I was thinking to myself as I prepared to come over here that I had to be crazy. That this wasn't right."

Confused, I grimaced, "That what wasn't right?"

For the first time since I met him, he was at a loss for words, then he continued, "Today is your twenty second birthday, and I have a daughter who is eighteen years old...I'm forty-two years old."

Remaining quiet, I let him labor with his thoughts without interrupting. Tom looked at me and sighed heavily, "I look forward to seeing you at work, and that's my first thought as soon as I open my eyes. When I say my prayers at night, you're in them, and that's my last thoughts at night."

"Tom, you feel uncomfortable with us being friends?" I wasn't stupid, I knew what he meant. I just needed him to clarify himself.

Once again he sighed deeply then gave me a half smile, "To be honest Tamlyn, yes and no. For one thing sweetheart, I don't want you to think of me as some dirty old man."

We both had to laugh at that. "And?" I coaxed him along.

"And no. I'm an observer. When I watch you and whenever we converse, I see so much more...*way more* than a twenty-two year old girl."

"When you look at me, what do you see?"

His eyes penetrated mine. "I see someone who has been through a lot, which has seasoned her far past her years. I see a survivor. I see a good mother who is raising three children that she loves dearly." Tom softly felt my face. "I see so much in you that I care about."

I whispered. "Do you really care about me?"

Tom looked at my eyes, "Have no doubt, I care about you, Tamlyn. But I'm not going to try to rush things. I know you're still in a situation with your son's father that you need to deal with. So we'll take this slow and let things fall into place how they may." He took both of my hands. "I just want you to know that when you're ready for a real man, I'll be here." Then he pulled my hands to his lips.

"This may be one of the best birthdays I have ever had," I said, smiling at Tom.

"I'm glad I could be apart of it."

After Tom left and I was alone in my bed drifting off to sleep, I felt sooo *guilty*! For the first time I had stepped out on Hassan. Now, wasn't that a strange thought when he didn't even remember my birthday.

FOR THE LOVE OF MONEY

After doin' some serious diggin', we finally scored big in the business. Got connected with *The Man,* Antonio Tennanti. He was a big time supplier from New York City. We had arranged to join forces just as soon as we could get the kind of cash he asked for. It took us a while, but we did it.

I was sitting in my apartment feeling the effects of a natural high and counting and bagging up the profits for the week. Our association with Antonio was reaping tremendous profits. Sho Nuff, Chief Rocker, Fletch, Bubby, and I were moving mad product though Trenton. We were famous. We moved more for much less than the competition. People were walking, driving, catching the bus, just to get a bigger, better cut for less money. I didn't know where Antonio was getting that shit, but niggahs was going crazy for it. Mad lootchy was falling out of the sky, there was so much of it.

To show his appreciation, Antonio invited us into New York for a little celebration. And that weekend was the shit! I'm talkin' 'bout *big fun!* We were sharp if I had to say so myself. All of us brothahs dressed in our black suits. When we reached Antonio's yacht, he made it clear that there would be no business discussed that night. He said that night was just to celebrate our moving so much product for him. 'And for making him so fuckin' rich', he said lifting his flute filled with Dom Perignon.

It was the most erotic ride I ever took. There were maybe twenty other guests. Antonio had hired twelve of the loveliest ladies of the evening to entertain us. They all looked like super models, and entertain us they did.

With a big smile on my face and a cigarette hangin' from the side of my mouth, I tossed the last bag of money in my gym bag. Turning off my stereo, I was getting ready to take the cash to Uncle Roger for safe keeping, when the phone rang. "Hass here."

It was Tammy on the phone, and I swear, *every time* I talked to that girl she started some shit. Always cryin' about needin' something. And be pressin' me cause I don't come around. Huh, and she wonders why? I grimaced, listening to her goin' off about her rent being past due.

By law, when she started working, she had to report that income and have her welfare benefits adjusted. She wanted to move out of Domtar Courts, out of the projects, so I helped her find a new place. With all the other things she had to hold down, 'cause she wasn't gettin' no more food stamps, she couldn't afford it. So, I stepped in like a man to take up the slack. Told her I'd pay her rent. After all, she had my son and he needed a place to live. And I didn't want the girls to have to do without. But Tammy didn't understand the agreement. I *said* I would pay her *rent*. I'd give her money then she'd be comin' to me wanting more. *No*, I wasn't havin' it.

The way I saw it, she brought all of that shit on herself. I told her trying to take care of three kids was no joke. It didn't have to be like that. She could have handled her business, finished college and had a damn job makin' some real money. Instead of workin' in some *pretty ass* place that wasn't payin' shit. I don't have no time for her shit. I had Antonio, and makin' money on my mind.

So there we were arguin' over the same mess. I cut it short, "Look Tammy, if I get a chance I'll be over!" She got mad and hung up the phone.

SUNDER

This was the first Saturday in this month of August that I was able to just spend time with my children and concentrate solely on them. Kiara loves to read. Hateem was walking around pulling down everything that his little twenty-one month old hands could reach and Tianna loved to color. We all were in the living room under the air conditioner. I was on the floor and we were all enjoying each other, *until* I looked up and saw Hassan walking up the stairs, like wasn't nothing up. My pressure rose, eyes squinted, and I damn near bit my tongue off, not to get loud in front of the kids.

Kiara, Tianna and Hateem jumped on Hassan like he was Santa Claus, showering him with hugs and kisses, and the only thing I could think of was, 'You sorry ass muthah fuckah'. I was totally and finally fed up with Hassan, had out grown his games, his lies, everything about him. It was clear to me that I had just become another bitch to Hass. He had no respect for me nor did he care about the welfare of my children. And when he simply did not care if we were put out on the streets, that was the last straw.

"Why are you here now?" I asked between clenched teeth. "Kiara, take Hateem. You and Tianna go and play in your room."

Hassan looked at me like, *here we go again.* "Why they got to go to their rooms? I came by to spend some time with 'em."

I waited until I heard the bedroom door close before I exploded. "I needed you last week when the damn owner threatened to put my ass out on the streets and you didn't show up. So why are you here now?"

Hassan threw one hundred and fifty dollars on the table. "I ain't come here to argue wi'cho ass. If you don't want that money then I'll just keep it."

"Go ahead and keep it Hassan. You're not doing me no big favor by giving me guilt money!"

"What guilt money? I ain't got nothing to be guilty about. I gave you some money before the rent was due. If you don't save it that's your fault."

"That money you gave me, Hassan, I brought food with it and what was left over, I brought some things for the house. You're trying to give me a hundred and fifty dollars. The rent is six hundred and fifty dollars, *Hassan!*"

"Well you're working now. How come you can't pay your own damn rent?"

"Hassan, I do not make enough to pay for rent, house bills, clothes and food. I just don't make enough and you know that!" I was so, so very tired of arguing with someone who didn't care to understand what I was trying to tell him. I would have been better off talking to the wall. With my hands covering my face, I tried to gather myself and get the strength to tell him what I should have said a long time ago, "Look Hassan I'll tell you what. I'm gonna make this easy for you okay. You don't *ever*, and I mean *ever* have to give me another damn dime a long as you live. You see, I'm not one of your bitches out there in the streets. If you can't treat me with the respect that I deserve, then don't come around here no more. We're through!"

"What are you talking about, we're through?"

"I'm saying that I don't want you in my life no more! Don't come over here, don't call me, don't write me, when you see me in the streets just walk right past me, 'cause I am sick of you and all your bull shit!" My neck and my finger were working double time, "You have put me through too much and I'm ending this right now."

"If that's the way you want it, two tears in a bucket." Hassan looked at me like he hated me.

Hateem had found his way out of the girls room was standing at my legs crying for me to pick him up. "No, that's the way you made it," I snapped back at Hassan.

"You ain't keeping me from my son!"

"Just get the fuck out, Hassan!" I yelled, bending down to pick Hateem up, putting him on my hip. "The only thing you good for is upsetting everybody. We were fine until you come up here and just upset everybody. You need to grow up Hassan, 'cause the world don't revolve around you."

"Yeah, fuck you, Tammy." Hassan walked out and left.

By mid-September I was so burnt out from going through the same old routine. Go to work, come home fix dinner, get the kids ready for bed and start the day all over again, and again, and again. I was going crazy, and I felt myself going into another depression. Tom was still trying to be with me, but that's not what I wanted. Hassan was still in my system and I needed time to get him out. Even though we weren't even on speaking terms right now, he was constantly on my mind. The children were over at my mom's for the weekend. Instead of putting the time alone to good uses, all I did was think of Hassan and I when we first got together. How good we were then. I analyzed how things went so wrong. Why they went wrong was what puzzled me.

.I picked up the phone and beeped Sho Nuff, to see if he had time to pick me up. Over the years we developed almost a brother/sister relationship. He was always around Hassan, therefore, we spent a lot of time around each other too. He *was* as shot out as everyone said he was, but Sho Nuff was seriously fun to be around. He came right away.

I needed to talk to someone who knew what Hassan thought about. Why he was the way he was, and why he hated *me* so much? Before I could completely let him go, I had questions that I needed answers to. And who knew him better than his own cousin?

Sho Nuff came over and we went driving around in his BMW. It was a warm night. Sho Nuff with his music pumping, got on I-95 South and kept driving. We wound up in Philly at Penns Landings. And *sho nuff,* Sho Nuff knew everything. He knew how deep my feelings ran for Hassan and he knew what was troubling him.

Penns Landings is where Hassan and I would come when we just wanted to shoot the breeze. Everything about this place reminded me of him, the waves that rocked back and forth, the sea gulls flew overhead, the lovers walking hand-in-hand across the pier, *everything.* And such a deep sadness filled my heart. Sho Nuff and I sat on the edge of the waterside, taking in the big full white moon reflecting off the water.

"Why does he hate me so much? I can't understand, why he hates me?"

We had agreed to be straight up with each other.

"Tammy, he don't hate you. He loves you and it makes him feel less than a man, because he can't be there for you like he wants to be."

"What do you mean, he can't be there for me?"

"He said that you're the kind of lady that needed a man around her all the time. He's in the life, and he believes you need a man that got a straight-up job. He *has* to be there for Debbie, Erkell and Jas." He hit a nerve when he mentioned that. My eyes rolled up in the sky. "Look Tammy, whether you like it or not, that shit is reality. Hassan is always gonna be with Debbie. See how you gettin' fed up with Hass and you ready to leave. Debbie don't do that. Whatever Hassan tells her to do, she'll do and he knows that. And you know how he feels about his kids. Only thing she gotta do is act like she takin 'em and his ass is in line. They know how to control each other."

"Does he love her?" This was one of those questions I've tried to ask Hassan, but he would never give me a straight answer.

"Yeah. But it's a different kind of love than he has for you. With Debbie, he's used to having her around. She's like someone constant that's always there for him. But he loves you in a more romantic kind of way. I remember when the brothah first saw you. You were on your way to the bus stop one morning. He asked you if you wanted a ride and you just switched on by, talkin' 'bout, *no thank you.*"

"I remember that!" I laughed because Sho Nuff was standing up switching with his pinky in the air, trying to imitate me.

"From that moment on, he was struck. He told me then. He said, 'man that's my wife.' I told him, 'man, you ain't gettin that,' and I'll be damned if he didn't get you."

"What happened, Sho Nuff, why did he turn against me?" I looked up at the big beautiful bridge that was lit up. Not sure if I was ready for the truth, I focused on the cars that drove along it. But I knew I needed to hear it.

"He had a lot of resentment against you for keeping the baby and not having an abortion when he told you to."

That hurt! That really hurt! "What, he don't love his son?" I jumped up in a stance, staring him down.

Looking up at me Sho Nuff continued, "I didn't say that. Yes, he loves his son. What I said was when he found out that Debbie was pregnant, dude got scared. He was afraid that you would find out and dis him."

"Well did he ask her to get an abortion?"

"No, but that's different."

"How is that different?" I demanded.

"You're not listening to me. It's different because she's not going anywhere. He knows that he's gonna be the only father Erkell and Jas are gonna have. You know how he be trippin' cause his dad left him and my aunt when he was a kid. But before he had any kids with you, he wanted to make sure everything was straight first. Now his nightmare is coming true. You're leaving him and you got his kid."

"That's bull shit."

"No, that's the facts, baby."

We talked for a long time. All of my questions were answered except one. I asked Sho Nuff if Hassan had my brother jumped, but he pleaded the Fifth.

Movin' On

When Hassan and I split up, his mom sort of got put on the back burner too. I didn't mean for it to happen, but with work, I hadn't had much time for anything else. Mrs. Colbirth called and asked if she could keep the children for a night during the weekend, *after* she chewed me out for not calling her in a while. So on Saturday, I rounded up the children, and we all drove to Grandma Judy's house. That's what Erkell called her and that's what she wanted all her grandchildren to call her.

"Hi Grandma Judy."

"Hi, sweethearts."

I laughed giving her a kiss on the cheek and said, "Now you know you're too young and pretty for anyone to be calling you grandma."

"Oh really?" she smiled, "Well, that's what I am." She scooped Hateem into her arms.

"How's grandma's big boy?" She looked at me, "My, this child looks more like Erkell everyday." I didn't mind the comparison. "What you feeding him, Tammy? He's as heavy as a ton of bricks." She laughed. The girls ran past us and went right for the toy box. It was a great big colorful toy box that used to be filled with only Erkell's toys, but since I've known Hassan, Mrs. Colbirth bought dolls and other toys for Kiara, Tianna and the babies.

"I had Erkell and Jasmine last weekend..." We walked inside of the immaculate house. Mrs. Colbirth and my mother, both had their furniture protected with the custom fitted plastic covers. But of course my mom made her own. "... and this weekend I have Kiara, Tianna, and Hateem. When the babies get a little older I'm gonna get all of them together. I can't handle the two babies at the same time by myself," she explained. "Have you seen Jasmine yet?"

Even though it had been almost two years, I had not seen her. "No I haven't. Hassan never brought her over." She must have sensed something in my body language when I answered the question and she responded.

"I'm gonna tell you Tammy the same thing I sat right here and told Debbie. Hassan is my son. I love him dearly, and I tried to raise him the best I could. I couldn't stay home and keep an eye on him all the time 'cause I had to work. Now that he's grown I try to stay out of his business. You three, Debbie, you, and Hassan got my grandkids, so I *do* consider that my business. Never mind your differences, and I'm telling you just like I told her, I don't want none of my grand babies to be mistreated." Her tone was easy but stern.

"I would never do that." I grimaced.

"I'm not saying you would, but I'm letting you know those children are going to be raised as sisters and brothers. All of them. Because they are. And like I said, when those babies get a little older, I'm going to get all the children together so they all can get to know one another. Those children don't have anything to do with any decisions that you three adults might have made." She had conviction in her eyes. I knew she meant well. Hassan told me how when she was a young girl that her mother passed away and she and Sho Nuff's father, which is her older brother were raised by their stepmother. She had three other kids, but loved them all the same.

"So how's the new job coming along?" She changed the subject. Mrs. Colbirth and I caught up with each other's current events. We also talked about Hassan. She reminded me that it was important to do what was best for me. She said that Hassan had a little of John in him. "Hassan's father ran the streets, and he never got used to the idea of being a family man. Finally, one day when Hassan was thirteen, he just left and never came back. And I do believe that was the best thing he ever did for me. But it took Hassan a long time to get over it, though. Look, I know you love Hass, but you have to make plans for your children. I don't think Hassan is ready to settle down yet, but I think you are. So leave yourself open for some other options." She patted my knee.

Sunday evening. I had to pick up my children from Mrs. Colbirth's house. It's funny, not as in ha ha, but as in *daymn!*. You *think* you know yourself only to be faced with a situation and have your own feelings turn around on you. Hassan's Lexus was parked outside and all I could think of was, I felt it was time to talk things out with him and work on getting past all of the hurt and bitterness. After all, he was the father of my son. He practically raised my daughters. And yes, I *still* loved him. I accepted the fact that our relationship was over, but it didn't make any sense for us not to even speak to each other, and that's what it had come down to. If he did speak to me, it was just to let me know that he was coming by to get Hateem and to have him ready. Sometimes he would take the girls along too. This animosity between us was ridiculous. As the saying goes, 'if we can't be lovers, we can still be friends'.

Checking myself in the rear view mirror, I wanted to make sure I looked good before I got out of the car. When I knocked on the door, Erkell opened it, which kind of threw me cause I wasn't expecting to see him. But what *really* got to me was when I saw Hassan holding Jasmine. Here I was thinking I was strong and had moved on, but *daymn!* This whole scene knocked me off of my feet. And as if that wasn't bad enough, on the other side of the room, Debbie came walking out of the kitchen and went over and stood next to Hass. They were getting ready to leave.

'Hold it together girl!' I said to myself. Trying not to choke on my own words, I breathed in deeply. "Hello, everyone."

My kids ran up to me. "Mommy, Mommy."

"Hello, Tammy," Mrs. Colbirth said, staying neutral.

Debbie rolled her eyes at me and Hassan looked like he swallowed a canary. He tried to appear cool, but I knew he felt just as awkward as I did. I wanted to go over and snatch every one of those extensions out of Debbie's damn hair. I hated her!

Into the kitchen I went and sat down until they left. To see Hassan standing there with his other family was too much for me to deal with. No matter what, he was a part of me. Debbie took Erkell and Jasmine, and left the house, then Hassan came into the kitchen where I was seated at the table.

"What's up, Tammy?" he asked almost sounding sincere.

I was hurting. To hell with that *friend* shit. Friends don't rip each other's heart out and stomp them on the ground. "You ain't all of that, Hassan. So, why don't you catch up with your wife and kids and get the hell out my face," I said angrily.

"I didn't come back here to argue with you." There he went again with that sincere sounding shit.

"Well, leave then!"

He gestured as if to say *forget it*, then walked out.

I came back into the living room and hurriedly got the kids ready to go. "I can't take no more of this." I was swelling up with tears. Tianna put her sweet little arms around my waist. Mrs. Colbirth just looked at me and shook her head. I thanked her for keeping the children and left for home. Later on that night, Hassan called and asked if Hateem needed anything. I didn't want to talk to him so I told him that I had to go and hung up.

The next morning I couldn't even bring myself to go to work. Something inside of me, *deep, deep, deep* down inside of me mourned. It was a hurt that wasn't there before. It was the feeling that let me know that we were *really* through. I called Brenda Matthews and took a few days off.

All day long I purged! I cried myself silly, and when the tears dried, I went from room to room removing all of Hassan's belongings. In a large plastic garbage bag I dumped his pictures, clothes, everything I could find of his, and walked them outside to the dumpster. I didn't want to leave it to chance that I might change my mind and put the stuff back in their original places.

The next two days I spent time with myself. After I took the girls to school in the mornings, and Hateem to daycare I went to the museum and to the park. I even went for a run and later to the beauty salon for a wash and set. It was the first time in a while I spent time solely on myself. I also renewed a ritual that my mother had us to do twice a day. It was something that took next to no time, yet had a major impact on the day's outcome- I prayed.

When I returned to work on Thursday morning, I was glad to see Tom. He dropped what he was doing and immediately came over to me. That made me feel good. "Tamlyn, I been trying to call your house, I even stopped by to see you but you weren't home. When I asked Brenda about you she told me you weren't feeling well. You had me worried, lady."

"I'm sorry. I just had to stop the world for a couple of days. I had a lot of things to sort out." It felt nice having him fuss over me like that.

"Well, while you were sorting things out, did you think about me? Because I sure thought about you."

"Tom," Mrs. Atkinson called to get his attention. She was Mr. Schmidt's secretary. He looked at her and motioned 'one minute' with his finger then turned his full attention back to me.

"Do you think that you could get a babysitter for the kids tonight? I think you could use some TLC."

I smiled.

"See, it's working already. And bring a change of clothes for tomorrow. We could pick up something for dinner, and just hang out at my house for the night." To assure me, he added, "I'll set the guest bedroom up for you."

It seemed like forever for the work-day to finally end. I could not wait to take Tom up on his invitation. Once at home, daddy picked the kids up for the night. I jumped into the shower, then packed my overnight bag. As soon as I finished, Tom was already at the door.

It was seven o'clock in the evening, and pitch black as we drove down the highway. Sunk deep into Tom's car seats and relaxing, the rain, the jazz playing and his smooth conversation made for a cozy drive. Tom's sophistication was intoxicating. I felt so at ease around him. We stopped at the China Kitchen for a take-out meal and then stopped at a video store to pick up a couple of movies. On our way to Tom's house it started to pour. From the moment we left the highway and drove into this ritzy neighborhood, I couldn't believe my eyes. It was nothing like I had ever seen before. In a word, *rich*!

Since it was night time I could see straight through some of the people's houses. And I was seeing chandeliers hanging down in the front entrance, spiral stair cases, and *huge* lawns! It was breathtaking!

When we pulled up in front of his door my mouth fell open. Thukella had said she heard that Tom had a nice house, but I would have never imagined that it was so beautiful. All I could think of was this brothah *got bank*! Tom turned into his drive way with the *three*-car garage, and opened one with his remote that he had tucked above his visor. We drove safely in from the rain and walked into his house. It was laid!

Tom took my purse and overnight bag and put them upstairs in his guest room and told me to take my shoes off and get comfortable. Then he came back downstairs, set things up in the kitchen and brought our take-out meal into the den.

On the off-white carpeted floor we ate and watched videos on his wide-screen TV built into the wall. Needless to say, I was extra careful not to spill anything. There also was a huge stone fireplace that divided two rooms. It was gorgeous, and I would have loved to see it lit. I had never seen one like it. I was enjoying myself, and Tom looked happy, as well.

He said that he didn't get much company, except for when his kids, a daughter and son, came home from college, mostly on holidays.

Tom was drinking wine. He said he found it relaxing. I looked at him sitting there with just the light of the wide screen lighting the room. His shoes were off and his shirt was opened and hanging out of his pants.

"Tamlyn, I want to kiss you."

And I wanted his kiss too. I wanted to be special to someone again, and to have someone special for me. Tom reached out to me and our lips met. We kissed like we were starving for it- love, affection, companionship, acceptance. All the *its* out there that leave you incomplete. And we just indulged ourselves until we were full. We stayed up until twelve-thirty in the morning, talking and cuddling.

We went upstairs to his bedroom suite. Tom said I could stay in there and he'd stay in the guest room. Just before he started to leave we struck up another conversation that lasted for the next two hours until Tom fell asleep.

As he slept, I jumped into the master bedroom's shower. It was like being in some fancy hotel, complete with the double sink, and sunken jacuzzi. Drying myself off, I put on my night gown. Pulling the covers back as not to disturb Tom, I climbed underneath the sheets of his king size bed. He was lying ontop of the comforter still wearing his work clothes. As my eyes adjusted to the dark, I stayed up for awhile staring at the ceiling wondering what would become of this relationship. Tom had a kind soul, and he was definitely a special person. Placing my hands up to my face, I thought, what if things between us didn't work out. Was he just like the rest? What if come tomorrow his whole attitude toward me changes for the worse? My mind started playing all of these negative games with me and I started to tense with anxiety. What if....What if? Sitting up in the bed, my thoughts began to take on a life of their own.

Tom opened his eyes. "Tamlyn...is everything alright?" I guess my moving around in the bed woke him.

Looking down at him I whispered, "I'll be fine."

He yawned and stood up. "Let me take my behind in my room so I can get some sleep."

"Tom," I called out to him as he reached the door.

"Yes sweetheart, what is it?" He yawned again.

"Can you just hold me? I mean...all I want you to do is just hold me. Would that be alright?"

Tom walked back to the bed and got on top of the covers with open arms. I rested my head on his heart and he kissed my forehead, stroking my hair. His body temperature was warm against mine. It was like he could read my mind. "I'm here now," he said, as if claiming his spot in my life. I closed my eyes and drifted off to sleep.

A week went by. Hassan came over to get Hateem for the weekend. I found that I had no feelings for him left. Even the anger was gone. I felt nothing. Tom came over and took me and the girls out to dinner and for a drive. After we returned, he and I sat on my couch and talked.

"Thank you, Tom," I said leaning my head on his shoulder.

"For what?"

"For being such a good friend. For taking time out for my children. For everything about you." My feelings were just overflowing in the best kind of way.

"Thank you."

"For what?" I looked at him with a half smile.

"For coming into my life," he said, slowly leaning into me for a kiss.

I hadn't had sex with Hassan in months and I wanted Tom to make love to me right here, right now. "Tom, let's go into my room," I said all frisky like.

"No, love. It wouldn't be right for us to do that here with the kids home. What would you do if they woke up and found me in your bedroom? They're young but they are keeping track of everything that you do, and you can't let them see you sleeping with other men."

Dejected and puzzled by his reaction I sat straight up staring at him sharply, "What other men? There are no other men. What are you trying to say?"

"Tamlyn, you just got out of a relationship with Hateem's father. That's all I'm saying. Just calm down. We have all the time in the world for each other," Tom said, so sure of himself. And his words *we have all the time in the world for each other*, just instantly chilled me out. Made me feel silly, even, and a bit out of my league.

For the rest of the evening we listened to the radio, cuddled, and talked. After I thought about it, I liked Tom respecting my children. He was a real step up for me, and I knew I had to step up to the challenge if I wanted things to go right.

Tom and I were relaxing over a pizza dinner one Friday night after work. He insisted that I come home with him this weekend. I had just intended to catch up on some overdue cleaning around the house. We began to spend a lot of time together. It never crossed my mind that I could have such a close relationship with a man so much older than me. Tom had me by almost twenty years, but when I was with him, God, it didn't matter. I just loved to listen to him speak. His deep voice just rocked softly in my ears and through my body. Jeannette told me that I must be looking for a father figure, but I quickly corrected her on that, no man could ever take the place of my daddy. He's the best.

Some of the same things that I loved so much in Hassan I found in Tom, even though they couldn't be more different. Hassan had a confidence about him that commanded attention. Tom had a quiet confidence. Then out of the blue it dawned on me, Tom's house was spotless. "How do you keep this big ole house clean?" I asked swallowing my last piece of pizza.

Tom laughed. "It's only me here, so I don't make much of a mess. Plus once a week, I have a lady who comes to mop and dust and clean the bathrooms. All the tough stuff."

"Oh you have a maid, do you? Well, that's cheating." I giggled. "You have to do it the hard way like I do it. On your hands and knees."

Tom looked at me with his big brown eyes and thick black brows smiling boyishly "Not me."

I got up and cleared the kitchen bar, ripped the pizza box and threw it into the trash disposal then washed our two glasses.

"I see you like to clean."

"No, I hate it. But I hate a nasty house even more. It's how my mama raised us."

Tom got up from the table and put his arm around me as I stood at the sink wiping down his counter top. "You ever been on a boat before?"

"Years ago, I was on the Spirit of Philadelphia." I said remembering my nineteenth birthday celebration, compliments of Hassan. "Why?" I turned to face him.

"Because if the weather's nice tomorrow, I thought you might enjoy cruising around on the water."

"Did you buy tickets?"

Tom seemed amused at my enthusiasm. "No, I didn't buy tickets, I have my own boat docked down at the marina." He gave me a little squeeze in his arms and kissed me tenderly on the forehead.

"Tom, you have your own boat?" I was truly surprised, delightfully so.

"Yeah, would you like to see it?" he asked, full of pride. Tom held my hand tightly and lead me into the living room. He pulled a big white photo album out from underneath his end table showing me his photos.

"Damn, Tom, that's beautiful." Once again, I was in awe over one of Tom's possessions. It was a high gloss black boat with grey designs and a grey canopy top.

I could make out the words on the side of the boat, *Amor Negro*.

"What does that mean?" I'm Spanish illiterate. Besides, I was pronouncing it incorrectly.

"*Amor Negro*," the words just rolled off of Tom's lips, "Means *black love*." He spoke deep and sweet. His eyes penetrated mine. Feeling a tingle go down my spine, I blushed then turned my attention back to the photos. As I turned the pages, I came to a picture of a younger Tom accompanied by a very attractive woman and two small children, a boy and a girl.

"Is this your ex-wife?"

"Yes, that's her."

"She's pretty. Tom, can I ask you a question?

"Sure."

"How can you afford this house, your boat, your car and all those designer suits on a chauffeur's salary?"

There was that boyish grin again. "Wow, and I thought you were going to ask me something about my ex-wife," he said kidding. "I wasn't always a chauffeur, you know, hon," Tom said going into the kitchen and coming out with a glass of white wine. I placed the photo album back under the table where he kept it. He sat down next to me on the couch and continued his conversation. "I've been a chauffeur for Biggron for about seven years. Before that I worked in Manhattan's financial district."

"Get out of here!" I screamed, "Wall Street?" Without realizing it I had literally jumped out of my seat. "Oh my God, you worked on Wall Street?"

"I see that you're impressed."

"Yes. We studied Wall Street in my business class when I was attending Mercer Community College. It just intrigued me the volume of money, all the power. Oh my God, Tom, I don't believe it," I said sitting back down next to him.

"I started working straight out of college with a reputable black-owned financial firm. Four years of Howard University, then my first year on the street, I made close to two hundred thousand dollars."

"Get out of here!"

"No kidding." Tom took a sip of his wine.

"Can I ask you another question?"

"You got the floor, my sweet." Tom gestured for me to speak as he extended his arm with the glass in his hand.

"Why are you working now, and of all things as a chauffeur? Don't get me wrong, there's nothing wrong with being a chauffeur, but you could work at Biggron in so many other capacities."

"Tamlyn, financially I'm set for the rest of my life. I never have to work for another paycheck as long as I live."

"Well, why do you?"

"For companionship. To get out of this house and do something useful with myself. The Street was high pressure. I had to be married to it, devoted to it, and always on call. After a while, it tore me down. I started planning for myself, and invested in a few choice stocks. When I reached my financial goal, I left the business and got the most stress-free job I could find." Tom turned the glass to his head and swallowed the last drop of wine.

"Do you ever miss the wheeling and dealing?"

"Well, I still dabble. I showed you my office in the study. I have my own little business up and running, as a small financial advisory service. One of my clients is Schmidt."

"You mean Mr. Schmidt, the big wheel, really?" I asked, smiling, "Now I'm really impressed."

FOR KEEPS

Tom and I drove down to the marina. This was a first for me. As we boarded his boat, I felt such an excitement. We were both dressed in jeans and carried a picnic style lunch with some sandwiches, chips and juice. I looked forward to our journey. He started the engine and we began to cruise. The day was overcast, but it didn't ruin the mood at all. More than anything it set the mood. We had a good time laughing and playing around with each other. He even let me take over the wheel, teaching me how to drive the boat. Tom sailed us into a New York marina and docked. It began to rain, and the drops hitting up against the canopy rooftop sounded like drum beats. Relaxing underneath the deck, I sat between Tom's legs with my head leaned back against his chest. He was stretched out on the leather couch-like seat.

Thinking about Jeannette and her crazy behind and remembering our last conversation, I had to smile. 'T, you mean to tell me that as many times as you've stayed over that man's house y'all ain't never fucked?' then she looked at me strange, 'Well is he gay? What's wrong with him? Yeah, I know, his old ass probably can't even get it up no more.' Then I told her that as many times as I felt his hard-on when we kissed, I knew he could definitely get it up. Then she said, 'Well, it's probably small as hell since he don't wanna use it. Somethin' ain't right, girl.'

Tom was older, yeah, but more importantly, from the old school. When I brought up us never having sex, he stated that he believed in treating women like women. And even though he has had sexual affairs, he wanted to show me that there was a different side to relationships that I've never experienced before. He said that he wanted me to know what it was like to be courted by a man, not just used by a man.

Tom kissed the side of my neck. "Tamlyn, you ever think about getting married?" he asked with his arms circled around me.

"Marriage...humm," I responded thinking it was just another one of his getting to know you questions. "I use to think about it when I was a kid. But I've come to the reality that it's not in the stars for me. Like my mother said, I made my bed, now I have to lie in it."

"What do you mean by that?"

"I'm a package deal, a woman with three children, and a lot of hurt feelings. That's a lot to bring to the table."

Tom's embrace became tighter and he whispered, "I want to marry you."

Shocked, I sat up looking at him puzzled. I cared for him and we had been seeing each other for a while, but I didn't think it was this serious. Marriage? "Tom, we haven't known each other all that long."

"That doesn't matter. I know what I feel. You're a good woman, Tamlyn. I want to be a part of your life. I want you to be a part of mine."

"Tom, I have to be honest with you." I carefully chose my words. "I enjoy your company and I love how you are when you're around my kids, but is that enough? Don't you want me to be in love with you?" And I couldn't lie. I wasn't in love with him.

"What is love to you?" he asked. "You told me that you were in love with your daughters' father and he played around, and after the girls were born he left. When your son was born it was pretty much the same scenario with his father. You told me that you were in love with him, too. Tamlyn, from what I can see, I don't think you've ever experienced true love. I love you, Tamlyn. And I know that within time you will begin to accept and return the love I feel for you. If we were married I would raise your children as my own. I know that you still have unresolved feelings about your past. But you and I, we get along good, your children are beautiful, and they need a full-time father...and...and

"Please, Tom, I need time to think this out. Are you sure that you are ready to take on this kind of responsibility. My kids can be loud. They get into things," I reminded him.

"At my house, they'll have all the room they need."

"Your house...I can't even imagine living in such a beautiful place."

"You won't be just living there, it would be your home too." Tom took my hand. "You know Tamlyn, some people might call me a fool for wanting to marry a young, lovely woman whom I haven't dated a whole year, but people marry for different reasons. If you marry me I can offer you a better place to live, more money, and a home with a full-time father to help you raise your children. But you and the kids will be offering me something too, a life. I get so lonesome in that house all alone. You and

the kids are a dream come true, and you are so beautiful," he said, holding my face in his hands. "Tell me you'll marry me and make me the happiest man in the world."
It was plain to see that this didn't just come from the top of his head. With everything he had said. He had to have thought this out. But I was totally thrown. "Right now, I really don't know what to say. I need to think."

"Don't think, just say yes, and I promise I'll never hurt you, not ever. And I'll never let anyone hurt you again." Tom took me in his arms and held me close to his heart. I felt safe and loved.

"Tamlyn whatever you want, I want to be the one to give it to you." He took my hands and bent down on one knee, "Tamlyn, will you give me the privilege of letting me love you for the rest of my life."

I thought about the points that he was making, what I had to gain, and what my children had to gain. There was nothing to lose and everything to gain, and I whispered, "Yes, yes, I'll marry you."

"You said, yes?" Tom stood, picking me up in his arms, and we kissed long and deep. His lips tasted different than any others I had ever tasted. Those lips tasted like the lips of my husband. The lips that I would be kissing for the rest of my life, and they tasted so good.

I had been going to Dr. Shirmanski's Wednesday night "talk" sessions off and on for three years now. Ever since the time I was in the hospital after giving birth to my son. She was right talking out your problems did work if you gave it a chance.

One of the things she encouraged me to do was to have more heart-to-hearts with my mom. At first it wasn't easy. There were a lot of tears and hurt feelings. My mom is from the old school and does not believe in psychologist. She says you should just pray about it, or talk with the preacher. So when Dr. Shirmanski suggested that my mother join me in a few of my sessions to help me deal with some issues that dealt with her, it was no easy job getting her there. Believe it or not, daddy put his foot down and made her go.

Three very productive sessions later, and even though my mother and I still had a lot of healing to do from the emotional damage that we inflicted on each other, we were now able to get pass it and have what Dr. Shirmanski calls a healthy relationship. She helped my mother and I work through some tough issues by seeing each other's point of view. The deep part of the session was when she had us explain our motives for doing certain things then the listener would paraphrase what they thought the other said. What was so deep about the whole experience was that nine times out of ten, my mother and I were saying and hearing two different things. As Dr. Shirmanski put it, we were not communicating, at all! She brought out the point that when we tried to speak to each other, we already had pre-established bad attitudes and negative expectations, before a single word was ever spoken.

With Dr. Shirmanski's permission, I invited my mother to a recent session to tell her about Tom. It was very important for me to start my relationship with Tom on a positive note. My family is a necessity in my life. They complete me, and living these last few years with all this tension between us had to come to an end. Even though I didn't expect a marriage proposal from Tom, I knew he was a good man. It mattered to me that my relationship with Tom be open to my family, unlike my past relationship with Mark and Hassan. Love him or hate him, I wanted to bring Tom to my family and introduce them to one another. I wanted to let the world know that this is the man I choose to be with. My mother took the news of me seeing a man closer to her age than mine hard, just as I expected her to, but with Dr. Shirmanski sitting near by, it gave me the courage to tell her.

FAMILY TIES

After I told Tom I would marry him everything started moving fast. He met my family, and to my surprise, everyone got along well. Mom cooked a big dinner on the day that Tom brought my ring and invited the whole family over. I was more nervous than Tom, who was very cool. And wouldn't you know it, he and Jimmy hit it off right from the start.

Now, it was my turn to meet his. Early Sunday morning, Tom picked us up for church and introduced the children and me to the congregation as his soon-to-be new family. After the church service was over we drove up to Jersey City to meet Tom's father and children. Brian was nineteen and a freshman at NYU, and very nice. Tom's daughter, Angie was twenty and also a college student at New York University. She didn't show us any love.

Tom's father lived in a brick row home in a worn neighborhood. With all the money Tom had, I wasn't expecting it. Mentally, I made a note to ask him about that later. Mr. Lester was a high spirited, nice old man who lived alone. Tom had told me that his mother died eighteen years ago in her sleep. He told me how devastating it was because there was no warning. He just got a phone call saying that she was gone. The room was real dim inside, even though the ceiling light was on which made it difficult to get a good look at the place. His decor was simple, old furniture with striped knitted throws covering the back of his chairs.

Mr. Lester fixed us lunch, and we watched wrestling on TV. He said he never missed it on Sundays. Angie was still giving off bad vibes. It was obvious that she wasn't interested in the wrestling or in me and my family by the way she totally ignored us. Brian played with the children, and Mr. Lester and I entertained each other while baby girl monopolized Tom's time. When Tom asked his children to be a part of our wedding ceremony, they both agreed. Angie did so reluctantly. He had to coax her bratty ass into it. We stayed until nine-thirty p.m. and I was all too glad to have the day come to an end. If it had not been for his daughter I would have had a nice time.

Getting ready for my big day kept me so busy and it was so much fun to plan. At work they threw me a surprise shower. Thukella grabbed my hand and led me to my seat. Some of Biggron's executives were also there, out of loyalty to Tom. My supervisor Brenda Matthews was the Master of Ceremony. Even Mr. Schmidt raised his cup filled with punch and wished us well. We received lots of presents and they bought me a beautiful cake. The whole time, Tom was right by my side. That was the most special part of all.

A week later we went to mom's to make wedding plans. Could you believe it, I finally would wear mom's wedding gown? The same fairytale gown I dreamed of wearing ever since I was a child. Mom agreed to make the alterations. She called Reverend Brown, who gladly agreed to perform the ceremony, insisting that he would not charge a fee. And Tom said that he wanted to use the lodge where he's a member for the reception.

Jeannette was going to be my matron of honor not only because she was my best friend, but also because I didn't want to have to choose between my sisters.

HEAR SAY

Chief rolled over to my crib to talk and take care of some business, when clear out the blue he asked me, "Hey man, you still kickin' it with Tammy?"

"Naw, man, why?"

"Because I ain't see her around."

"We still talk, every now and then about the kids."

"What's up wit that, man? She was nice."

"Lot a shit man," I said, wishing he would drop the subject.

Since we broke up, I can't lie. I had been with several females, but I wasn't feelin' none of 'em. Most of them fake ass ho's just wanted to be down, so they could say they been with the Furious Five's Hassan Ali. The notorious Hass. They wasn't 'bout nothin'...Stank bitches!

But the more I was out there, the more I seen what I had in Tammy. That girl loved me. And she ain't give a damn 'bout what I was drivin'. How much money I had, or that I was fuckin' Hassan Ali. She loved me...the man.

Couple nights ago around eleven o'clock, I went over there to see how they were doin'. All partied out, I was like the prodigal son, ready to come back home. Missin' Tammy real bad, I knew I fucked up! And believe me I was willing to make it up to her. Swear to her I wasn't gonna leave no more. Wasn't gonna hurt her no more, none of that bull shit. I wanted to make love to her like I used to do. Kiss that pretty brown skin. When I got there she wasn't home. I tried to use my key, but she had the locks changed. Just as I was getting ready to pull off, this beige Buick pull in the spot next to me. Inside was Tammy the kids and some dude.

I was stunned. It felt like someone had knocked the air out of me. When they got out, I stepped out of my car, walked over to Tammy and took Hateem out of her arms. He was sleeping. Kiara jumped out of the car half-sleep, came over to me and hung herself around my waist. Then that punk, way older than Tammy, gonna carry Tianna and stand right in front of me.

Tammy took Tianna out of his arms, put her on the ground and shook her to wake her up. All this time, I was squarin' his ass up. Tammy looked like she didn't know what else to do so she introduced us. But the shit that made me want to go off was that old bastard had the nerve to kiss her on the lips, then asked if she was gonna be alright! My nostrils flared, fist balled, and I swear I could have knocked him dead on his ass.

He left. I went up into the apartment with them, thinkin' I was gonna at least be able to tell her how I felt. That I was sorry, but she went off cause I tried to hold her. All I wanted was to be close to her. But she come screamin' in my face 'bout her gettin' married. Married! She even had the rock to prove it. Hurt me to my heart.

Chief left after I told him the whole story. I began to think about Tammy with another man. The thought just ate at me. I could picture his hands all over her sweet little brown body. The more I thought about it the more I felt like hurting something. My world felt like it had come to an end.

PUPPET MASTER

It was Friday night, and Tom was due to pick me up in a half an hour. The children were spending the weekend with Mrs. Colbirth, and I was to spend a romantic weekend with Tom. We made plans to go to a play in Philadelphia and to dinner tomorrow night and I couldn't wait. My overnight bag was open. I danced around the room to the tunes on the radio. As I threw in my last few items, the phone began to ring. I let the answering machine pick up, turned off the radio and went into the living room.

"Tammy, it's Hassan. Pick up! I know you're home. Pick up the phone! Tammy, I'm sorry. Tammy, I'll change, give me another chance. Tammy don't do me like this, baby. Please baby, pick up the phone." CLICK.

L-o-v-e, what a crazy thing...just like an alcoholic loved his booze, I loved Hassan. And NOBODY wanted to be an alcoholic! I stood there, frozen, as the sound of his voice enticed me to fall off the wagon. In a flash of a second- I remembered the good times, the first time we made love, us united- standing at Hateem's incubator. I remembered his explanation for Hateem's name. I remembered him accepting my daughters' love and giving it back, and the first time he said I love you and the first time I knew I loved him. I remembered...I remembered...I remembered!

The answering machine cut Hassan off, but he called right back, "Tammy, I just need to hear your voice baby please. Why are you punishing me like this girl!" He yelled into the phone, then his voice cracked, piercing my heart. "I love you. Pick up the damn phone, Tammy. You're my world, girl. Don't marry that man, Tammy. You don't love him. You love me. We got a son together. Don't take that away from me. Please." CLICK. Hassan was disconnected in more ways than one.

He was the puppet master. He yanked on my strings and I danced. I stared at the phone paralyzed, biting my nails as tears ran down my eyes. Somehow, Hassan had got the word that my wedding day was near. Either Jeannette or his mother could have let it slip. Since last week, he's been calling me at home and on the job regularly, talking about how much he loved me, and that he couldn't eat and couldn't sleep. He would ask me if we could go out and have lunch and talk, or if he could come over and spend time with the kids, or anything- just as long as we could be together. Hassan even paid my rent two months in advance. He knew how desperately I loved him. He also must have known that if he kept begging me, he would once again have my heart. But that week I stopped accepting any of his calls. I had been feeling too weak.

My soul ached. I wanted to pick up the phone and comfort Hassan, but I knew that his love was a poison. Hassan's love was painful, inconsiderate and selfish. But he was every bit as sweet, compassionate and caring. Maybe he did learn his lesson. Maybe we could make our relationship work...Maybe? Contradicting emotions collided inside me, as I stood there hypnotized by the blinking red light and with such bad timing, Tom knocked on the door.

Drying my eyes, I needed some time to think and clear my head. Taking a few deep breaths I must have waited at least two minutes before I opened up the door.

"Sugar, what took you so long?" Tom asked concerned, then moved in for a kiss. Coldly, I turned away from him and he looked stunned. "What's wrong?"

"Nothing, I'm just not in the mood to go away with you this weekend," I said half-heartedly.

"What? Why? I just spoke to you on the phone not more than an hour ago and you were happy then. What's going on?"

My head started to swirl as I turned my back to him and marched away. "Why are you asking me all these damn questions? I just don't want to go with you. Leave me alone!"

"I'm sorry but I just can't do that," he said sternly as he followed me. "See for one thing I didn't drive all this way, at this time of night just to leave. Second of all, if something is bothering you I think we should talk about it."

"Look, Tom, just leave me alone." I started to cry. I didn't want him to see me like this. Since we talked about everything, he knew that I was having a tough time getting over my relationship with Hassan. Tom wanted to help me through it because he had fallen as deeply in love with me as I was with Hassan.

"Is it Hassan? Did he say something to you?" Tom touched my arm.

Turning away from him, I didn't want Tom to see my reaction. He stepped up behind me and put his hands on my shoulders. I couldn't help it, but I shrugged from his embrace.

"Don't do this. Talk to me!"

The flashing red light on the answering machine tormented my soul. I felt so torn! Should I go with my heart and go back to Hassan? Should I give in to common sense, knowing my history with Hassan, and devote myself to Tom who loved me and the children and who wanted to take me away from all this madness?

Tom stared at me. He just stood there watching me stare at the blinking light trying to figure out what had put me in this state of mind. Then it dawned on him, "What's on that tape, Tammy?"

"Nothing," I quickly responded, liar written all over my face.

"Play the tape," he insisted.

"No, Tom, just leave me alone!

He walked over to the answering machine. I was right behind him.

"Don't turn that on, Tom!" I demanded.

He reached for the machine, and I was so angry that I flew into a rage. He had no right to invade that painful part of my life. And besides that, I couldn't bear to listen to that tape again. We started struggling. Tom grabbed me and held me in one of his strong arms just long enough to turn the machine on with the other. He used both hands to back me up far enough as to where I couldn't reach the machine. The greeting came on, then Hassan's voice begging.

"Why are you making me listen to this? You have no business turning that on! I don't want to hear him!" Striking out at him in the only way I knew how, I started to swing. He didn't move a muscle, just kept his face out of striking distance.

"I love you. You can't hurt me! If you have to punch me to get rid of the hurt that brother put in you, then here I am, punch me!" I kept on punching and punching until my arms gave out. He put his strong yet loving arms around me as I cried my frustrations away. "You're going to be alright, Tamlyn. It seems like you'll never get over him, but you will. I know what you're going through because I was there once. It's going to take time. Trust me. I'm here for you, but you got to talk to me."

"I don't know how, Tom. I don't know how," I cried. "I don't know how to love a man anymore, and I don't know how to talk about it."

"You're doing a good job of it right now. Just don't ever stop." Tom held on to me. "Go wash your face and get your bags so we can go."

Here I was crying over another man and instead of getting mad and walking out, Tom held onto me. He didn't make me feel bad or throw up his hands and leave. He was just there, for me.

While I was in my room I could hear the screeching of the tape as Tom erased

Hassan's message from the answering machine. I washed my face, lightly sprayed on some perfume, and walked bag-in-hand into the living room, where Tom was sitting on the sofa deep in thought. He stared at me as I walked over to him. Standing up, he took my bag, and walked out the apartment leaving me behind.

It was a quiet ride to Tom's house, and a very quiet evening. He fixed dinner but I wasn't very hungry. After I bathed, I slipped into my eggshell white, silk nightgown and went to the bed to watch television. At least half an hour I stayed there and in all that time, Tom didn't even come upstairs to check on me which was not like him. For the first time, I felt that he was hurt.

I got off of the bed and walked downstairs into the darkened room where he was seated. Kneeling between his legs, I looked into his distant face and my heart sank. "Tom, I don't want to lose you. I'm sorry for what happened, but I'm not good at handling all this pressure."

"Am I pressuring you, Tamlyn?"

"No. You've been so sweet to me. I don't know what I'd do without you."

With doubt in his eyes he looked down at me. "Will you be my wife?"

"Yes, Tom, I told you I would. Why are you asking me this?"

"Do you need time away from me?" he whispered.

"No." I could feel a lump in my throat.

"Do you want Hassan back?"

"I want you."

"Do-you-want-Hassan-back?"

"No, Tom, I want you."

I felt like a child being scolded. His icy tone made me tremble with uncertainties of my own. It also made me realize that if I didn't shape up, he might not be around much longer. Unbuttoning his shirt, I kissed his hairy chest and his neck. "I love you, Tom."

He leaned his head back and closed his eyes. I didn't know if he was ignoring me or feeling my pain. Pressing my mouth up against his, I hungrily swallowed his tongue. Fumbling to unzip his pants, I reached inside and for the first time felt his thick, warm erection in my hand. Slowly, I kissed down his body, apologizing and pleading my case. With my hair in the tight grips of his fist, Tom moaned from the depths of his soul. I know this wasn't what he planned for our first time making love together, but I needed him now. Just before he accepted my apology, he picked me up and sat me facing him on his lap. My legs where spread open over each side of him. Holding on tight, I screamed as Tom thrust inside of me letting me know that all had been forgiven. Quickly the pain I felt turned into ecstasy. "Tom don't leave me...don't leave me...don't leave me," I said over and over again in his ear as I came.

"I'll never leave you. Never," he said softly to me with his strong arms wrapped around my back.

The weekend turned out really nice even though we cancelled our plans for the play and dinner. Instead we spent time together doing nothing but snuggling, exchanging stories, and getting to know each other better.

Sunday evening when I picked up my children from Mrs. Colbirth's house, I was all smiles and she seemed genuinely happy for me. We were sitting on her couch eating some apple, raisin and walnut pie that she said she made with the help of Kiara and Tianna. "You look so happy, Tammy. That Tom must be some kind of man."

"He's all that and some more, Mrs. Colbirth. He's everything a man is suppose to be." My eyes sparkled when I talked about Tom to her.

"And how are the wedding plans coming along?"

"Everything's set, only two more weeks. You are coming, I hope? I didn't want to send an invitation because I didn't want to upset Hassan."

"Well, honey, you're too late for that because Hassan's plenty upset already. He comes around here, crying about how can you do this to him. I told him to shut up his mouth. All the trouble he done put you through. Just like his father. I love my boy, but he ain't' no good sometimes. You're doing the right thing. You got you a good man who's gonna marry you and take care of those kids, and that's all that matters.

The phone rang and Mrs. Colbirth picked it up.

"Hello...Yes Hassan, she's here." While she spoke, I shook my head so she wouldn't say anything else. Of course she didn't get it. She just hung up the phone, "That was Hassan, speak of the devil. He said that he's around the corner and he'll be right over."

I started to panic "I don't want to see him. Y'all get your stuff, and come on!" I said to Kiara and Tianna. Rushing, I snatched Hateem up by the arm. Something inside of me knew it would not be a pleasant encounter. When Tom dropped me off home that morning, Hassan had left several more angry messages on my machine saying that, we were gonna talk! I just wanted to be long gone by the time he got there.

"No, Tammy, don't run from Hassan. Stand your ground and tell him face to face to stop bothering you!"

"Mrs. Colbirth, you don't understand how Hassan can get." I explained while I zipped up Hateem's jacket. After the drama I went through over the weekend, I just couldn't deal with any more. Emotionally drained, I just wanted to get behind my apartment doors and confront Hassan at another time when I felt stronger. I grabbed the kids' bags and took them to the car. By the time I went back in the house and came out with the children, Hassan was parking his car.

And oh Lord, when I saw his face, he looked angry. I opened the car door and the kids were piling inside when he approached me.

"Tammy, how come you didn't call me back?" He stood over my shoulder.

"Get in, Hateem!" When he saw his dad, Hateem started to turn around and get back out of the car. Hassan grabbed me by the arm, "What! You just gonna ignore me?"

"Stop, Hassan! Don't be grabbing on my arm!"

"Look!" Hassan said with his hands up, backing away from me, "Why don't you come back to my place? Let's talk and work this shit out." He had been drinking. His eyes were blood-shot red, and his breath was ripe from alcohol.

"No, Hassan, I have to go home!"

"Why, your other niggah there?" He got all indignant. "I pay for that place remember!" He pushed me up gainst the car and I got scared. I wasn't prepared for this. "Your ass owe me. I want all my money back that I ever gave you! Let that punk mothah fuckah buy your shit for you!"

"Fuck you Hassan!" Slamming the back door, I attempted to get to the driver's side of the car.

"Fuck me? Fuck me? How you gonna say fuck me?" Hassan started pushing me as I turned to walk away, "You musta' forgot who I am already. You need me to remind you?"

Trying to get him away from me, I swung, hitting him in the face, and he went off. Hassan beat me in the street for the entire neighborhood to see. Two men ran over and wrestled Hassan away from me.

Mrs. Colbirth came running out of the house screaming, "Stop it! Stop it, Hassan! You leave her alone!" She put her arms around me yelling, "You get away from here! You better leave before I call the cops on you myself! I'm ashamed of you!"

We walked back into the house, and I went into Mrs. Colbirth's room where I laid down. She went back out and tended to the kids. I was so shaken that Mrs. Colbirth had to drive us home.

The next morning at work Tom came over to my station with a mug of hot coffee loaded with cream and sugar, just the way I liked it. But he had a bagel instead of the danish. Still rattled from the events of the weekend, I thought about whether or not to take the day off. Work was the best choice because at home, I would have driven myself nuts. Staying busy was the best thing.

Keeping my head tilted slightly to the right, I was trying to hide the scratch going down the side of my face. But just like radar, Tom zeroed right in on it. His smile faded into a sharp glare, "How did that happen?" As Tom touched my arm to pull me closer to him, I flinched in pain. "What happened to you, Tamlyn?" he repeated.

"Tom, I don't want you getting mixed up in this. It's my problem. I'll handle it."

"Did he do this to you?" I could see rage building in Tom's eyes. "Thukella!" He yelled across the lobby.

Thukella came over to my station. "What's up lovebirds?" she asked playfully

"Cover for Tamlyn, a minute."

"Sure. Is everything alright?" Her smile dropped as she noticed Tom's urgency. He led me out of the lobby and down the hall to a conference room. There he closed and locked the door behind us.

"Take your arm out of that dress." I unzipped the back of my dress and slowly pulled my arm out. My muscle was still tight from where Hassan hit me. It was black and purple.

"Take your dress off!" Tom was furious.

"It's just my arm."

"Do it!" Taking my other arm out, I stepped out of my dress. He examined my chest, my back, and he looked down at my legs through my stockings. There were no other visible bruises on my body. I'm glad he couldn't see my broken heart. "Where does he live?"

"Tom, please, don't go over there. I don't want you to fight."

"I don't need to be protected, Tamlyn. I hope it is not your intent to make me feel less than a man." I looked into Tom's face and he meant it, he wanted Hassan's address. Out of respect for Tom I gave it to him.

I went back to my workstation, and he left the building.

"Girl, what happened? I have never seen Tom so serious before."

"Thukella everything is so messed up. Hassan and I got into a fight last night and..."

"A fist fight?" Her eyes stretched wide in disbelief.

"Yeah," I said showing her the scratch on my face.

"Tom's upset and now he's going to confront Hassan. I don't know what to do." I was worried.

"Tom will be alright. You just got to trust that he knows what he's doing."

"I do trust Tom. But I don't trust Hassan." I sat down and answered the ringing phone.

MAN TO MAN

I was sitting with my feet propped up on the coffee table suffering from a massive hangover. Before I met up with Tammy over at my mom's crib, I was sitting here at my place getting tore down. Trying to drown out the shit that was in my head. I had a woman that I loved and I turned around and fuckin' let her slip right through my hands. Feeling stupid, I knew I didn't have any one to blame but myself. I came to love Kiara and Tianna as my own blood. Might as well say I was their daddy, I was there for them most of their lives.

Now, they say when a woman lay down to have a child, she's laying down her life. I ain't no religious man. What I mean is that I believe in a higher power. My name ain't on nobody's church roll, but I don't know how else to explain it. I never intended to be in the room when Tammy had the baby. Purposely I wasn't there in the room when Debbie had Erkell, just like with Jasmine. I was at the hospital, just not in the same room. Just my choice. Some like that kinda shit, I didn't. But how the whole thing went down when my son, Hateem, came into this world was just like that. Being right there at Tammy's head as she pushed our child into this world, it had to be what some people call, divine intervention. Out of my three biologicals, Hateem is the only one I bonded to like that. Why? 'Cause something in the stars must have known that I wouldn't always be in his life. I needed something stronger from that child, so I would never forget where he came from and who he belonged to.

The more I thought about it, the more I drank. Then I said, fuck it, I'll make her come back to me and that's when I jumped in my ride called moms on the cell phone and confronted Tammy. It was not my plan to break ill and beat her down like that. Not at all! But the shit just started escalating and that damned Jack Daniels started takin' over. By the time I got back into my apartment later on that night, I picked up where I left off and drank until I fell the fuck to sleep.

As I sulked in my stupidity, someone started bangin' on my door. I wasn't going to answer it, but they just wouldn't go away.

"Aw'ight, Aw'right!"

When I answered it, I remembered the dude's face. It was Tammy's old man. I knew what he was here for. "What's up?" Aggressively, I stared him down.

"I've come to talk to you."

"If you come to do some damage old man, we can take this shit outside."

"I came to talk to you like a man, to a man." He said staring me down.

The vessels in my head were throbbing, so damn bad. My eyes were squinted. Grabbing the side of my head, I walked back inside my apartment. He followed behind me. I sat down, lit a cigarette and reached under the couch and pulled out my .38, laying it on the coffee table in front of me. I was in no condition to fight, so if this mothah fuckah wanted to act ill, I would have to bust a cap in his ass.

He remained standing, reminding me of one of them Muslim brothah's, all suited down with his legs apart and his hands cupped behind him. He was rattling off some shit about how he saw what I had done to Tammy, and that she was all bruised. He told me don't ever bother her again, because he claimed her as his wife now, and if I touched her again, I'll have him to deal with. Sitting there I looked at him while I inhaled on my cig. I didn't have nothin' to say to him cause I couldn't believe that I took it to that foul level either. My father's ghost was staring me right in the face. The same thing I did to Tammy was the same ill thing I despised my old man for doing to my mom. So what did that say about me? Did my one night of insanity validate my father's actions toward me, toward my mother. Was my one night of standing in his shoes suppose to be enough to make me understand his rage?

Even though Kiara and Tianna might remember that shit, I prayed that my son wouldn't. I don't want him to grow up hating me, thinking of me as some punk mothah fuckah who beat up on his mother. So yeah, I came to the same conclusion- stay the hell away from Tammy. His point was made and I wanted him to step. "You through?" I interrupted nonchalantly.

He looked at me, aggravated like he had more on his mind, "Yeah, I'm through."

I motioned my head toward the door.

"Peace," he said, staring me in my eyes in a defiant kind of way.

Smashing the butt into the ashtray, I flicked it to the other side of the room. "Peace to you too," I snarled.

WITH THIS RING

I spent the night over my parents' house so mom could help me and the children get dressed. My dad, Jimmy, Tim and all the other men gave Tom a bachelor party last night after the wedding rehearsal was over. Too excited to sleep, I heard daddy come in the house around midnight. I was hoping everything was alright with Tom, because I didn't want anything to mess up our day.

Alone in mom's bedroom with the door closed, I sat at her vanity table dressed in my stockings and slip, taking the curlers out of my hair. Even with all of the noise from everyone in the house, a stillness existed in mom's room. People were all over the place. Mom's family was from Georgia and South Carolina. Dad's people were from Washington and Boston. And the bridesmaids were all starting to arrive. The phone rang and on the first ring I picked it up.

"How you making out, sugar?"

At the sound of his voice, I exhaled. Speaking softly I confessed, "I'm so scared, Tom."

"I know you are, baby."

"You do?"

"Yeah, but believe me sweetheart, you'll be fine."

I can't wait to see you," I said from the bottom of my heart.

"I love you, beautiful."

I felt very blessed to have such a wonderful man. I thought about the life that my children would have, growing up in such a beautiful home with a father to look up to and learn from. I thought about how much better their education would be. And I thought about the two-week honeymoon cruise to the islands Tom and I were going on after the reception. I felt like Cinderella. Tom and I talked on the phone for ten minutes. By the time I hung up, I was more than ready to become Mrs. Thomas Lester.

Slipping on my white beaded wedding gown, I stood in front of the full-length mirror that hung on my mother's closet door. I took my time and stared at the beautiful African Queen that stared back at me. Mom had out done herself altering the white gown she wore when she and daddy married. This was my day, indeed.

"The limousines are here! Put a move on it up there!" Daddy yelled. Mom walked in all dressed up in her 'mother of the bride' gown and sat on the bed with tears of joy in her eyes.

"Baby, you look so very beautiful. Tom's a good man. You deserve the best, and God's giving it to you." She walked over to me and helped straighten my headdress and we hugged. "You be happy. And I pray for you to know the love from your husband, like I know from mine." We hugged and wiped each other's tears away.

Just then Jeannette walked in. "Ooh, Tammy, you look so beautiful," she said with her arms stretched out. I hugged her tight. She was my home team. Jeannette was my best friend. She stuck with me when everyone else turned their backs.

"I love you, Jeannette."

"I love you too, Auntie."

"Auntie?" I gave her a quizzical glance, then it dawned on me -a baby! I screamed.

"Shhh!" Jeannette said, "I'll talk to you later. Let's go get you all married, girl."

Mom walked downstairs first. I was behind her and Jeannette held my train. The photographer snapped pictures and everyone clapped and whistled.

I was shocked, but it was nice to hear when Tom's daughter Angela said "You look nice, Tamlyn."

"Thank you." I gave her a kiss on the cheek as a gesture of a hopeful new beginning between us. I knew it must have taken a lot for her to say that, but like it or not, we were family. And I did want peace between us.

While heading to the church, the limousine drove past Domtar Courts. I truly felt that I would wake up and that the limo would turn back into my broken down Subaru, and that it would drive me back into Domtar Courts. But that didn't happen. I did a double take because I thought I saw Hassan's Lexus. I turned around and looked long enough to notice that it was a different type of car all together.

It was a perfect sunny day for a wedding. The flowers and the trees were in bloom. There was a warm breeze in the air. Once at the church, Mom went in the back to let Rev. Brown know that we were here and ready. The pianist began to play and the vocalist began to sing Stevie Wonder's Ribbon in the Sky. Sharon lined everyone up, instructing them to keep in step. Hateem announced that he had to go to the bathroom, now. I panicked. Daddy grabbed him and took care of him. Sharon went to the pianist and told him to add another verse.

Finally, the back doors opened, and the show was on. The couples marched down the aisle to the beat of the music. After they were all at the altar, Jimmy and Tim rolled out a white liner, and Hateem walked straight down the aisle without turning around or dropping the pillow. Then the organ blasted Here Comes the Bride and six year-old Kiara and five year-old Tianna sprinkled flowers in my path. The congregation of around one hundred friends and family members stood as I entered holding daddy's arm.

Tom seemed so proud. I looked at his face smiling at me so confidently. His son, Brian was his best man. Daddy walked me three quarters of the way down the aisle then Tom held his hand out to me, for our walk together to the altar. Daddy placed my hand in Tom's and walked behind us.

The women in my wedding party were dressed in African style mint green, trimmed in gold dresses that mom made. The men wore black tuxedos, except for Tom who looked so fine in his white long tail tux.

"Who giveth this woman to marry this man?" Reverend Brown asked.

"I do," said daddy. He kissed me and shook Tom's hand, then joined mom on the front bench.

As Reverend Brown read scriptures from the Bible, I looked into Tom's eyes. From deep down inside my soul, I knew that everything would be alright. Tom stared back at me and whispered, "I love you." And I returned his sentiments, and this time with all my heart I meant it, "I love you too." We smiled at each other.

After the service, the wedding party and guests threw rice as we rushed toward the limousine. Tom and I laughed and kissed, as we waited for the driver to return. My husband. I rolled the idea around in my head. I was someone's wife, and I had a husband. All I could think about was, I wanted to be a good wife, and give my children a stable home like they deserved.

I turned around into the back window waving at the smiling crowd. Tom and I and our wedding party went the Trenton Annex to take pictures. They always had the largest variety of beautiful flowers in the spring. I squeezed Tom's hand, and he kissed me on the cheek. Thank you Lord for letting this happen to me, I prayed.

WAKE UP CALL

One Year Later

After Tammy got married on me, it took me a while to get myself straight. All that drinkin' and shit fucked my system up, 'cause I ain't no big time drinker. Yeah, I loved my forties and something harder every now and then. But not like I was putting it away. At first the drinking numbed me. Didn't make me forget, just took the edge off of all the things I couldn't control. But after awhile I got to the place where I didn't care 'bout nothin'. Which for a while was cool 'cause I stopped thinking about Tammy. But the only problem with that was the shit wasn't selective. Couldn't say, 'aw'ight booze, I want you to freeze up memory a, b, and c, but leave the rest of that shit alone'. It don't work like that. That booze told my ass, 'fuck you, I'm takin' everthing out, and when I'm through you ain't gonna be caring 'bout a damn thang'. And I didn't. Not about myself, not about Tammy, my money, not even my kids. That's when Debbie stepped in to wake a brothah up, making me take a good look at what I was doing to myself. Helping me dry out.

For the first week and a half of her help Hassan mission I stayed at her crib. Then for two months straight after that, every single day she mother-henned me. Making sure I didn't slip up, 'Hassan promise me you won't drink today? Hassan did you go work out today? Hassan did you talk to your mom today cause you know she's worried about you? Hassan, I love you'. Most of the time the shit just got on my nerves, but it did keep me on track, and for that I was thankful.

As if that wasn't bad enough, things with my business were fallin' apart. The Five was getting some serious heat from the cops. Thank goodness for my girl, Cheryl who worked down at the Commissioner's office. She tipped me off that there was a sting team organizing to find out who was behind the drug explosion, and that the Furious Five was one of the rings targeted for a shake down. I knew this would happen sooner or later, but I was hoping for later. With her inside help I was able to keep one step ahead of the game.

To keep our business tight, I called a Five-Five and everyone gathered at my crib. A Five-five was a code that me and the fellas came up with that meant something serious was going on with the business, that demanded we stop whatever we were doing and meet! I told them what was going down with the drug investigations and warned everyone NOT to be spending money like crazy until Cheryl gave us the okay. That's all we had to do...chill. But for Sho Nuff, that was too much to ask. That fool caught an attitude sayin' if he makin' his money, he gonna spend his money. Then went out and brought himself a brand new Mercedes Benz. We got into a fight. He dropped out of the Five, sayin' he was starting his own business.

His ass was riding high for exactly two weeks after he bought that car. He went up to New York in his new ride to pick up his product and on his way back from the city, he got pulled over by the NJ State Troopers, for speeding. How fuckin' stupid can you get? Uncle Roger called to inform me that Sho Nuff and some other knuckleheads were locked up. We went down to the station, where the cops were big time uncooperative, rude, and making it quite clear that they were going to nail Sho Nuff's ass to the wall. They told us that he was being held without bail, and that his car had been impounded. That shit was the beginning of the end for the Five-Five.

It was Friday night, and I was over Debbie's house visiting my kids. She wanted me to go and get a couple of videos for her and the kids to watch. Erkell and I were cruisin' in my ride with the tunes playing in my CD. I had to go back to my place to pick up my video card, and return a tape that I rented last night for myself. I had on my FUBU baseball shirt and cap. Erkell had on his little FUBU gear that I picked up when I got mine and our shit was tight. Hassan Ali, and Hassan Erkell, chillin'! Looking down at my boy it was strange how eight years flew by. One day you're buying them diapers and the next day you're buying them matching clothes. When we pulled into Blockbusters, Erkell was telling me about this girl in his class that he had a crush on named Sharee. Had to laugh 'cause third grade was when I had my first crush- on this girl named Donna. He told me he liked her because she was smart, which was good. The only thing I cared about was if they were fine, which let me know there was something higher he was reaching for than I was at that age.

I let Kell pick out a movie for himself and some cartoon mess for Jas. After that we swung on by KFC picked up a bucket of chicken so Debbie wouldn't have to cook, and I would be ready for some of her lovin' later on. Man, I felt good!

On my way back to the bridge, I noticed this cop car following me. I was cruising, and he was still on my tail. I moved into the right lane, then he moved into the right lane. I turned the corner then he turned the corner. Then he flashed his lights and made a quick sound with his siren. I couldn't believe that shit. My heart started pumping juice, because I didn't want anything to go down in front of Erkell.

"What is it dad?"

"It's nothing, just sit tight."

Opening the car door, I got out and closed it behind me. "Is there a problem officer?" I asked.

"Step away from the car and put your hands up high where I can see them."

"What for? What's this about?"

"Step away from the car and put your hands up where I can see them, please," he said again.

My man started patting me down then two more cop cars came pulling up.

"What's going on? What the hell did you stop me for?"

"Mr. Hassan A. Colbirth," the cop said reading my name off of my driver's license. He had pulled my wallet from my back pocket. I had seen him before and this was no routine stop. "We have reason to believe that you are in possession of drugs."

"What?" Then from the corner of my eye another cop caught my attention. "Take your hands off of my son!"

One of the other cops had opened my car door and pulled Erkell out by the arm. Erkell looked scared. They had me hand cuffed, leaning face down on the hood of my ride. The cop took Erkell and pushed him onto somebody's front lawn. He told him sharply, "You sit here boy and don't you move."

Two other cops checked my glove compartment, under the seats, in my trunk. One of the mothah fuckahs even stuck his hands in my bucket of chicken.

"Nothing, Lieutenant."

"Did you check the boy? Maybe he's hiding for his pappy."

No! What are you doing? Leave him out of this! Leave him out of this!"

"Pat 'im down."

The officer then went to Erkell, grabbed him by the arm and pulled him up. "You know what this is about, boy?"

"No! Get your fuckin' hands off my son!"

"Your daddy's a big time drug dealer."

Trying to stop them from harassing my son, I was yelling when the officer, who was dealing with me, hit me square in the middle of my back with his club, forcing me back onto the hood of the car.

"See, he sells dope to pregnant women and little kids like you. Did you know that?"

Erkell had his head down crying out loud. And I couldn't help him.

"Fuck you, you bastards!" I was yelling and cursing. Spit was flying out of my mouth and I could feel the sweat breaking out all over my body.

"Look at him! Look at him," that pig said turning Erkell to face me, making sure he saw me stripped and degraded. "If you choose to go into the family business boy, that's going to be you, remember that. He's clean."

The fucked up thing about it was I never told my son what I really did for a living. As far as he knew, I worked for Uncle Roger as a roofer. That's what I told him when he was little and I never went back to change the story. Always figured I'd make me some serious money, get out the drug life and he would never have to know. The cop removed his club from my back.

"Now, I think you've had about enough for tonight. I'm gonna take these cuffs off you, and you and your kid can go. But, if you try anything when your hands are free, I'll haul your butt right down to the station quicker than you can say dumb drug dealer. The choice is yours."

I could have killed him with my bare hands, but I held back.

"We're gonna be watchin' you," he said tossing my wallet at me. Catching it with one hand, I hulk-spit on the ground keeping my eyes fixed on him.

"Come here, Kell." Grabbing my son from behind the neck I kissed him on top of the head, pulling him into me for some much needed comforting. Furious! My shit was thrown all over the place. That fuckin' greasy ass chicken was all over my leather seats. When I got into my car, they were just pulling off. I put the pieces of chicken back in the bucket and slung it out the window at the back of the cop car, then gassed the fuck up on out of there. I thought they were gonna stop me again. If they did, they would have had to beat me down that time, 'cause I was in a fightin' mood.

All the way to Debbie's place, Erkell was quiet as a mouse. He kept his head down, looking like he was gonna cry, but he didn't. I was cursing, ranting and raving about the nerve of them cops. To attack me was one thing, but to search my boy. That shit was foul. We pulled up to Debbie's building and I parked the car. Before I could get the key out of the ignition, Erkell jumped out, slammed the door and ran into the apartment complex.

When Debbie opened the door, she was all smiles ready for fun. "Your daughter is so crazy Hassan! That little girl only in nursery school, but know all the words to that damn Barney tape. You should hear her. She..."

Erkell grabbed her holding on as if his life depended on it. Then he started to cry.

"What's wrong with him?" Debbie was stunned and looking at me for an answer.

"I got pulled over by the cops."

"Again?"

"They searched Kell, Debbie," I said looking away from her. Guilt wouldn't allow me to face her.

"What! You let them search my son?"

"I ain't let them do nothin'! They had my ass handcuffed, face down on the hood of my car. So you tell me what I could do!" I blasted, slamming the door behind me. My hostility was not directed at her, but at the incident that just happened.

"Sit down," Debbie said guiding Erkell to a chair. "So what are you gonna do about this? Them mothah-fuckahs ain't have no goddamned rights searchin' my chile! You just gonna let them get away with that?" Debbie searched for her shoes.

"Stall, Debbie," I said holding my hands out to reach for her.

"Stall my ass, Hassan. I'm going down to that police station and find out why the fuck they felt the need to search my baby. They gonna give me some answers or I'm gonna turn that fuckin' place out!"

Grabbing her in my arms, I held her tight so she couldn't go any place. "Stall, Debbie, stall. Baby, please stall." My heart was in pain over what just took place, and I needed her there with me. Erkell needed her too.

Debbie put her arms around me and burst into tears. She cried out loud, "That's my son, Hassan. They can't do that to my son."

"If you go down there you just gonna be making matters worse, not better. They want me. And, they gonna hound anybody they can to get to me," I said with my lips pressed against her neck. "Now go on over there and take care of Kell."

Since Sho Nuff got busted, I been pulled over and searched four times but this time upset the hell out of my system. Debbie talked me into chillin' at her crib for the night. She and I have been getting closer over the last several months.

When I woke up the next morning Debbie was already cooking. Smelled like pancakes or waffles, whatever it was, the shit was smellin' good! In no real rush to get up, I laid there in her bed listening to the noise from the television coming from the living room. With my hand cupped behind my head, I replayed the tape of last night in my mind. How scared Erkell looked, and how scared I was that things were going to get totally out of hand. The shades were pulled down to the bedroom windows and it was so peaceful. What a shame I had to get up and face the day.

I jumped into the shower, dressed and joined Debbie in the kitchen. She was on the phone.

"Morning baby," she said puckering for a kiss. She was dressed in a bathrobe and slippers. Then she laughed real loud at a comment made by the person on the phone. Picking up the newspaper from the table, I peeked into the living room where the kids were on the floor still in their pj's watching cartoons. Erkell was on his stomach with his head propped in his hands and Jasmine had her wooly uncombed head of hair laid on his back with her finger stuck down her throat.

"Jasy, take your fingers out of your mouth."

She jumped up and ran over to me and gave me a kiss. I picked her up in my arms. On my knee, I sat her then thumbed through the morning paper to see if there was anything in there about what happened last night, or to see if there was anything in there about the latest happenings of Sho Nuff's case. Thank God there wasn't.

Debbie laughed again, "Hassan, Dametta wants to know if you still got them polyester pants mama got you."

I had to laugh my self at that one. "Tell her hell no. Now Cathy knows that ain't my style. I don't wear no tight country ass lookin' pants." Debbie's mom Cathy was sweet as can be. The woman drank, smoked, and cursed like a dude, but she was still good people. She just didn't know shit about shopping for me.

"Well, sister dear, I'll keep you posted. Love you, 'bye." She hung up the phone then yelled for Kell to come eat. Debbie placed the plates of pancakes, cheesy eggs, beef sausage and grits on the table. Jasmine had her very own Barney place mat with the plate, cup, and utensil set. The girl wouldn't eat without it being all set up for her. She jumped off of my lap and climbed in her own chair with the booster seat.

"What was Dametta talkin' about this morning?" I inhaled the flavor, ready to get my hungry on.

"Well to tell the truth, Hassan, I called her this time," she said pouring juice into all of the cups. "I was asking her how she and Rock liked their new home, and she was telling me how nice the development is where they are. She said that they're still building a lot of new homes." There was more to this, I could tell by the way she was delivering it to me. "Hassan, why don't we move down to Virginia?" Whoop there it is!

"Girl, are you crazy? I ain't movin' to no fuckin' Virginia, and you can drop this subject right now."

"Hassan, think about it. Why don't you and I take the kids and move? There's so much going wrong here, but there, we can start fresh, and leave all this madness behind."

Looking at her, it was apparent that she wasn't going to let me eat in peace.

"Hassan, Dametta said that they have a good financial program for first time home buyers, and that we have a good chance of getting approved."

"Buy a house?" Dropping my fork on the plate, I wiped my mouth with the napkin, "Buy what damn house? I done told you that I ain't movin' to no fuckin' Virginia." I got up from the table and walked into the living room where the TV was still blasting the Looney Tunes.

Debbie followed me. "Hassan, I have lived in this apartment for seven years. I'm ready to make some major changes in my life and I made up my mind. I'm moving to Virginia with or without you, love. Monday morning, I'm giving my job two months notice. That should be enough time for me to get my finances in order so I can move my shit." She stared at me defiantly. I knew she was serious.

"How the fuck you just gonna take my kids away from me, Debbie?"

"I'm not taking them away from you Hassan. As their mother I have to do what I feel is best for them."

"And what about me as their father, huh? I guess that don't mean shit then, right?" I asked, all up in her face.

"Erkell could have gotten hurt last night, Hassan, and you know that. Them cops want y'all bad, and I'm not gonna stand around here and wait for one of them to kill your ass, or possibly one of my kids in the process."

Fuckin' women! All I could think about was how Tammy left and took Hateem and the girls away from me. Now Debbie was getting ready to do the same damn thing.

"Hassan," Debbie called to me as I walked toward the front door.

"Fuck it, Debbie."

"Hassan." She walked ahead of me blocking the exit preventing me from leaving. "Hassan, I don't want to take the kids away from their father. I want more than life itself for us to be a family. I love you, man. You should know that by now Hassan. Come with us," she pleaded.

"I don't get this. All of a sudden you just gonna leave your job, this apartment. Me? And move to Virginia?" I asked suspiciously 'cause the shit just didn't make sense.

With her arms folded she paused, dropping her head, then looked back at me, "I been thinking about this for a while, almost a year. Ever since Rock and Dametta moved. I just had to make a decision."

My forehead balled tight as my eyes narrowed, "You been thinkin' about takin' my kids away from me for a fuckin' year, and I'm just hearin' about it, now!" I couldn't believe the betrayal. "Thanks a lot Debbie. You, of all people."

"Hassan," she said, trying to hold my hand. The look on her face was like she wished she could say something to reach me.

"Fuck it, Debbie, take 'em. I can always make more." I grabbed her and shoved her from in front of the door.

"Hassan, don't go! Hassan?" She grabbed at my clothes. I managed to get away from her and I left.

Since Tammy got married a year ago everything changed. It just wasn't the same around the way no more. The women were tired and worn out. My blood Sho Nuff was looking at 15 years and cops were riding The Furious Five. Every week they had one of us at the station. The cops beat Bubby so bad. I went to bail him out. It scared the shit out of me, and I don't scare easily. He had a busted lip, his eyes were swollen, one of them shut, and this cracker cop kept looking at me as-if-to-say, 'you next'.

Shit was just going from bad to worse. Coming in late last night only two blocks from my house, I got pulled over for the fifth time, and searched for no reason at all, then they let me go. For the rest of the night I stayed up thinking and thinking about my kids and Debbie's threats to take them away from me. My eyes were stinging, and I was light-headed from lack of sleep. I had smoked up almost two packs of cigarettes and I still had on the same clothes from the day before. It was six forty-five a.m. and I was going back over Debbie's to let her know that if she thought she was taking my kids away from me that she done lost her damn mind.

By the time I walked into her apartment at seven-ten, Erkell was running past me with his book bag strapped on his back. He gave me some love then ran outside to catch the bus. Debbie was running from room to room, rushing trying to get herself ready for work. In the kitchen, Jasmine was all dressed, sitting at the table eating what looked like oatmeal.

"Hi dadee," she was smiling and had food all over her face.

Hey Jasy." I snatched a piece of hand towel from off the roll, wet it and cleaned her up. Holding the cup of milk to her mouth, I watched as she put her little hand over mine and took her time drinking. When she was finished, I picked my doll up from the chair and held her in my arms. Jasmine wrapped her arms around my neck squeezing tightly, and with her cold lips pecked me on the cheek. Continuing to hold my baby girl, I felt like my insides were coming apart. Debbie came rushing into the kitchen, Hassan I gotta go. I have to drop her off at the nursery and get to work," she said, checking the watch on her wrist. Kissing Jasmine on the cheek, I put her down on the floor and Debbie grabbed her by her arm, "Go put your sweater on Jasmine." She looked up at me as if it were the first time she actually noticed my pain. "What's wrong with you?"

My eyes were misted. I stood there in my stance, arms folded looking at her. "You ain't taking my kids away from me."

Debbie sighed, checking her watch again. "Hassan, I can't talk about this now. I'm gonna be late."

"You right, ain't nothing to talk about cause you ain't takin' 'em." My glare narrowed.

Debbie slammed her hand down on the kitchen counter, "Hassan, I'm gonna be real with you. It's only a matter of time before they get you, too. They got Sho Nuff. They got Bubby. Chief said a detective was surveilling his pad. They done stopped and searched you over a hundred times already. Y'all so damn hot, you can't run your business like you need to."

"Yeah, so what you saying Debbie? I done told you I ain't movin' to no fuckin' Virginia. You can hang that shit up." Pissed off, I walked into the living room and Debbie was right behind me.

"No, I ain't gonna hang it up. What are you waiting for, a mountain to drop on your head? If you're not gonna think about yourself, think about Erkell, Jas, and me. Hassan you owe me!" She put her hand on her hip and pointed at me.

"Owe you what? What do I owe you Debbie?"

"You owe me the consideration to at least think about what I'm saying to you before you shoot me down. I waited for you since we were in high school. I had your children, and I have been there for you always, but I'm getting too old for this shit. Time ain't waiting for nobody. Soon Erkell and Jasmine will be big, and we'll still be waiting for you to get yourself together. News flash, Hassan, if you go to jail, I ain't gonna be waiting no damn ten years for your ass to be getting out. In ten years, I'll be pushing forty, and I hope to be settled down by then."

She was right, even though I didn't want to hear what she was saying. And by the way Debbie looked at me, she could tell that I agreed with her, but I wasn't ready to give in yet. Debbie walked up to me, placing her hands on my arms. "Come on Hassan, think about it. I talked with Dametta, and she said she'll help us get settled if we move."

Frowning at the whole idea, I smoothed my hand across the top of my head, "You know, I ain't crazy about living with your twin."

"I know, baby, but it will only be for a little while, until we get our own place."

I walked off to the other side of the room, "What you gonna do about a job? And be for real, I ain't got no fuckin' skills. Where am I gonna work at?" I asked throwing my hands in the air.

"Oh that's no problem, I can find a nursing assistant job any place. Dametta said there's lots of temp agencies down in Richmond. And Rock works down at the dock repairing ships. He can get you on with him. They make pretty good money." Debbie walked up close to me. "Hassan, we can do this."

"You really thought this out, huh?"

"Yes, I have, Hass." Her eyes were begging me.

"I don't know, Debbie. What about my mom? What about Hateem?"

"Your mother is a grown woman. She'll be just fine. And from what I see, Hateem is very well taken care of even better than my children are. Hateem lives in the suburbs, in a nice big house, with a good school system, with his mom and his stepfather. And my kids are barely making it, and their father won't quit until he winds up in jail or dead." Debbie reached over taking her purse and Jasmine's hand.

I just stood there looking at her without saying a word. Wasn't nothin' left to say. She walked up placing her soft lips on mine then whispered, "Baby, please come with us."

"I'll call you tonight. I have some thinking to do." Seemed like there was no place else for me to be except in Virginia with Debbie and the kids.

BITTER SWEET GOODBYE

Spent the rest of the day at my crib thinking. Memories rolling in my mind like big wheels, they just kept on turning. Seeing Tammy's sexy face smiling at me. I thought about the way she use to snuggle up like a kitten under my neck. Then I thought about all the pain I put her through. Finally, I realized if I wanted any true peace, I had to accept the blame for the way Hateem came into the world. And the pain he endured the first couple of months in his life. Freaked me out, how was I so reckless and still Tammy loved me so fully? I blew it. I'm a man and I can admit that. Tammy should have been my wife. It should have been her I'm packing up and moving away with.

Too late for Tammy and me, but I still had time to make things right between Debbie and me. I ain't in love with her, but I can't risk losing my kids. They are all that matters to me.

One thing I definitely didn't like was the idea of getting a 9 to 5 and answerin' to the man. But Debbie was right, if I stayed here with the heat up like it was, I was headed for jail or an early grave. The fellahs and I could go back to hustlin for nickels and dimes, but that's some back-in-the-day shit. If I can't make the big bucks, fuck it. It wasn't worth the time or the risk.

As the day ticked on, my dad popped into my mind, and that was the best reason for me to take my ass to Virginia. Just to prove that I wasn't no punk like him.

When I couldn't stand another thought in my head, I drove over to mom's house and stayed there until she came home from work. My mind was set, but I had to square everything with her first. She was my right hand. I love her. Around three o'clock she came strollin' in the house. She looked exhausted. "Hello, son. What brings you here?" Her briefcase was in one hand and a brown bag filled with groceries was in the other.

Taking the bag out of her hand, I gave her a peck on the cheek laughing 'cause ole girl knew me too well. "Dag, mom, I can't come to see you?" Walking into the kitchen, I placed the bag on the table then came back into the living room where she was kicking off her shoes.

"Sure you can, but I know that look. So cut through the crap and tell your mama what's on your mind."

I looked long and hard at my mother and I took her by the hand. "I love you, you know."

"Boy, I know that. What's wrong? Did something happen? Are you in trouble again Hassan? Are..."

"Mama, I'm gonna take Debbie and the kids and we're gonna move to Richmond, Virginia." After I said my piece, I stood there waiting for her reaction but there was none. No words, only silence, and mom's silence was piercing. She walked to the screen door and stared out, with one arm folded across her chest and the other under her chin then, she spoke softly. "You know, ever since you were a little boy and I used to watch you play outside, so intense, so competitive..." She turned and looked at me, "I knew that one day you would grow into a man and have to leave me. You see, son, God gives us gifts to hold only for a little while, then he removes them from us. The lesson being- while you have it, cherish it before it's gone. I'm going to miss you and my babies, but you're doing the right thing. She nodded her head. "You are doing the right thing."

"How you gonna make out, ma?" Leaving her concerned me because I always looked out for my mom. Uncle Roger was here, but he was always so caught up into his own thang.

"Now I don't want you worrying about me. I'll be alright. I'll be just fine," she said to reassure me. I walked over to her and we held each other.

After I left mom's I had to take care of my business. With two hours to kill before visiting hours at Trenton State prison, I drove down to Willingboro to see Hateem and the girls. Usually I'd call before coming, but today, what the fuck. I knocked on the door and Tammy's husband answered it. Offering my hand, we exchanged a gentleman's greeting. I didn't have any beef with him, because now he was the keeper of the gate. He was in charge of four very special hearts, and sad to say, he was the one who would teach my son to become a man.

"How you doing, man? I came to see the kids for a minute."

"They're inside doing homework right now, but I'll get them."

He had come to the door dressed in a pair of blue jeans and a Polo golf shirt holding a cooking fork in his hand. The smell of fried chicken filled my nostrils so I guess he was Mr. Mom for tonight.

Walking to the edge of the driveway, I waited by the car checkin' out their neighborhood. Closest thing I ever came to this was watching the Fresh Prince of Bel Air. Even though you only get to see the one house, I guess this is what the rest of the neighborhood would have looked like. Reaching in my car I was going to get a cigarette from the pack, but decided against it. I could wait.

One by one the kids ran out the house excited to see me, and that made my day.

"Daddy! Daddy! Daddy!" They all yelled, with Hateem taking up the rear. I opened my arms wide as Kiara and Tianna filled them. After I squeezed all the juice out of them, I squatted down and swooped my little man up in my arms. For fifteen minutes or so I rapped to them about school, how they been, if they were happy. Took everything out of me not to say how's your mom, but I wasn't gonna put them in the middle of no shit. At seven, six, and four, I knew they wouldn't understand my leaving town. How do you tell your kids goodbye? Instead, I just told them to always remember that Daddy loved them.

Kiara and Tianna were growing tall and skinny, looking a whole lot like Tammy. Hateem looked so much like Erkell when he was that age, seems like they could have had the same mama. Before I left I gave each one of them twenty dollars, hugs and much love.

By the time I got into Trenton, it was visiting hours at the prison. "I'm here to see Roger Holmes," I told the guard at the front desk. After I was searched and issued a visitor's badge, he told me to be seated at window number 12. These facilities never fail to depress the hell out of me. It's like I stop breathing every time I come in this place, and it don't matter what side of the glass I was sitting on. Sho Nuff came walking in, sportin' his prison gear and had his hair in cornrows. Picking up the black phone, I pressed it to my ear and we put our fists up next to the thick glass that separated us.

"Peace bro."

"Damn, Hass, man. It's good to see your face. These niggahs up here 'bout to drive me crazy."

"Yo, man, five-five," I said seriously.

"What's up?"

I had Sho Nuff's complete attention.

"I'm getting out of the business, Sho."

"What?" Sho Nuff looked at me like I was crazy. "Hass, man, what's up wit dat?

I thought we was five strong. Ain't nobody ever got out before." He switched the phone to his other ear acting like he forgot he dropped out of the five before his ass got locked up.

"Look man, ain't nothing here for me no more. I done slept with every ho in town. I got the heat on my ass, Debbie sweating me to move, and Tammy...Hateem. Man, I just got to break the fuck out of Trenton." Sho Nuff was crushed. He didn't say a word, just kept his head down staring at the table. "Sho Nuff, I don't have enough to buy my way out. I got six thousand in the pot, but I'm still short four thousand dollars. Can you spot me the four G's? I'll get it back to you somehow."

"Yeah, whatever you need. You know that."

Yeah, I did know that. My cousin and I have had many fights and disagreements with each other in our lives. But we were family and always managed to see past that shit. In order not to interrupt the flow of the business, we agreed that if one of the five was to leave the organization we had to buy our way out at a price tag of ten thousand dollars. Sure, I could have just skipped town, but that's not how I wanted to be remembered.

After I left the prison, on my way to Uncle Roger's house, I used my car phone to call up Debbie and told her to call Bubby, Chief, and Fletch and tell them it's a five-five at my place in exactly one hour. With all ten G's in my hand I was gonna tell them 'I'm out'.

SIGNED, LOVE ALWAYS

A couple of weeks before we left, I dreamt about Tammy. Lately, I couldn't get her off my mind. She stood on one side of a pond with her arms stretched out to me, calling my name. Jumping into the pond, I swam with all my might to reach her, but when I got in the middle she disappeared. I could still hear her calling for me. Then I woke up. All day I thought about her. I needed to see her. More than anything, wanted to hold her and tell her how much I loved and missed her. Just one hour alone with her was all I needed. Shit, I would even settle for a few minutes.

Over to Domtar Courts I drove and parked my ride. Sitting there I reminisced about how Tammy dissed me the first time we met and then came back to apologize. And how I had it in my mind to dog her, but wound up falling in love. Looking over at Tower A, I remembered how she and the kids would wait for me. Kiara and Tianna would be running around looking all cute and she would be holding Hateem in her arms. Then we would jump in my ride and chill out at mom's for a while, like a real family. If I knew then what I know now.

Soon as I stepped out of the car I heard shouts from my fan club, "Hey, Hassan!"

"Whas up Jim Jim."

With his army green duffel bag thrown across his shoulder he said, "I got that smell good man. Only two dollars a bottle. Egyptian Musk, Obsession. I even got some new oils; wanna check 'em out?"

"Later, man. I'm kinda in a rush right now."

"You want me to wash your car, Hassan?" another asked.

"Naw, Mr. Alex, man. Not today."

"Come on, Hass, man. Things a little tight right now. I could use a ten spot, my brothah."

"See me when I get back, and I'll hook you up. I'm kinda in a rush right now," I said that shit hoping he'd be gone by then. I ain't got no money to be just giving away.

"Naw, that's not it man. I don't want nobody givin' me nothin'. I works for my money," Mr. Alex insisted.

I had to laugh. This old mothah fuckah ain't never worked a day in his life, and since when don't he accept handouts. "Mr. Alex, I'll tell you what. You watch my ride and make sure nobody don't mess wit it. When I get back I'll pay you for your services. Is that a deal?"

"It's a deal." Mr. Alex tipped his ragged old Hess hat at me.

Knocking on Jeannette's door, all I could think about was Tammy and the times we had in apartment 917. Jeannette opened up the door, "Hey Hassan! What a surprise!" She hugged me. I gave her a kiss on the cheek.

"So what brings you here?" Stepping to the side, she motioned for me to come in.

"Just droppin' through. So how you been?" We sat down in the living room. The place looked the same, nothing new, but did she pick up a little weight.

"You're not going to believe this, but I'm a mothah."

"No kiddin'! You?" I smiled. Somehow I can't picture that." The Jeannette I knew was too much of a free spirit to be anyone's mother.

"Me neither, but yup, I am." She laughed

"Congratulations. What did you have?"

"A little boy. His name is Tahj." Jeannette took me in her bedroom to look at the little man. Cute little fellah. We walked back into the living room.

"Damn, I can remember when mine were that small."

"How's your kids?" she asked.

"They're fine, but you probably seen Hateem and the girls since the last time I seen them."

"I don't know. I might have."

I couldn't hold it in any longer. "So, you seen Tammy lately?"

Jeannette smiled. "There, you feel better now, Hassan?"

"What you talkin' about?" I smiled.

"I knew that's what you came over here for. Yeah, as a matter of fact, I talked to her yesterday."

"How's she doin'? You know, is she happy?"

"Happy? Hey this is real life. You're up one minute, down the next, but she's rollin'. You know she's back in college now?"

"Yeah, my mom mentioned it. They keep in touch."

"Hassan, I heard about your cousin. What's up with that?"

"Don't look too good for him." My beeper went off in the middle of my sentence. Recognizing the number, I asked to use her phone and was off real quick. "I got to run, but first, I need you to do me a favor?"

"That depends on what it is."

"Jeannette, I need to see Tammy. I might be leavin' town in a few. I haven't made up my mind yet, but one thing's for sure, I need to see her before I go."

"I don't know Hassan. I mean, how you gonna be comin' off on her? What are your intentions?"

I got pissed off. What she mean, she don't know. "I just want to see her J."

"Yeah, you said that already, but she don't need you messin' around with her head. She and Tom are doing fine, but if you come around puttin' ideas in her head, Hassan, that might tear her apart."

"Don't you think, I thought about that already. I got some things I need to tell her, things that she should hear from me. Messin' her head up is not in my plans."

"Hassan, you still in love with Tammy, aren't you?"

I sighed and took my time answering, "For a while, after she got pregnant I lost sight of that shit, you know, but now it's all up in my face, crystal clear. Yeah, I still love her, and I miss the hell out of her. Come on, J, you gonna hook me up?"

"Hassan, you got to promise me that you ain't gonna be gettin' all deep on her, 'cause I know for a fact that she's still in love with you too."

"No shit, for real, she be talkin' about me?"

"Oh boy, here comes the ego."

"Naw baby, ego ain't got nothin' to do with this. Straight up, she talks about me like she still care?"

"Yeah." Jeannette nodded her head. "So when you want me to hook this up?"

"Set it up for this afternoon, and I'll be here."

"Hold on Hassan! I'll call her now." Jeannette dialed the phone. "Hello, can I speak to Tamlyn Lester? This is Jeannette Ford." Jeannette changed back to her around-the-way voice, and made her need sound urgent. "Tammy something happened, and I need to talk to you. Well, I can't talk to you over the phone, but it's important. No, don't take off from work, I have a doctor's appointment now anyway, but if you come after work, that'll be good. Yeah, I'm sure I don't want you to come now. I'll be strong. See you later Tammy, 'bye." Jeannette smiled at me.

"Thanks babe, this means a lot. You need anything?" I asked as I headed out the door.

"Always in need my brothah, but this one's on the house."

I reached in my pockets and dug out a fifty. "Go ahead, take it. That baby is gonna be expensive, so put this up for him."

At 5:30 there was a knock at Jeannette's door. I waited in her bedroom.

"Hey girl, you alright?"

The sound of Tammy's voice made my heart quickened.

"Come on in, Tammy."

As she walked in Jeannette closed the door behind her, then I appeared. "Hey babe."

Tammy's mouth fell opened. She was totally unprepared to see me. She glared at Jeannette.

"Girl, I'm sorry about this, but Tammy, he begged me to get you over here. You know how he is," Jeannette babbled, took her baby and made a quick exit out of the apartment.

Tammy looked so fine. Her hair was on her shoulders, and she was dressed all pretty and smellin' good.

"Look at you, girl." I was nervous as hell. "You lookin' mighty fine. Marriage must really agree with you." Tammy looked uncomfortable, she didn't seem happy to be alone with me. The last time we were alone together I was drunk and went off on her, so I understood her anxiety. As for me, it was like the year and a half had erased all of the ill shit and left only the love behind. If only I could turn back the clock and make things right again.

"Why am I here?"

"Tammy, I just had to see you again. I'm not gonna cause you no problems. I just wanted to tell you a few things." Now that she was here, I couldn't collect my thoughts. "I stopped by the house last week to see the kids."

"Yeah, Tom told me."

"Y'all are doin' a good job. They seem happy." I walked close to her wanting to just touch her soft skin. Kiara and Tianna are looking more and more beautiful, like you."

In a whisper she said, "And Hateem like you."

"Tammy, I been thinking so much about you lately." I was drownin' in her big brown eyes. "I know this is too little too late, but I'm so sorry, baby, for ever hurting you. I just needed you to know that."

"I needed to hear it," She said, beginning to let her guard down.

Reaching out, I ran my fingers against her arm. "Tom's a lucky man, and I'm a damned fool. I should have never let you go. You know, even though what we had is over, you're still in me girl."

Tammy walked toward the window and changed the subject. "How's Erkell and Jasmine?"

"They're fine. Tammy, I'm about to make some major changes in my life. But before I do, I need to clear up a few things."

She turned toward me. "Changes, like what?"

"I'm leaving town in a few days. Movin' down to Virginia to clean myself up, you know. Get a real job, and all that shit."

"Virginia? Are you going by yourself?" The tone in Tammy's voice was all too familiar.

I hesitated. "Naw, ah, no. Debbie and the kids are coming too."

Tammy turned back toward the window, "Would you have gone away with me, if I'd asked you to?" She asked sarcastically, "Never mind, don't answer that," I could see the hurt in her face. "She did say that she would always be there for you, Hassan." Tammy tried to sound nonchalant, but her body language told another story. I took her by the hand and pulled her to me. I just wanted to put her in my arms and let her feel things I didn't have the words to say.

Again, she walked away. "What's the point? What did you bring me here for? You should have just slipped away, and I would have never known that you were even gone." Tammy's eyes started to water.

I desperately wanted her to understand. "I told you. I just had to see you. I been doing some serious soul searching. I'm trying to do the right things for myself, for my kids. I done fucked up with us, Tammy. If I could change all that, girl I would, in a heartbeat, but I can't. The only thing left for me to do now is to play the fuck out of the cards I have left. Walking closer to her, I gathered her back in my arms. "Baby, I wish it was with you. I wish it was with you, Tammy. You gotta believe me." Resting my lips on her face, I held her tightly so she couldn't slip away. Closing my eyes, I never needed anything so much in my life. I know I don't deserve it, but I gotta know." I whispered, "Do you still love me?"

She whispered back, "I never stopped. Do you still love me?"

"Until I die!" I buried my face into her neck with my eyes close. She released tears on my arms and inside my heart, I cried with her. I held her in my arms until she let it all out. "I miss you so much girl," I said from the depths of my soul.

Tammy walked away from me holding up one hand, "Let's not do this." She wiped her face.

Walking up behind her, I wrapped myself around her body caressing the back of her neck with my lips, nipping her ear with my teeth. "I miss the way you use to call my name, Tammy." I caressed her sides, gently fondling her breast. "I remember everything you like, baby." I kept working those sensitive places on the back of her neck that Tom probably knew nothing about. Breathlessly my name escaped from her lips. From that moment on we both were gone. It was all about us. "Did you miss me, Tammy? Did you miss your man?"

"Uuuh," she moaned as I touched all of her secret places.

Right there on the spot I was ready to explode. "Let me make love to you, Tammy. Just one more time. Please, baby girl."

Her body trembled. And just like old times, I picked her up in my arms and carried her into the bedroom. I snatched off my shirt and slacks, then threw my draws in the corner. Tammy wasted no time removin' her clothes to receive me. Kissing the softness of her brown skin, I couldn't wait to feel her once more.

Hassan, how you gonna be comin' off on her? I mean what are your intentions? Hassan you got to promise me that you ain't gonna be gettin' all deep on her now. Jeannette's fuckin' voice began ringin' in my head. *Hassan, how you gonna be comin' off on her?* It took every ounce of strength, discipline and willpower I had inside of me, but I jumped up out of the bed. My hard-on was sticking straight up in the air.

"You better go." I was out of breath, sweating, with my heart pounding wildly in my chest.

"Ha-ssa-n," she cried out my name, just like in the dream.

"Look at us. This shit ain't real, Tammy."

"Hassan, I want you, please, please."

"I just needed to see you before I left, babe."

"Hassan, please." Tammy begged me to make love to her and at that point I wanted to be up inside of her more than I wanted my next breath. I knew I wouldn't be able to resist her cries for me much longer, so I grabbed her by the arms and stood her to her feet.

"Fix yourself up and leave, Tammy!" Don't ever leave me is what I really wanted to say. I wanted to grab her by the hand, run to the nearest Greyhound bus station and disappear without a trace.

"What did you get me here for! I think about you constantly. I can't get you out of my mind. Sometimes I think about you so much it feels like I'm gonna go crazy."

"Don't be thinkin' about me! You hear? Don't be thinkin' about me! I'm nowhere, Tammy. My life is fucked! You got a good thang going on. Don't fuck that up for nobody. You hear me, nobody!"

"But, Hassan, I love you."

"Look, you go to your husband and our kids, and you make that shit work!" Stepping into my pants, I walked back into the living room. Tammy dressed then followed. I couldn't look at her. It hurt too much.

"Hassan, Hassan." Her eyes were filled with tears. Mine were too. We held each other, both crying over the love that we once shared and mourned the love we'd never have. Putting my mouth over hers, I tasted the sweetness of her tongue for the last time. Letting go was the worst fuckin' feelin' in my life. She put her head down, as she started walking out, then she stopped.

"Don't look back baby," I said as she started to turn around.

With fist balled, I listened to the clicking of Tammy's heels. She walked further and further away from me. In my life I wanted her. Needed her! But all I could do was stand there and let her walk out forever. 'How am I going to live without you, babe?' Pain, rage, and helplessness swelled inside me. I took aim and punched a hole into Jeannette's living room wall.

WE ARE FAMILY

After work and night school, I came back home exhausted. I drove my bomb and parked it next to Tom's car in the garage. I opened the door leading into the house. It was a different world from the one had I left. The house was noisy. Tianna and Hateem were running around laughing and shouting at one another. The television was on and some Disney cartoon was playing on the VCR. And Kiara and Tom were making a chocolate cake in the kitchen.

"What is this?" I asked in disbelief. I had expected everyone to be in bed. It was nearing 9:30 at night.

"Hi, Mommy!" Hateem said, running and diving into my hip.

"Hi Ma!" Tianna yelled, waving her hand in a figure eight.

"Mom, come here, come here. Taste this. Me and Tom made this cake mix without even using the box." She shoved a spoonful of chocolate batter in my mouth.

Tom was looking at me with a naughty smile, "I figured if I tired them out, they'll sleep late and give us a late Saturday morning."

"If you say so." Some extra time would be nice, I thought.

During my lunch break, I had gone to the mall to pick up new comforter sets for the bedrooms. Tom and I had been talking about making the house feel more like a home for all of us. Not that I was ungrateful, but when I moved in, he suggested that I leave my things behind. I didn't like that idea one bit, but when I expressed my feelings to my mother she said, 'Look, chile don't go making no big deal about that ole stuff. That man has a dream house. He's probably telling you in a nice way that he don't want that junk cluttering up his place. Honey, sometimes you just have to compromise.' True indeed, a compromise was one thing, but even the beds the kids slept in belonged to his children.

I walked through the house putting the shopping bags away, when I noticed a lot of things missing. I went back into the kitchen. "What did you do? Where's your Chinese vase, your Ivory elephant?" I asked walking around Kiara to wash my hands at the sink.

"I moved all the valuable things that the kids might damage into my study. Now you can take the leash off of them, and let them enjoy this house, too."

Another thing Tom and I had talked about was his gripe that I didn't let the kids relax when they are at home. I just didn't want them to break any of his stuff.

I can't lie. This last year and a half has been a big adjustment period for all of us. Sometimes, I'd wake up and feel like the luckiest woman in the world. Other times I'd yearn for yesterday, for the good times I spent with Hassan. Sometimes, I'd get into such a funk wondering, what if? What if we would have given it one more try?

But what has mended my heart is what I saw and felt every day when I walked into this house- my children's faces, content and happy. They were making new friends in the neighborhood, and they loved their new school. And there was no denying, when we were all together, there was a completeness that I had always prayed for. The kind that my brother, Jimmy and his wife shared. The kind that my parents shared. Tom constantly reminded me that ours was a permanent bond. For keeps! And every time he said it, I believed him more and more.

Tying my apron in place, I puckered for a kiss from my husband. While Tom, Kiara, and I prepared a late dinner together, Tianna and Hateem continued to run around the house. I felt so blessed. Tom was such a good husband and father. I thanked God for my new family.

A FISH OUT OF WATER

For three months Debbie, the kids, and I have been in Virginia living with Dametta, Rock, and their son Christian. Two weeks after we moved down Debbie and I went to the realtor so we could get a house of our own. We both were nervous as hell, but we did manage to put one under contract. Debbie was the one who actually applied for the loan, but I made sure my name would be on the deed.

All the houses in the development were different, from one level homes, to split-levels. We placed a bid for a split-level. It was just like Dametta and Rock's place, but ours would have a deck on the back. From the outside the deck looked to be on the second floor, but it was actually attached to the kitchen. The bedrooms were on the first floor and the living room and kitchen were on the second.

Dametta's side of the complex had a pool and tennis court. The complex plans to build a mini-park area for the kids with swings and a basketball court on the side near our home.

All of that house stuff excited Debbie. But I had Trenton on my mind and was starting to catch a real attitude, wondering why I even agreed to move out of my apartment in the first damn place. I missed my bed. I missed going to my own bathroom and cooking on my own fuckin' stove, but most of all, I missed my freedom. I couldn't believe that every night, I went to bed, and every morning, I woke up next to Debbie. I felt like getting in my ride and going back home. I was out of my element here.

Debbie was on it. She came down here and on her first job interview she was hired full-time at a nursing home. That damn position working at the docks with Rock hadn't come through yet. I was steamed, 'cause I wasn't bout to be depending on Debbie for no money. Friday rolled around and I was fuckin' depressed, and bored to death.

When night fell, I hopped in the shower threw on my Paco Raban cologne, slipped on my trousers, and what do you know, Debbie started putting on her dress. She was looking for her stockings talking about she felt like hangin' out with me tonight. True dat, I been out every night that week but I needed space.

"Where we going tonight, Hass?"

"I don't know where you going but I'm going by myself."

"Hassan you been out every damn night this week. You can't take me with you one night? What, you done met someone down here that fast?"

"There you go, why it got to be somebody? Why can't it be that I got a lot on my mind and just need to get out to clear my head?"

"There ain't that much clearing your head in the world. Let me rephrase that, exactly which head are you trying to clear?"

"Just leave it alone Debbie, this ain't the time or the place."

"How you think it's making me look to Dametta and Rock, you being gone all the time. You my man and you in the streets and can't even take me."

"You lookin' like you always been lookin'. You the one insisted we come down here, now we here, but while we're here I ain't frontin' for no damn body. You should know that."

"I ain't askin' you to front Hassan. I'm just askin' you to respect me."

"Respect yo self."

"Hassan, I want you to respect me by not making me look like a fool in front of my family."

"How am I doing that Debbie? Do I be cussing you out in front of them? Do I put my hands on you in front of them? Do I leave you hangin' for money or things that you and the kids need? Do I? Didn't I drive your ass down here and pay for everything? When you wanted to buy a house, instead of gettin' an apartment, like I wanted, didn't I go along with it and give you the down payment? Didn't I do that? I can't hear you. Didn't I do that?"

"Yeah!"

"So where the hell you come off tellin' me I'm dissin' you?" I was steaming. After I finished dressing, I pushed pass her and headed out the door. Everyone was in the living room watching television. I didn't say a word. Just got in my car and drove off.

By now I knew the surrounding vicinity well enough to get around the city by myself- to the supermarket, to the gym, and Rock took me around to some of the clubs in town. He's more of a homebody, so I would go out by myself, just to get away. While driving, I turned on the radio and what was playing but Mint Condition's You Send Me Swingin' and my mind immediately went on Tammy. Umm, how we use to make love to that song. I don't remember if she liked it cause I liked it, or I liked it because she did, but somehow it became our song. Not wanting to be reminded of what I couldn't have, I turned my radio off, listening only to the hum of my car's engine.

Tonight I needed to be someplace that was all mine, where I could cool out and be Hass. Nobody's man or dad. I, damn sure, didn't want to be looking in Debbie's face in the morning. Pulling into a Slumber Inn hotel, I got myself a room. It was on the seventh floor and the scenery was all that. It had a balcony facing the highway. Now I ain't one to be gettin' all emotional, but I swear I could have screamed my fuckin' head off. I felt so free, like a bird sitting in the highest fuckin' tree. Flicking on the television, without the volume, I walked over to the patio doors. Opening up the curtains and the door wide, I let the night breeze in. Stripping down to my underwear, I got on the bed, chillin', collectin' my thoughts. Before I came here, I stopped by the liquor store and brought myself the only companions I wanted for the night, a fifth of Jack Daniels, and a forty. I was about to get nice!

The next morning when I got back to the house, I knew the attitudes were gonna be raw, so I prepared myself for it. As I walked in the room, Debbie was sitting on the bed. She didn't say a word to me, but she gave me mad attitude. I didn't say anything to her either. I just wanted her to know that I was back.

A LONG TIME COMING

As I walked into the Dean's office, I felt vindicated as he placed my Associate's Degree of Business in my hand. I wanted to stand on his desk and yell, 'Victory is mine!' and give off one of those psycho laughs of a mad scientist. That was on the far side, but on the real, I felt blessed.

I had requested to have my certificate now versus waiting until after the graduation ceremony. Tom and my mother tried to encourage me to graduate with my class and do the whole cap and gown thing, but that's not what I wanted. Schoolwork was never difficult for me. I'm a natural student. I enjoyed it. To me, books were like treasure boxes full of knowledge, and I could take as much of it as I like. My third grade teacher, Mr. Grice gave my class that analogy once. It's been something that I lived by ever since. What has come hard for me was being able to stay on that educational track. I never dreamed about having children as a teenager, or having three significant men in my life. All those detours kept me from my one true aspiration- my education. So today was personal.

I took my certificate from Dean Bailey, and he handed me a citation for making the Dean's List. I thanked him and walked to my car. As I sat inside, I studied the piece of paper that read Associate Degree of Business, Tamlyn A. Blake-Lester. Running my fingers over the raised seal, emotions built up inside of me. This was the day I've waited so long for.

"I did it. I really did it."

Bending my head, I said a silent prayer of thanks to my Father God for blessing me to prove to myself, that I had the right stuff. For giving me the determination to fulfill my desire of becoming a college graduate. No ceremony in the world could have made me feel more warm and complete as having this time of atonement with myself. Tears ran down my eyes than I burst into a laugh. I remembered Hassan and I sitting in my apartment, reminiscing about the first time we met, and how he said he knew I had the right stuff, and that he was proud of me for trying so hard to better my condition in life.

"I did it baby," I said softly, wishing that he could hear me, knowing in my heart that he did. I placed my certificate and citation on the passenger seat, and headed to the stationary store to buy myself a frame to hang my prize on my wall.

I didn't have too much time to gloat, because my Bachelor's studies start next semester.

A HOUSE, A HOME

Closing, and not a day too soon. It wasn't much to it at all. We went to the realtor's office, and sat down with our lawyer and the developer. Debbie signed papers for about twenty minutes, and they handed her the key to our new home- 76 Cherry Heights Lane, right around the street from Dametta and Rock. Debbie turned to me and put the key in the palm of my hand.

Much props to Rock, for helping me refocus. I knew it took a lot for him to open his home to us like he did. If I knew Dametta, it was all her idea. He and I were rappin' on evening after the night I stayed at the hotel and simply put he said, 'While you're here, be here'. And his words hit hard but he said it so nonchalantly. I knew he didn't give a fuck whether I took his advice or not, but I did. I had my second chance, and I was gonna make it work.

After the closing, Debbie and I drove over to our house. She went on several walkthroughs with the realtor making sure that everything was right. I was only in the house the one time for the very first walkthrough. I didn't want to get my hopes up all high, just in case things didn't go right. I had to give it to her. Debbie really outdid herself. I had never been around this much newness in my entire life. The house came complete with all of the major appliances, washer/dryer, range top, big-ass refrigerator, microwave and oven built into the wall. Shit, we even had central air and heat.
Never would I have envisioned this for us, but I'm glad she did.

I JUST CALLED TO SAY...

I was sitting at my desk when the phone rang. It was Regina, the new receptionist/secretary. After I earned my degree, I applied for and was promoted into an entry-level position in Biggron's Marketing and Planning Division. She announced that I had an incoming phone call by a gentleman named Mr. Colbirth. Nearly dropping my cup of coffee all over my papers, I cleared my throat and tried to restrain the excitement that was surging inside of me. "Put him on."

"Hey stranger." Hassan's voice melted me where I sat.

"Hey yourself. How are you?" I said in a low melody. I felt like running around the office screaming, Yes! Yes! Yes!

"I just called to say congratulations to the college graduate. I always knew you could do it Tammy."

"Thank you, Hassan. I'm so happy about it. You know how much my schooling means to me." I laughed. "It took me long enough."

"But you did it, girl, and I'm so proud of you. You my superstar." I couldn't stop blushing. Hassan sounded so good to me. "How the kid's doing?"

"They're fine. Kiara's starting to get two little bumps, and you can't tell her nothing. Tianna's still acting like the baby, and you won't believe how big Hateem is getting. Hassan, I swear, it's like he's taking hormones or something. And he's developed quite an appetite."

"I miss all y'all."

"You're missed too. How's my handsome Erkell, and Jazzy girl doing?"

"They're fine. Both of them are getting big. Kell just turned ten."

"Dag Hassan, where has the time gone? I still remember the first time you brought him over to meet me. He was only three then. Now he's almost a teenager. We're getting old Hassan."

"Like a bottle of wine. Hey, how's Jeannette?"

"She's great, and Tahj is so sweet."

"How she handling the whole motherhood thang?"

"She's happier than I ever thought she could be."

"How's life treating you? You find whatever it was you've been searching for? Tom treating you good?"

My mind wondered back to my graduation night. When I got home Tom had planned a big surprise for me. He took the kids and me out for seafood. Instead of going home afterward, we dropped the little ones off at my mother's house. We then headed straight for the airport. We had a three-night, two-day mini vacation in the Bahamas. "I never knew life could be this good to me. Lord knows I've had my share of bad times. Being married to Tom makes me grounded. Yes, he is real good to us. But you know what I'm most proud of?"

"What's that?"

"Getting my degree. There is no feeling like it in this world. I've worked so hard for it." I began to laugh, "And guess what else?"

"What?"

"I finally got myself a new car. I bought a Camry."

Hassan laughed out loud, "It's about time. You sure got your money's worth out of the Subaru."

"You ain't kidding. I held that car together with band-aids. But it lasted." Tom wanted to buy me a car ever since we got married, but I wouldn't let him. Even though he could afford to buy me any car I desired, I explained to him how important it was for me to have a certain amount of control over my life. And getting a car was something that I wanted to do for myself. Tom respected that. "Well, tell me about you, Hassan. How are you and Debbie making out in your new house? Your mom told me all about it."

"Good, good. A lot better than I expected. She's a lot more together than I ever gave her credit for." He laughed almost to himself.

"She loves you, I can say that for sure. If she stayed with your butt all this time, it's got to be love." I chuckled. "So when are y'all getting married?" I asked sarcastically.

"I'ma marry you."

"You can't marry me. I'm already married."

Hassan started laughing. "I'm gonna wait until that old geezah of yours kicks it, then I'm comin' for you."

"That's not funny. Seriously though, are you happy?"

"Hey, I'm livin'. It ain't how I thought I'd end up, but all-in-all I'm Okay. I got a job now. It's a dirty, ball buster, but all-and-all, it's chill. I mean, least I ain't in jail or dead, right?" Hassan's voice faded. "You know baby girl, there's not a day that I don't think about you. Without you in my life, I'll never be complete."

"That's so deep Hassan, 'cause I feel the same way. I can't explain it. Tom makes me so happy, and I love the life that we share, but there is a part of me that is so empty with out you."

"Damn, why couldn't we..."

"Don't say it! We can't change the way things are. Let's just be happy for each other. You have someone who cares for you. I have someone who cares for me. All of our children are fine and in homes with two parents."

"That's all well and fine, but what about love, Tammy? Can you tell me that you are in love with Tom? I know you love him for being there for you, but are you in love with him?"

"You stole that part of my soul away. That part of me will always be yours, but that still doesn't change a thing."

"If you can't be with the one you love," Hassan said.

"Then you have to love the one you're with." I finished his sentence. "But you'll always be in my heart."

"And you in mine, until I die."

One of the fellahs from the mailroom brought a package to my desk. I signed for it.

"Hassan, I have to get off the phone."

"Tammy, it was so good hearing your voice again, girl. I miss y'all so much." He paused for a second. "Kiss the kids and tell them I love them, and that I'll try to come up and see them real soon. Will you do that for me?"

"Yes, of course. I love you."

"I love you too. Peace, lovely," he said.

"Bye," I said softly.

About The Author

Undra E. Biggs is a native of Trenton, NJ. She is co-founder of the Trenton Writers' Guild, a member of Black Women in Publishing and Toastmaster International.

Undra is also a devoted wife, and mother of two children, Miya and Alvin, Jr. To learn more about her other endeavors, contact her at http://www.undraebiggs.com